THE RANSOM

THE RANSOM

A NOVEL

KATHI MILLS-MACIAS

BROADMAN
&HOLMAN
PUBLISHERS

NASHVILLE, TENNESSEE

Published by Broadman & Holman,
Nashville, Tennessee

0-8054-3051-2

Dewey Decimal Classification: 813
Subject Heading: MYSTERY—FICTION

1 2 3 4 5 6 7 8 9 10 08 07 06 05 04

To *Yeshua*—as always,
the same yesterday, today, and forever.
To my husband, Al,
my hero and best friend.
To my dad:
I miss you and can't wait for our heavenly reunion.
To Uncle Werner:
Thank you for everything. You will always be very special to me.

CHAPTER 1

It was scarcely noon and Sophie Jacobson was exhausted, though her trip hadn't yet begun. The seventy-four-year-old woman had enjoyed her two weeks in Orlando visiting her lifelong friend, Leah Goldberg, but she vowed never again to come back to Florida until well into the winter months. The sticky heat of early September, combined with her friend's insistence that they "do" or "see" something every single day, had drained her, and she was anxious to return to the cool seclusion of her Centralia, Washington, hillside home. Sophie was almost relieved when Leah had dropped her off at the airport, apologizing because she would not be able to wait with her, as she had scheduled another appointment and didn't want to be late.

Slumped in the waiting-room chair, Sophie gazed at her swollen ankles as she listened for the first boarding call. Her plane wasn't scheduled to depart for at least thirty more minutes, but she liked to take advantage of early boarding. At her age she believed she was entitled to a few extra perks now and then, including taking her time getting on the plane before the crush of the crowd thrust her forward at a pace that aggravated her already aching feet.

She sighed, reminding herself that Leah was more like a sister to her than a friend, particularly since her only real sister, Rachel, had died in a car accident years earlier. But it would be nice, she thought, if Leah could learn to slow down and relax a little now and then. It was as if, since her husband had died only months after they'd retired and moved to Florida from New York, she'd been trying to outrun the pain by filling up every moment of her life with something new and exciting. Sophie doubted that it had worked. She too had lost her beloved husband, David, almost twenty years earlier, and she still missed him terribly. They'd never had children of their own, but they'd always doted on their nephew, Avraham—Abe, as everyone else called him. Now, of course, he was married to the *goy*, the Gentile.

She sighed again and shook her head. She must stop thinking of Toni so negatively. True, she was a *goy*, but she was also a sweet girl who obviously loved Avraham deeply. For that Sophie was grateful, though it still would have been much easier if he'd just married a nice Jewish girl. But, Sophie supposed, Avraham was undoubtedly influenced by his mother, Sophie's only sister, who had also married a *goy*. A family curse, Sophie imagined, getting worse with each successive generation. But at least Rachel, unlike her only son, hadn't converted.

That had been the hardest part for Sophie, a devout Jew who had prayed fervently for years that Avraham would not follow in his mother's footsteps but would return to the faith of his fathers. Instead, he had become a *Christian.* Sophie still had trouble thinking the word, let alone saying it out loud. It had been so hard for her in the beginning that she had written her nephew off as dead, going as far as to sit *shivah* for him, observing a period of grief after the death of a loved one. But in the end her deep affection for him had won out, and she had attended his wedding. How pleased she was, though a bit confused, that he and Toni had at least incorporated a few of the Jewish traditions into the ceremony. And she had to admit that, in the slightly more than five months since the wedding, they had bent over backward to make her feel welcome and wanted, something she needed desperately now that Avraham was her last close, living relative.

The memory of Sol—Shlomo, her only brother—twisted her heart with shame and longing. How she missed him! And yet, though he had died trying to protect Avraham from a criminal's bullet, it was Shlomo himself who had been involved in the crime ring that had been responsible for at least two murders and the kidnapping of Toni's younger sister, Melissa. *It was because he, too, turned his back on you, Adonai. Of that I have no doubt. My own brother refused to believe in the God of our fathers. What a price he paid for his defection.*

And so there was no one left but she and Avraham. Now that he had converted, what would become of the family heritage once she died? Who would be left to pray for her only nephew? Would the tiny remnant of the once faithful Levitz family pass into oblivion, lost in the paganism of the *goyim,* the Gentiles to whom they had joined themselves?

Sophie frowned. She had to admit that, though she still considered Christianity a pagan religion, one that had persecuted her people for centuries, this Jesus—*Yeshua,* as her nephew called him—had her puzzled. She had heard varying accounts of this supposed Jewish rabbi and was herself unsure whether she believed he had ever lived. Avraham, on the other hand, spoke of him as the Messiah of Israel—and of the *goyim*, as well. How was that possible? A dead Messiah, living again— even coming again, if she were to accept the claims of these Christians—and the Messiah not only to God's chosen people but also to the pagans? Ridiculous. And yet, lately, each time she heard *Yeshua's* name, she felt a strange tugging at her heart.

"Ladies and gentlemen, flight 1327 to Dallas and Seattle will begin preboarding in approximately ten minutes."

The announcement interrupted Sophie's reverie. How glad she would be to finally be home. And, she grudgingly admitted, she would even be glad to see Avraham and his bride when they picked her up at the airport. *Goy* or no *goy*, much like Avraham's *goy* father, Toni was a nice person—kind, honest, quite religious in her own pagan way, and lovely besides. Sophie had often imagined that Toni and Avraham would someday have beautiful children together. Was it possible that Adonai would allow her enough time on this earth to influence their little ones toward the true faith? It would be so nice to hold a child again, to bounce a baby on her knee and sing to him the song of Moshe—Moses, the great lawgiver of their people.

Catching herself before her thoughts drifted off once more, she checked her ticket and boarding pass. Everything was in order. Six more hours and she would be home.

Don't go.

Sophie jumped as if someone had slapped her. Anxiously she looked around. The seats to her left and right, as well as directly across from her, were still empty. Who had spoken? She had heard the words so clearly, and yet . . .

Don't go. Wait until later.

Sophie's eyes opened wide. Was it Adonai, the Lord himself, who had spoken to her? Was it possible? Certainly in the days of Avraham and Moshe, God had communicated directly to his people . . . but now? Today, in the year 2000? And to her, Sophie Jacobson?

She shook her head. No, it was not possible. It could not be. Adonai no longer spoke directly to anyone, even his chosen people, so why should she be an exception? She clutched her purse, checking once again for the ticket and boarding pass that were carefully tucked into the side pocket, then raised herself from her chair and began, slowly, to make her way toward the door that would soon open and allow her an early entrance to the jetway leading to her plane. Two elderly ladies in wheelchairs were already waiting there, along with a young mother and three small children. The preboarders were gathering, and soon they would be allowed to enter.

Don't go.

The warning came again, even as the door swung open and the smiling attendant picked up the handheld microphone and announced pre-boarding for the flight. Nervously Sophie pulled her boarding pass from her purse. The wheelchair passengers were already being pushed through the doorway, and the attendant was examining the boarding passes for the mother and her children. Sophie was next.

Wait for another flight.

Sophie's hand began to shake, and she dropped her pass. Before she could bend over to retrieve it, the attendant picked it up for her. "Are you all right?" she asked, her smile warm.

"I . . . yes," Sophie answered, swallowing and trying to keep her voice calm. "I'm fine. I just . . ."

The attendant tore off the perforated portion of the pass and handed it back to Sophie. "Take your time boarding," she said. "And if you'd like some help—"

Sophie shook her head. "No, I . . . I don't need any help, thank you." She forced a smile and stepped past the attendant.

Don't go.

This time the voice was so loud she turned to see if anyone else had heard it. But nothing had changed; no one appeared to have heard or sensed anything out of the ordinary.

"Excuse me," Sophie said, shaking once again as she reached out and touched the attendant's arm. "I think maybe . . . maybe I'm not feeling so well after all. Is it possible to . . . exchange my ticket for a later flight?"

The woman's face mirrored her concern. "Why don't you sit down right here," she suggested, indicating a chair to her right. "I'll have someone help you in just a moment."

Sophie nodded and sank into the chair, wondering if she looked as pale as she felt. She wondered how soon she could get another flight for home. She wondered what she would tell Avraham and Toni about why she had changed her plans at the last moment. Most of all she wondered if she might be losing her mind.

~~~

Abe frowned when Toni told him of Sophie's call. "Did she say why? Is there some sort of problem with the airline, or . . . ?"

Toni shook her head. "No. She just said she'd explain when she got here. But she sounded . . . I don't know, shaky or confused, maybe even a bit frightened. But that's all I could get out of her. She said the next available flight won't get her in until after nine this evening." She paused, touched by the depth of concern she saw in her husband's dark eyes. Reaching up, she laid her palm against his cheek. "She'll be fine, sweetheart."

"I know." Abe smiled down at her. "It's just that . . . I worry about her. Especially because she doesn't know *Yeshua.*"

Toni nodded. "But she will. I'm sure of it. We've been praying, and we've seen her soften so much in the last months."

"True. And I guess if God can get hold of me, he can get through to anybody."

Toni laughed. "That's for sure. So quit worrying and let's think of something to do, now that we've got all this extra time on our hands before we have to leave for the airport."

Abe's eyes sparkled and he pulled Toni close. "I like the sound of that, Mrs. Matthews. And I think I know exactly what we can do to pass the time."

≈≈≈

It was nearly two-thirty and Sophie was dozing fitfully in her chair. The airlines had been cooperative in helping her arrange a later flight, even offering her a place to lie down for a while, which she had declined. Instead, she had called Abe's number and talked briefly to Toni, then grabbed a bite to eat and bought a book to read while she waited. But her eyes had grown heavy, and she had felt herself slipping back and forth into a half sleep several times. As she did, she began to wonder whether the many thoughts and images dancing through her head were dreams or reality. They seemed to be running together and were, for the most part, relatively unclear.

Except for the face—strong yet gentle, wounded yet compassionate. He wasn't particularly attractive, yet he drew her to himself, especially when he held out his hands—scarred hands, beckoning her to come closer. But she resisted because deep inside she knew who he was. She had seen the face, the outstretched hands, on previous occasions, calling her, wooing her, but always she refused his invitation. Today would be no different, she vowed. She had no place in her life, or in her heart, for this *Yeshua*, the God of the *goyim*.

She was jolted awake by the sound of her name—not over the loudspeaker but almost directly in her ear.

"Sophie! Sophie, *baruch Hashem*! Praise be to God! I thought you were on the plane."

Sophie blinked as the round face, framed with curly, dyed red hair, came into focus. Leah. What was she doing here? Had something happened? Was something wrong?

Before she could open her mouth to voice her questions, her friend began to speak again. Her brown eyes were open wide, and her lips moved rapidly, as did her manicured hands. "I heard it on the radio when I was driving home. They didn't give any details, and I was nearly frantic with worry. I thought about going home to see what I could learn from the television, but then I thought I might be able to find out more by coming here, back to the gate where you would have boarded. That's when I saw you sitting here. Oh, Sophie, praise be to Adonai, he has spared you!"

Sophie still didn't understand what was going on. What did Leah mean, she had "heard it on the radio"? Heard what? What was she talking about?

She shook her head, sat up straight, and peered into her friend's anxious face. "I'm sorry, Leah. I don't know what you mean."

Leah's painted eyebrows shot up. "You don't know? No one has said anything about the plane crash?"

This time it was Sophie's turn to widen her eyes. A plane crash? What plane? Surely she didn't mean . . . "What are you talking about? What plane?"

Leah grabbed Sophie's arm and leaned closer as she spoke. "Yours. The one you were supposed to take home. At least, I thought that was the one. But . . . why are you still here?"

Sophie felt her heart leap, and she swallowed before she spoke. "My plane? The one I was supposed to be on? Flight 1327?"

Leah nodded, still leaning toward Sophie as if waiting for an explanation.

Sophie looked around. She noticed what appeared to be an anxious-looking group of people huddled around the check-in counter and wondered if it had anything to do with the tragic news Leah had just told her. Was it true? Could it be that, had she not listened to the warning voice a few hours earlier, she might be dead at this moment, ushered into the presence of Adonai himself?

She shuddered. Why should she have been spared? Why would God—for surely it had been his voice she had heard—warn her about the flight? What possible reason could there have been for him to spare her life? What purpose could an old woman have that would be important enough for the creator of the universe to intervene and speak to her? Did he want something from her? If so, what could it be?

Suddenly she remembered the image of Yeshua, beckoning her to come to him. She closed her eyes, terrified at the implications, trying desperately to will the image from her mind. But it would not go. And in that instant she knew that she was going to have to investigate the claims of this Yeshua once and for all.

"Sophie." Leah's grip on her arm grew tighter, bringing her back to the present. "Sophie, are you all right?"

Sophie opened her eyes and swallowed again, nodding slowly. "Yes," she whispered. "I'm all right. Thank you, Leah. Thank you for coming here, and thank you for telling me."

Leah relaxed her grip and patted her friend's arm. "I think you should come home with me—stay a few more days, until you've had time to get over the shock. You can't go home now."

Sophie was surprised at her own answer, but she knew it was right even as she spoke it. "I must go home, Leah. Today. I have things to do that just can't wait." She tried to smile reassuringly. "Please don't worry about me, Leah dear. I'll be fine. Avraham and his wife will be waiting for me when I arrive."

CHAPTER 2

Abe was doing his best to stay focused on the overweight, middle-aged man from Texas who filled up the chair on the other side of the desk, but his mind kept wandering to his surprise plans for Toni. Today was their six-month wedding anniversary, and he had made reservations for dinner at her favorite restaurant overlooking the Columbia River. The evening out was no surprise to his not-so-subtle wife, who had specifically requested the occasion, but the tickets for a four-day getaway in Southern California were strictly his idea—one he was sure she would love once he presented them to her over dinner.

The memories of their two-week honeymoon in Hawaii had convinced Abe to splurge and plan another vacation for the two of them—one where they could once again walk along a warm beach and listen to the surf pounding at night. Their honeymoon had ended far too quickly, as far as he was concerned, and he was eager for at least a mini-repeat of the occasion. The travel agent had assured him that early fall was one of the best times to visit the world-renowned San Diego beaches, and she had gotten him a package deal that included a quaint bed and breakfast overlooking the Pacific.

"So, what about it, Mr. Matthews?" The man sitting across from him was eyeing him intently. "Can y'all help me find my brother? It would mean a lot to me—to *all* our family."

Abe hoped he hadn't missed too much of the man's monologue, but it was that annoying, droning drawl that had helped induce Abe's daydreaming in the first place. It was as if . . . as if the man were reading an invisible script, one that lacked sincerity and passion. Still, he was a prospective client, and Abe needed to get a clear picture of what the Texan wanted from him. Determined to pay closer attention, he put on his most serious face.

"I'll have to talk it over with the other half of the Matthews and Matthews team," he said, "my partner, who also happens to be my wife. We've only recently started doing this together full-time, and we've agreed not to take on any cases without discussing them first. But if you don't mind checking back with me on Monday or Tuesday—or if you want to leave me a number where I can reach you, then I'll call you after Toni and I have had a chance to talk about it."

The man's facial expression didn't change, but he shrugged his shoulders. "Sure. Why not? I'll give y'all a call the first of the week." He stood and offered his hand. Abe took it, thinking that it felt as meaty and lifeless as it had when they first shook hands in greeting. Abe wondered briefly why the man hadn't offered to leave him a phone number or tell him where he was staying, but dismissed it as unimportant and followed him into the front office to grab a cup of stale coffee, reheated from the night before.

As the front door closed behind his would-be client, Abe poured the dark liquid into his favorite cup, then glanced at his wife's desk. It was buried in stacks of paperwork, as usual. He felt guilty that she got stuck with so much of the bookkeeping and correspondence, but by mutual agreement they had decided that she should be the one to handle that aspect of the business, as he'd never had a knack for that sort of thing. He was a stickler for details when researching a case, but something as mundane as the details involved in balancing books or paying bills held no interest for him whatsoever. Toni had teased him more than once that they'd be bankrupt in a week if she let him handle the finances. Still, the pile on her desk looked overwhelming, possibly worse than normal because she'd been called to substitute teach the day before, something she seldom did anymore now that they'd decided to keep the agency open. But Toni had agreed to fill in for one day, until the district had time to find someone else.

Abe was glad she had opted to spend the majority of her time working at his side, particularly now that he had decided not to go back to the police force. It had been a tough decision, one that had been at least partially influenced by the sad memories Abe's former job evoked regarding his late uncle Sol, who had served on the force for many years before becoming involved in the criminal activities that finally claimed his life. But Abe's decision not to return to the police force had also been one that he and Toni had prayed about for months, finally coming to the mutual conclusion that this was where they both needed to be—running the Matthews and Matthews detective agency together, just as Toni's parents had done for many years.

The second Matthews and Matthews detective team, Abe mused. He smiled as he remembered telling Toni that she should marry him if for no other reason than she wouldn't have to change the name on her driver's license. He had wondered more than once if Toni's father's decision to keep the Matthews and Matthews name for the agency after his wife died had been more than slightly prophetic.

Now, of course, Toni had lost both her mother and father—her mother to cancer nearly fourteen years earlier and her father to murder less than two years ago. Abe's parents, too, were gone—killed in a car accident while Abe was still in college. At that point Sol Levitz, Abe's uncle, had stepped in as father and advisor, and the two had grown close. It had been devastating to Abe to learn of his uncle's involvement in a lucrative but illegal baby-selling ring, particularly when Sol was killed as a result. That left Sol's sister, Sophie, as Abe's only living blood relative. How glad he was to have her home from her trip to Florida. It had been two weeks now, and he still hadn't gotten over the shock of learning that her originally scheduled plane had crashed soon after leaving the Orlando airport. The accident had been attributed to pilot error, and there had been no survivors. By the time Sophie had arrived at the Portland airport that night, the three of them had collapsed into one another's arms in tears.

She's doing a lot of thinking now, Abe reminded himself. *I'd already seen some changes in her before, but now that she realizes her life was miraculously spared. . . .*

He shook his head. He had to stop getting sidetracked and get back to work. He wished Toni were already there. He knew she was planning to come in to the office soon, but maybe until she arrived he could at least help her sort through some of the mail sitting on her desk.

He plunked down in her chair and wondered if they'd ever get to the place that they could hire a part-time secretary. Toni insisted they didn't need one, that her parents had handled the agency on their own, her father having hired a secretary-receptionist only after her mother died. And, of course, Toni had been quick to remind Abe that the second woman her dad hired to fill that position had been instrumental in arranging his death. So for now the topic of hired help was off-limits, and Toni had opted to keep her actual "sleuthing" to part-time, spending the rest of her office hours on correspondence and balancing the books.

The mail looked as uninteresting as the pile they accumulated daily at home—lots of ads, a couple of bills, and nothing in the way of personal letters. But underneath the three days' worth of mail, Abe discovered what appeared to be the first two chapters of a manuscript: *Storm on the Horizon* by Toni Matthews. Abe's heart swelled with pride as he realized his wife had finally begun the novel she'd been talking about writing for as long as he'd known her. He was also a bit hurt that she hadn't confided in him about starting the actual writing. In fact, as much as she'd talked about writing a novel, she'd never really told him the plot. His curiosity urged him to read the printed pages, but respect for his wife convinced him otherwise. He'd wait until she presented it to him, though he hoped it wouldn't be long.

Abe took a swig of his coffee, grimaced, and decided he wasn't desperate enough to drink it. Rising from Toni's chair, he walked into the bathroom and dumped the remaining liquid down the sink, then rinsed the cup. As he exited the bathroom, he heard the front door open.

"Abe?"

"In here," he answered, walking back toward the front office. "I sure am glad you're finally here. It's been lonely without you."

His voice trailed off as his wife came into view. Toni's short blonde curls seemed to shine more than usual in the office's overhead lights, and her blue eyes drew him as they had the first time they'd met, right here in this office. Setting his cup down on Toni's desk, he reached out and pulled her into his arms. She smelled clean and fresh, and his heart raced with anticipation of the trip he would surprise her with tonight.

"I missed you," he murmured, his face buried in her hair.

"I missed you too," she said, turning her face up to his. "It's been almost three hours."

He nodded, thinking once again that he had married the most beautiful woman on earth. *Thank you, God*, he prayed silently, even as he bent to kiss her. They'd been through a lot in the year and a half since they'd first come to know each other, but it had been worth every minute. Things had never been better in Abe's thirty-two years of life, and he prayed constantly that nothing would ever happen to interfere in their relationship. He couldn't imagine living a day without her ever again.

"So, detective," Toni said, pulling back slightly, "what have you been up to these past three hours? Solving lots of crimes while I was away?"

Abe smiled. "Nothing that exciting, I'm afraid. I made a few phone calls on some of our active cases, but that's about it. Except for Mr. Landry, that is."

Toni raised her eyebrows. "Mr. Landry? Who's that?"

"Some guy from Texas, looking for his brother. Seems no one in the family has seen him in years. The last contact anyone had with him was when he called his mother about two years ago. Didn't say much, just that he was all right and would be in touch again when he could. That was it."

"Where was he when he called?"

"That's why the brother—George Landry—was here. It seems the call was made from right here in River View."

"Hmm. And that's why he landed on our doorstep." She frowned. "But why now? If the call was two years ago, why didn't they come looking for him then? Why wait so long?"

"I wondered the same thing. He said it was because their mother had just passed away and they wanted to find him and tell him about it."

Toni shrugged. "Makes sense. So what did you tell him?"

"That I had to talk it over with my partner."

"Good thinking, detective."

Abe smiled. "I'm learning. Give me another six months and I'll have this being-a-good-husband thing mastered."

"You think so?"

"Absolutely."

"So what do you want to do? About the case, I mean. Shall we take it?"

"I don't see why not. Don't know what we'll find after all this time, though. If the guy doesn't want to be located, I doubt he's still hanging around here."

"True. But we're not exactly overloaded with cases right now. Maybe we should go ahead and take it."

"That's what I was thinking. Can't be that big a deal, can it? A missing person's case . . ." Abe's voice trailed off, and he watched Toni's reaction to his words. The pain was fleeting but obvious, even before she spoke.

"You know what I'm thinking, don't you?"

Abe nodded and pulled her closer. "The missing person's case your dad was on when he died—Julie Green's. He was murdered trying to solve it."

Toni hesitated before speaking again. "Well, this one certainly can't be anything like Julie's. If it's all right with you, sweetheart, let's go ahead and take on Mr. Landry and his missing brother. It sounds like a run-of-the-mill, garden-variety missing person's case to me. Nothing to worry about, I'm sure."

Abe kissed the top of her head. "OK, then. It's settled. Now all I have to do is get through the rest of the day so we can hurry up and go out for our anniversary dinner tonight. I can't wait."

Toni looked up again and smiled. "You're an incurable romantic, Abe Matthews, do you know that?"

Abe nodded. "That's right. And don't you forget it—ever."

$$\sim\sim\sim$$

Melissa marveled at how quickly she could shift from feeling like an almost grown-up woman to a frightened child and then back again. It was as if her emotions were on a never-ending roller-coaster ride, one that she wouldn't mind getting off of now and then, just so she could relax and catch her breath for a little while. But this was hardly the time.

It had started this morning. Abe had already left for the office, and she and Toni had been sitting at the kitchen table, munching on toast and sipping orange juice. The topic of college had come up, and Toni had asked her if she'd given any thought to where she might want to go or what she might want to do after high school graduation.

"After all," Toni had said, "your sixteenth birthday is right around the corner, and you're a junior in high school now. You'll be amazed at how fast these last two years fly by, believe me. The next thing you know you'll be marching across the stage to receive your diploma. It's never too soon to start planning for that next step, you know."

Melissa had nodded, admitting to her sister that she had often thought about that topic lately. "I think I'd like to stay right here in the

Northwest," she'd said. "Close enough to come home for weekends and holidays but not close enough to live here. Nothing personal, of course. I just think it would do me good to spread my wings a little and try living on campus."

Toni had laughed. "I think you're right. And don't worry. I won't take it personally. I'm just glad you're already looking ahead and starting to make some plans. It's a responsible sign."

As they'd continued to discuss the possibilities of different campuses, scholarships, majors, and career opportunities, Melissa had found herself feeling mature, almost on an equal par with her older sister. The feeling was only slightly intimidating, and she'd decided it was one she could easily get used to.

And then she'd headed off to school, still caught up in her future plans, when she suddenly realized she was walking right past the park where she'd been kidnapped just slightly over one year earlier. Despite the warm autumn sunshine, she shivered at the memory, trying to block out the feelings of terror and helplessness that always accompanied any reference to that nightmarish event.

I don't have to be frightened anymore, she reminded herself. *Abe and Toni rescued me before those horrible people could carry out their plan to "sell me to the highest bidder" for things I can't even stand to think about.* But her reminder did little to dispel her sudden sense that she was once again a young, foolish, vulnerable girl who needed the protection of others on a daily basis. How glad she was that she had both Toni and Abe as her protectors, now that she no longer had parents to fulfill those roles.

Fighting tears at the thought of her beloved father, who had died a year and a half before, she trudged on to school, all thoughts of being a grown-up now banished from her mind. And then she'd arrived on campus and seen Eric a few steps ahead of her, his dark hair gleaming in the sun, and the roller-coaster ride was swirling at full tilt once again.

This must be what growing up is all about, she thought. *Planning for college, noticing boys*—really *noticing them, especially one as cute as Eric Fullbright. If Carrie were here, she'd remind me right away that there's a lot more to it*—and I know that. *But this part is definitely the most fun so far . . . maybe the most embarrassing too. I wish I could be more like Carrie*—except for the wheelchair. *She's miles ahead of me on the maturity road. And spiritually, it's no contest. She's even ahead of most adults I know. But I am doing better, aren't I, Lord? At least, it seems that way most of the time.*

The jolt was so unexpected that Melissa dropped her books and binder. Flustered and humiliated by her clumsiness, she hurriedly bent to retrieve her belongings, letting her long auburn hair fall over her face to hide what she was sure were very pink cheeks.

"Let me help you," a male voice offered, as a strong, suntanned hand reached in to gather up her books.

Melissa swallowed as she looked up, recognizing the voice immediately and realizing whom she'd run into while lost in her thoughts. "I'm sorry," she stammered. "I didn't mean to run into you. I guess I just wasn't paying attention, and . . ."

Eric's smile was dazzling. "Hey, don't worry about it. I'm the one who wasn't paying attention." His voice lowered a notch, and his warm brown eyes sparkled mischievously. "But if running into beautiful girls like you is what I get for not paying attention, I guess I'll have to do it more often."

Melissa's cheeks grew hotter, and she suddenly realized how far she was from true maturity. A grown-up wouldn't blush like an idiot just because someone of the opposite sex—a good-looking someone, she reminded herself—gave her a compliment.

He helped her up and handed her the books, his eyes never leaving hers. "I'm Eric Fullbright," he said. "I just moved here from Nebraska with my family. What's your name?"

"I know. That you're Eric, I mean."

He waited, then said, "I'm impressed that you know my name, but does this mean you're not going to tell me yours? Do I have to discover your identity by asking all the other guys on campus? I guess I could just tell them I ran into the prettiest girl around and would like to know who you are. No doubt they'll know exactly which girl I'm talking about, but I'd really rather hear it from you."

Melissa was mortified. She wanted to tell him her name, but her mouth and brain just couldn't seem to get into sync. Just then she heard Carrie Bosworth's voice, calling to her from the entrance to the corridor. Melissa turned and saw her best friend sitting in her motorized wheelchair, her books in a backpack strapped to the back of her chair.

"Melissa," she called anxiously. "Come on, we're going to be late. Class starts in five minutes."

Melissa nodded and waved, then turned back to Eric. "My friend," she stammered. "I have to go."

Eric smiled again. "Melissa. OK, at least I know that much. It's a start."

Melissa swallowed again. "Matthews," she managed. "My name is Melissa Matthews."

"Thanks, Melissa Matthews. And I hope we run into each other again real soon."

Melissa chuckled in spite of herself. "It's a big campus," she said. "But who knows? As long as we don't start paying attention to where we're going, we probably will run into each other again."

Eric's eyes softened. "You have a nice laugh." Then he turned and walked away.

Melissa, the almost sixteen-year-old woman-child, watched him for a moment, then joined her friend and headed to class. She hoped Carrie would be in enough of a hurry maneuvering her wheelchair down the corridor that she wouldn't have time to ask Melissa about her conversation with Eric Fullbright, the recently arrived senior from Nebraska—the one with the gorgeous eyes and heart-stopping smile. The one who had just said she was the prettiest girl around. The one, Melissa hoped, she would "run into" again very soon.

~~~

Toni gazed out the window as the slowly setting sun stretched its sparkling rays across the waters of the mighty Columbia. This had been her father's favorite restaurant, and she never tired of coming here, especially now that she had Abe to come with her. Tearing her eyes from the beautiful scene, she turned her head and looked across the table at her handsome husband. She'd thought that he too had been enjoying the spectacular sunset, but apparently he'd been staring at her all along. She smiled, pleased that he would rather look at her than at the wonders of nature. She hoped it would always be so.

"Beautiful out there, isn't it?" she commented.

His eyes never left her face. "Not as beautiful as it is in here."

She smiled again. "You're quite the charmer, you know that, detective?"

"I try."

Toni reached across the table and took his hand, just as the waiter arrived with their salads. "Would you care for some fresh ground pepper?" he asked, smiling as he held out the huge wooden pepper mill. They declined, and he walked away.

Still holding hands, they bowed their heads and Abe offered thanks for the food. "Hungry?" he asked when she looked up.

Toni nodded. "Aren't you?"

"Have you ever known me not to be?"

She laughed as she picked up her fork. "No. And I doubt I ever will."

As they worked their way through the greens, alternately gazing out the window and at each other, Toni felt herself relaxing. It had been a long day, and it felt good to sit quietly with the man she loved and dream about their future. Lately she'd found herself wondering about children. They both wanted several, but how soon? She was, after all, almost twenty-eight years old, and Abe was thirty-two. Maybe they shouldn't wait too long—

"Earth to Toni. Come in . . ."

Toni flinched, suddenly drawn back to the reality of the restaurant and her husband sitting across from her, calling her name. How did she always manage to drift off so quickly and completely? She smiled.

"I was just thinking about kids."

Abe raised his eyebrows. "Kids? As in 'our kids'?"

She nodded.

His eyes began to twinkle. "You're not trying to tell me something, are you? You're not—"

Quickly she shook her head. "No. Not yet. But I was thinking that maybe we shouldn't wait too long to start our family."

Abe's grin spread from ear to ear. "Now that's the kind of thinking I like. Maybe we should just skip the main course and go home for dessert."

Toni laughed, as she felt her cheeks grow warm. "You're impossible, Abe Matthews. You know what I meant."

"Yes, I'm sure I do. And like I said, that's my kind of thinking."

Toni shook her head and took another bite of salad. Abe might be impossible, but he was also adorable. Even though she'd known him only a year and a half, she wondered, as she did so often, how she'd ever gotten through life without him. True, she'd been engaged to her high school sweetheart, Brad Anderson, when she'd first met Abe, but she realized now that she'd never known what love was before this good-looking detective had walked into her life.

For a brief moment her heart constricted with the painful memory of that time. It was right after her father had died, before she'd ever suspected that he'd been murdered. The day she'd first laid eyes on Abe had been the same day that she'd first found the clue in Julie Green's file—the clue that had begun the investigation that had led not only to the discovery of her father's killers but also to the uncovering of a huge baby-selling ring. The investigation had thrown her and Abe together, and it had also driven her and Brad apart. She'd felt badly about that but knew now that it was meant to be. Even her younger sister, Melissa, had come to the same conclusion, particularly after Abe had so daringly rescued her from her kidnappers—

"Hellooooo . . ."

Toni jumped. "I did it again, didn't I?"

"Yes, you did. What were you thinking of this time? Making babies again, I hope?"

"No, I'm afraid not—but something just as good. I was thinking about how we first met and wondering how I ever lived without you."

Abe's smile was back. "You're right. That's just about as good as making babies." This time it was he who reached across the table. Taking her hand he said, "Six months, Mrs. Matthews. It's really flown, hasn't it?"

She nodded. "Half a year as husband and wife. The best months of my life."

He squeezed her hand, then released it and reached into his pocket. "Happy anniversary, sweetheart," he said, handing her an envelope.

Toni frowned. "What's this?"

"Open it and find out."

Sliding the envelope open, she reached inside and pulled out an itinerary. San Diego. A bed and breakfast overlooking the ocean. Four days and nights.

"Oh, Abe," she gasped. "This is wonderful! But when? How?"

"Two weeks from today. And don't worry about the how. I've already taken care of the details."

"But Melissa. The office."

"Melissa is going to stay at Carrie's, and we'll just shut the office down for a long weekend. Nothing's so pressing that it can't wait a few days while we have a second honeymoon."

Toni's heart melted and she felt the tears threatening. "You're incredible," she whispered.

He was grinning again. "Does that mean you'll come?"

She laughed. "Try and stop me, detective." She returned his smile. "This is so perfect."

"Perfect for making babies—among other things, of course."

Before she could say another word, the waiter picked up their empty salad plates and poured more water before moving on. When he was out of earshot, Toni asked, "Are you sure there's nothing going on at the office that can't wait? What about that new case—George Landry, is it? The one with the missing brother?"

"He's going to call us back the first of the week, so I'll just tell him we'll go ahead and take the case but we probably won't get too much done on it until we return. Fair enough?"

"You're right. After all, it's just a routine case, at least from what he's told you so far. So there's no reason we can't go on our trip. All the other cases are pretty much on schedule."

Abe nodded. "You see? So there's no excuse." He lifted his glass. "Southern California, here we come!"

Toni touched her glass to his. "To our second honeymoon."

"And to making babies."

They laughed, and the waiter approached once more, this time bearing their main course. *Life is just about as perfect as it can get*, Toni thought. At last the danger and heartache that had so characterized the early months of their relationship were over. They were finally free to dream and plan their future together.

Thank you, Lord, Toni prayed silently. *Thank you for bringing us through such difficult times. And thank you that those times are behind us once and for all.*

CHAPTER 3

George Landry didn't like to be kept waiting; he'd already been waiting for more than two years. Sometimes it seemed as if he'd been waiting his entire life. Now that pretty-boy detective and his so-called partner wanted to put him off one more time. True, it was only another week, but one more wasted week in this two-bit hick town was not something he looked forward to—unless, of course, he could come up with some clue himself in the interim. For that reason alone he decided to stay, rather than catching the first available flight back to Dallas, where he would at least have something to do while he waited.

Two years, he thought, pacing the tiny motel room for what seemed the hundredth time. *All that time she knew where he was—or at least where he said he was when he called her—and she never told us.*

If she hadn't broken down and said something on her deathbed, we still wouldn't know where to look. But Jimmy always was her favorite.

Memories of his recently deceased mother threatened to unearth his long-buried emotions, but he steeled himself against them. She was gone, and that was that. She was better off anyway. All those months of suffering, and never once did good old Jimmy boy come to see her. Just one measly phone call, that's all he gave her—at least, as far as they knew. If there was any other contact, she'd taken the knowledge of it to her grave.

The worst part was that she had died with Jimmy's name on her lips. Not his, George's, the firstborn, or even Mindy's, her only daughter. Just Jimmy, her baby, the one she had bailed out of every problem he'd ever had. Well, Mama wasn't going to be around to run interference for him on this one. This time little Jimmy boy had bitten off more than he could chew, and he was going to pay—along with anyone else who got in the way of what had to be done. And that included the Matthews and Matthews team. George would use them however he had to in order to get to Jimmy, but if they became a problem along the way, he would simply have to eliminate them. This was just too big a deal to risk leaving any loose ends.

～～～

The flight had been quiet and uneventful, arriving at San Diego's Lindberg Field just before noon. The famous California sunshine had sparkled on the water below them as they'd come in low over the old downtown area for a near-perfect landing. "Welcome to America's finest city," the flight attendant had announced as they taxied to their gate. Being partial to River View, Toni wasn't sure she agreed with the attendant's assessment, but she was certainly looking forward to all their weekend getaway had to offer.

In less than thirty minutes she and Abe had claimed their luggage and stashed it in the trunk of their rental car, then headed out of the airport and past the marina toward the freeway entrance that would take them twenty miles north to their destination. Toni's stomach rumbled as she realized how long they'd been up without eating.

"I'm getting hungry, aren't you?" she asked, reaching across the console to lay her hand on Abe's arm. He looked at her briefly and smiled, his dark eyes twinkling mischievously, then turned his attention back to the busy freeway in front of him.

"Sorry," he said. "No time to stop. You'll have to be patient just a little longer. I've already made arrangements for a special lunch."

Toni raised her eyebrows. This husband of hers never ceased to amaze her. "Really? You didn't tell me about that part. Where are we going to eat? What have you got planned?"

Abe smiled but kept his eyes on the road. "Like I said, you'll just have to be patient. We're almost there."

Toni sighed and laid her head back against the seat. Closing her eyes, she returned Abe's smile, though they weren't looking at each other. They had been married only six months, but already she knew him well enough to realize there was no use trying to pry his surprise out of him. When his mind was made up, that was that. And so she would wait—not because she was being patient, as Abe had advised her, but because she had no choice.

Fifteen minutes later, when Abe announced they had arrived and Toni jumped at the sound of his voice penetrating her consciousness, she realized she had dozed off. Blinking slowly, she sat up straight and focused on the beautiful old two-story building in front of her. The sign above the front porch read "Maggie's Bed and Breakfast, Established 1908." Toni was impressed.

"How did you find this place?" she asked, turning toward her grinning husband. "It's absolutely charming."

"I knew you'd like it. When the travel agent showed me the brochure, I picked it right away."

"Has it really been a bed and breakfast for almost a hundred years?"

Abe shook his head. "Not really, although that's when the place was built. From what the agent told me, a young couple named Frank and Molly Greenfield were the original owners, and they passed it on to their only child, Maggie, who never married but stayed on in the house and eventually turned it into a bed and breakfast. She's long gone now, but a couple from Germany bought it about twenty years ago and opted to keep the name."

"I'm glad." Toni smiled. "Somehow the 'Oom-pah-pah Bed and Breakfast' just wouldn't have the same charm as 'Maggie's.' So is this where we're going to have lunch?"

Abe shook his head again. "Nope. But it's where we're picking it up. Come on, I'll show you."

Jumping out of his side of the car, Abe hurried to open the door for Toni. He then grabbed their bags from the trunk and carried them up the stairs, with Toni at his side. The blue-gray Cape Cod-style building with the white trim made her feel right at home from the moment she stepped onto the expansive porch with its three rocking chairs and a porch swing that swayed gently in the ocean breeze. Stopping to look behind her, Toni gasped at the view. The mighty Pacific spread out in front of her like a shiny blue emerald, beckoning her to come and get acquainted.

"This is nothing like the beaches up north," she said. "They have a stark beauty of their own, of course, but this—I mean, I've been to Southern California before, but . . ."

Abe came up behind her and slipped his arms around her waist. "Incredible, isn't it? I'm going to have to send a special thank-you note to that travel agent. We haven't even walked in the front door yet, and already it's more beautiful than she said it would be."

"Thank you," she said, leaning her head back against his chest, "for all of this. I didn't realize how much we needed it, but you did, didn't you?"

Abe kissed the top of her head. "Yes. Now what do you say we go inside and pick up that lunch I told you about?"

Her curiosity piqued again, Toni tore herself from the ocean view and walked with Abe into Maggie's Bed and Breakfast, excited to see the inside of this lovely old home. She wasn't disappointed.

"This is incredible," she whispered. "The blues and greens, the ocean motif—it's all so soothing and restful."

"As it's supposed to be," Abe assured her. "I told the agent I wanted to get you away from everything—worries, responsibilities, to-do lists, everything—except me, of course. And I think we've found just the right place."

Before she could voice her agreement, a large woman with glowing pink cheeks and an immaculate white apron came in from the next room and greeted them warmly in her gentle German accent. "Mr. and Mrs. Matthews, yah? So good you have come. I am Katrina Schmidt. My husband, Otto, and I are your hosts. You will meet him later, after he returns from town. Please, follow me and I show you your room. You will like it, yah?"

Toni found herself nodding, restraining herself from saying, "Yah, yah." There was no doubt in her mind that she would like the room.

And she did. It was spacious yet cozy, tastefully decorated but not overdone with too much "foo-foo," as Abe called anything frilly or lacey. The large four-poster bed was covered with a soft pink and peach comforter that looked inviting, but her stomach, which was rumbling once again, reminded her that the bed would just have to wait. She was relieved when Katrina left them to settle in, reminding them as she walked out the door that their lunch was waiting for them in the kitchen when they were ready.

Toni reached for one of the suitcases, determined to get the unpacking over with quickly, but Abe interrupted her. "Later," he said, his voice husky as he pulled her close to him. "We'll unpack when we get back from lunch. I know you're hungry, and besides, if we don't get out of this room right now, I just might not let you out at all."

Within minutes they had descended the stairs and found their way to the kitchen. True to her word, Katrina had left a large picnic basket with a note pinned to it sitting on the butcher-block table. On one side of the note was their name; on the other, a hand-drawn map.

"What's this?" Toni asked, frowning as she studied the note.

"Directions to our hideaway," Abe answered, taking it from her and picking up the basket. "Come on, let's go."

Checking the map only occasionally, Abe managed to lead them both to the most beautiful picnic spot Toni had ever seen. Just above the water on a sandy plateau surrounded on three sides by grassy dunes, they spread out their blanket and began to unload their bounty. The fried chicken didn't surprise Toni, as she'd smelled it ever since they entered the kitchen. In addition they found deviled eggs, crisp dill pickles, fresh fruit, homemade chocolate chip cookies, and a thermos of iced tea. Even the napkins were perfect—sky-blue with white initials: M's B&B.

"You sure know how to do things right, detective," Toni smiled. "Right down to the last detail."

Abe grinned. "I aim to please. Glad you like it."

Toni laughed. "How could I not like it? But if we eat like this for the next four days, I'm going to have to buy bigger clothes when we get back home."

"I was figuring on that soon anyway, since I'm hoping you'll be pregnant before this weekend is over."

"Aha. So you did have an ulterior motive in mind when you scheduled this getaway."

"Absolutely. So don't expect any sightseeing trips while we're here. I have other plans."

Toni smiled again, wondering if anyone could possibly be any happier than she was at this moment. "It's going to be a great weekend, Mr. Matthews."

~~~

It was a golden autumn Saturday in the Pacific Northwest, and Melissa and Carrie were sitting in the Bosworths' backyard, Melissa in a lawn chair, Carrie in her wheelchair, enjoying the sunshine and trying to convince each other that they really needed to quit daydreaming and get busy on their homework. So far it hadn't worked.

"So how is geometry going so far?" Carrie asked. "You said you were dreading it. Is it as bad as you thought?"

Melissa rolled her eyes. She'd wondered how long it would be before Carrie brought up this unwelcome subject. At least they'd made it through Friday night before she'd had to deal with it. "Worse," she answered. "I've never worried about flunking a class before, but this might be a first. I just don't get it—and I don't see the need for it. How is finding the area of a trapezoid or a parallelogram going to help me in my future? Have you ever known anyone who had to explain the Pythagorean theorem on a job application?"

Carrie laughed. "You never know. You just might end up becoming an engineer or something someday, and then all that stuff will come in handy."

"Oh, yeah, right. Big chance of that. That side of my brain shut down before I was ever born, believe me. I just wish I didn't have to take that class for college."

"But you do. So maybe we'd better get inside and get started. I'll be glad to help you with it."

"I know you will. And I appreciate it, believe me—even if I can't figure out why in the world you like that class. But can we wait just a few more minutes? It's so nice out here right now."

"It is, isn't it? OK, ten more minutes. And then we are going to go in and do our homework."

Melissa's sigh was exaggerated. "Yes, boss. Whatever you say. I guess, since I'm staying at your house all weekend, I'm at your mercy."

Carrie smiled. "Personally, I'm glad Toni and Abe are gone. It's fun having you here. Do you think they'll call you again before they get home?"

Melissa shrugged. "Maybe, but I doubt it. They get pretty caught up in each other, if you know what I mean. Not that I mind. I think it's great. It's just that they forget everyone else when they're together. I'm glad they at least remembered to give me a quick call yesterday to let me know they got there safely. Toni said she loves the bed and breakfast where they're staying. Abe picked it out. And then he took her on a picnic lunch by the ocean. She said they didn't get back to their room until late afternoon."

"He's very romantic, isn't he?"

"That's for sure. They're crazy about each other, and he's always doing little things to surprise her. This was kind of a big thing, though."

Carrie nodded. "They both seemed excited when I saw them the day before they left. No doubt they'll bring lots of pictures home with them."

Melissa started to say she doubted they'd spend much time taking pictures, but before she could speak, Carrie's mom came outside, carrying the portable phone.

"It's for you," she said, her eyebrows raised slightly as she handed the phone to Melissa.

"Really?" She glanced at Carrie. "I guess I was wrong about them not calling again." She put the phone to her ear. "Hello?"

Melissa clutched the phone tighter when she heard the rich male voice on the other end of the line. She could feel her palms growing clammy. "Hi, Melissa. It's Eric. I hope you don't mind me calling you at your friend's house, but I tried your home number and no one was there, and I know you and Carrie are always together, so . . ."

Melissa recognized the familiar flush creeping up her face. "No, I . . . it's OK. I . . ."

"So how are you? Are you busy?"

"Busy? Well, no, I . . ." Once again she glanced at Carrie, who was studying her with a confused expression. Melissa dropped her gaze. "No, we were just—I mean, I was—about to do some homework."

"Really? For which class?"

"Oh, well, several classes, really, but mostly geometry. I have a lot of problems with that subject."

"You're kidding! That was my favorite class last year—got straight As every quarter. Hey, how about us getting together sometime, and I can help you with it?"

Melissa swallowed. This was too good to be true. This good-looking senior was actually calling her and wanting to spend time with her— not that doing homework together was exactly a date, but . . .

"Melissa, are you there?"

"Yes. I just . . . I don't know. Carrie and I were about to go work on it together."

"No problem. Maybe next time. I really would like to spend some time with you though. Maybe we could go to a movie or out to eat or something. I have a car, you know. An '84 El Camino."

Melissa nodded, then realized he couldn't see her. "I know. I've seen it. It's really nice."

She could almost hear the smile in his voice. "Really? You like it? Then it's a date. We've got to go somewhere in it really soon. You name the time and place, and I'll be there."

Melissa could feel her friend staring at her, but she willed herself not to look up. "Well, I'm kind of tied up this weekend. My sister and her husband are gone, and . . ."

"No problem. Let's shoot for next weekend, OK? We can talk about it when I see you at school."

Once again Melissa found herself nodding. "OK. Sure. We'll talk about it when I see you."

As she clicked off the phone, she raised her eyes to meet Carrie's questioning stare. Until now they had always shared everything with each other. No secrets, not ever. But this? Somehow she sensed that her friend would not approve, even though she wasn't completely sure why.

~~~

Toni's head rested comfortably on Abe's shoulder as they lay in their four-poster bed, the soft comforter spread across them and the sound of the surf rising and falling outside the open French doors. Abe thought it had been the most perfect weekend imaginable. He only wished it didn't have to end so quickly. Still, he knew there was no point in trying to convince Toni to extend their trip; there were just too many responsibilities waiting for them at home.

"What's on your mind, detective?" Toni asked, rising up on her elbow to look down at him. The room was dark, but Abe could still see the outline of her face in the moonlight spilling in through the window and open door. He wondered if they would ever be married long enough that he would stop being overwhelmed with her beauty. He doubted it.

"You," he said, reaching up to trace the outline of her mouth. "I was just thinking about how much I love you, what a wonderful weekend we've had, how I wish it would never end."

She leaned down and kissed him. "It has been wonderful, hasn't it? Thanks to you."

"And a certain travel agent."

"True." She kissed him again. "I'll have to remember to put her name on my Christmas card list."

"Not a bad idea. Maybe we can get her to give us a discount next time."

"Next time? You plan to do this again?"

"Every chance I get."

"Hmm. We're going to have to find a way to make a lot of money so we can take all these trips."

"Maybe you could write a best-selling novel, and we'd be set for life."

Toni laughed. "Right. And maybe I'll buy a lotto ticket and win a million dollars."

"Hey, it could happen. The best seller, I mean. You haven't given up on your dream of writing, have you?"

Toni was silent for a moment before answering. "No, I haven't. In fact, I've actually started on a book. Would you like to see it?"

"You brought it with you?"

"Yes. I'm not sure why. Maybe I wanted to show it to you. I really don't know why I packed it."

Abe sat up and flipped on the lamp next to the bed. "So where is it? Bring it on. I'm ready to read."

Toni blinked at the sudden light. "Right now? You want to read it now?"

"Sure. Why not? It would be the perfect ending to a perfect weekend. And if I don't read it now, I won't have time before we leave."

"Are you sure you don't want to wait and read it on the plane?"

"I'm sure, I'm sure. Come on, Matthews, stop stalling. I want to see your masterpiece."

"Well, I don't know that I'd call it a masterpiece."

"I don't care what you call it. I just want to read it."

Toni got out of bed and padded over to the closet, where she pulled a large manila envelope from her suitcase. "Here it is," she said, coming back to bed and handing it to him. "I've titled it *Storm on the Horizon*. What do you think?"

"I think you're incredible," Abe answered, taking the envelope from her and pulling out the fifty or so sheets of paper. "I'll let you know what I think about *Storm on the Horizon* as soon as I'm finished reading it."

"It's only four chapters. I'm not done yet."

Abe didn't answer her. Leaning back on his pillow, he began to read the opening paragraph—and already he was hooked.

CHAPTER 4

Sophie sat in the living room in her favorite chair, a battered old rocker that had been in her family for years, and ignored the gathering darkness. It didn't even occur to her to get up and turn on a light or to think about fixing herself something to eat. Her dog-eared copy of the *Tanakh*, or Old Testament Scriptures, sat on her lap, still open to the passage in Isaiah that she'd read a couple of hours earlier. It was a familiar section of Scripture, particularly the final verse of chapter 35, one she had read hundreds of times through the years and even memorized as a child. But suddenly it had jumped out at her as if she were seeing it for the first time, and she couldn't understand why.

Those ransomed by ADONAI will return
And come with singing to Tziyon,

On their heads will be everlasting joy.
They will acquire gladness and joy,
While sorrow and sighing will flee.

The ransomed will return to Zion, she thought. *Yes, I know that. The remnant of Israel who have been faithful to Torah will once again live in the land. Even now, many have returned, and Israel lives once again. And yet most are not faithful to Torah. Many do not even believe in you, Adonai, and of those who do, few truly serve you. And sorrow and sighing certainly haven't ceased for those who live there. Daily there are murders, suicide bombings, rumors of wars, failed peace accords. And yet I know your Word is true. So what are you trying to tell me? Could it be that you are calling me to make* aliyah, *to return to Israel? Or is it something else? And what is it about the word* ransom? *I have come across it so often in the Scriptures lately, and I feel certain that the word is a key to what you want me to understand. Help me, Adonai. Open my understanding.*

∾∾∾

Melissa wasn't sure why she was sitting in the law office that Wednesday afternoon, waiting to see Brad Anderson. Even though they were close—big-brother, little-sister close—she still couldn't pinpoint why she felt the need to see Toni's former fiancé. But here she was, and she knew Brad would be glad to see her, as he always was.

Eric had been glad to see her too; that was obvious on Monday morning. He'd been waiting for her near her locker when she arrived at school, smiling his dazzling smile and insisting on walking her to class. She'd been relieved that Carrie wasn't with her that morning, as she still hadn't told her about her conversation with Eric the previous Saturday. After hanging up the phone that day, she knew Carrie had been waiting for an explanation of the call, but she had ignored her friend's silent questions and started chattering about the need to get busy on their homework right away. They had done so, and the subject of her phone call had not come up again, but Melissa knew it had caused a strain between them that had put a real damper on the rest of the weekend. And with Eric starting to show up at her locker fairly regularly and accompanying her to most of her classes, the strain between Melissa and Carrie was growing. She knew she was going to have to discuss it with her best friend sooner or later, but until she better understood what she was feeling about Eric Fullbright and what she was going to do about it, she had decided to keep it to herself.

Now, as she eyed the firm's new receptionist, she wondered if her emotional turmoil over Eric had something to do with her visit to Brad. She wondered, too, if she would have the nerve to bring up the subject with him and, if so, how she would broach it. She supposed she would just have to play it by ear and see where their conversation took them.

The receptionist smiled at her, and Melissa noticed how attractive she was. The petite redhead had worked for the firm for slightly more than a month now, but beyond a pleasant hello and a few other words of perfunctory conversation, they hadn't really talked much. All Melissa knew about her was that her name was Jeanine Simmons, she had just moved to the area from back east somewhere, and she didn't wear a wedding ring. She appeared to be in her mid-twenties, maybe slightly younger than Toni, and seemed to be efficient at her new job. Melissa returned her smile just as Brad walked into the reception area and made a beeline toward her with his arms outstretched.

"Melissa! What a great surprise."

She hugged him, then looked up as she pulled back. "I hope you don't mind. I was just heading home from school and thought I'd stop by."

Brad's warm smile lit up his hazel eyes. "Of course I don't mind. I'm always happy to see you. Come on in. You want a soda or something?"

Melissa shook her head. "No, I'm fine. It's warm outside, so I stopped and picked up some juice and drank it on the way over here."

Brad draped his arm across her shoulder. "Well, then, let's go into my office. I don't have another appointment for half an hour." He looked at the receptionist. "Hold my calls, will you, Jeanine?"

Jeanine's smile was more tentative than it had been earlier, and Melissa wondered if she imagined the flush on her cheeks and the slight tremor in her voice as she answered, "Yes, Mr. Anderson." Just as they reached Brad's office, Melissa turned back for a quick look. Jeanine was watching them, though she quickly turned away when Melissa caught her eye. So she was right—Jeanine was interested in Brad. She wondered if her "big brother" had figured that out yet.

"What's up with Jeanine?" she asked as soon as they'd closed the office door behind them and she was seated across the desk from Brad. She tried not to grin while she awaited his answer, but it didn't work.

Brad looked puzzled. "I don't understand. She's turning out to be a great employee, if that's what you mean, but . . ."

Melissa's grin widened. "But . . . ?"

"Sorry," Brad answered, shrugging his shoulders. "I'm afraid I just don't know what you're getting at."

"That's what I figured," she said. "You're real smart about some things, Bro, but when it comes to women," she said, shaking her head, "you're hopeless, you know."

Brad nodded. "No kidding. If I weren't, I might be your brother-in-law right now."

Melissa's smile faded. "That wasn't your fault. It just wasn't meant to be."

"True. I know that now. But it was a hard thing to accept, after all the years Toni and I . . ." He stopped, waving his hand as if to dismiss the topic. "Enough of that. No sense rehashing ancient history. So what were you trying to say about Jeanine?"

"I was trying to tell you the obvious—that she's got a thing for you."

Brad's eyebrows rose. "A 'thing'? As in, a crush?"

"Absolutely."

Brad shook his head. "No, I don't think so. Your imagination is just running away with you. I'm her boss—*one* of her three bosses here in the firm—and she's the employee. That's it. Nothing more."

"You really are hopeless, aren't you? You can't even see what's right in front of you. But I saw it—the way she looked at you. I'm telling you, Bro, she's interested."

"And I'm telling you she's not. So let's forget about my love life—or lack thereof—and talk about you. What are you up to today? You didn't just come down here to see if my receptionist had a 'thing' for me, did you?"

Melissa resisted the temptation to squirm in her chair. She hated it when she didn't have a direct answer for Brad. He always seemed to see right through her, and she wasn't sure she wanted to know what he saw right now. But if she didn't want to talk about Eric, why had she come?

"I don't know," she said. "Maybe I just missed you and wanted to say hello."

Brad eyed her for a moment before answering. "Maybe." Melissa remembered how Toni used to talk about Brad's "courtroom face," and she wondered if this was how a witness felt on the stand when Brad was doing the cross-examination. She was relieved when he changed the subject.

"So how are Toni and Abe? I heard they were away for a while."

"Yes. They went to San Diego for a long weekend. Just got back on Monday. They're fine. Said they had a great time."

"I'm glad."

The brief moment of silence made Melissa uncomfortable. She knew Brad hadn't let go of his initial question about her reason for being here, but he was letting her work up to telling him about it in her own time.

"And how's Carrie?" Brad asked. "Any change in her condition?"

"Not really. We all keep hoping, but . . ." She paused, shuddering as she remembered the day of the shooting less than a year earlier. She and Carrie had been on their way to a school assembly when the lone gunman, a former student named Tom Blevins, had opened fire, killing a teacher and wounding several students and faculty members, including Carrie, before he himself was shot and arrested by a couple of law enforcement officers who were at the school to do an antidrug, antiviolence presentation at the assembly. Thanks to some super-sleuthing on the part of Abe and Toni, it soon came to light that Tom had been involved with a female teacher who had a grudge against the principal for ending their affair. She had used Tom to get even, and now she and Tom were each serving a twenty-five-to-life sentence.

Carrie's injuries had left her in a wheelchair, paralyzed from the waist down. Because the bullet had not severed her spinal cord, the doctors held out a slim hope that the teenager might one day walk again. But to date there had been no improvement. In the meantime Tom Blevins, now eighteen, had become a Christian, thanks in great part to the combined efforts of Carrie and the jail chaplain. Carrie's ability to forgive Tom, even writing letters to tell him of her forgiveness and God's love for him, had impacted Melissa almost as deeply as it had Tom, and the memory made her feel even more guilty about not confiding in her best friend about her feelings for Eric.

"I . . ." She had no idea what she was going to say, or why, but she knew she could trust Brad to keep her words to himself. "I think maybe Carrie's a little bit upset with me right now."

Brad's eyes narrowed, mirroring his concern. "Really? Why?"

Melissa swallowed, wishing she'd accepted Brad's offer of a soda. Her mouth was dry, and she clasped her hands tightly in her lap. "There's this boy . . ."

Brad smiled. "Ah. Now I understand your obsession with romance. This isn't about Jeanine or me—it's about you and . . . who? Anyone I know?"

Melissa shook her head. "I don't think so. He's new here. Moved with his family from Nebraska. He's a senior."

"An older man. Does he have a name?"

"Eric Fullbright."

"Hmm. Well, you're right. I don't think I know him. Don't recognize the name anyway. But he must be special if he's got your attention."

"Oh, he is. Special, I mean. He's so good-looking, and . . ." Her voice trailed off as she realized how immature she sounded. Yes, Eric Fullbright was definitely good-looking. But what else did she know about him? He said he got straight As in geometry, and he had a cool car. Somehow she didn't think that would be enough to impress Brad.

"Does Toni know about Eric?"

Melissa shook her head. "No. I haven't said anything to anybody but you. He's been walking me to class, and he's called me a few times. He wants me to go somewhere with him sometime."

"A date."

"I guess so."

"Then you need to talk to Toni about it. You know that."

Melissa hesitated, then nodded. "I've been putting it off."

"Don't. Just tell her. She'll understand. And she'll give you good advice."

"I know."

Brad paused, then asked, "So why would Carrie be upset with you about this?"

"I'm not sure. I think it's because she knows I'm keeping it from her, but somehow I just sense she wouldn't approve."

"You and Carrie have been friends a long time. You trust her, don't you?"

"Completely. But . . ."

"So trust her on this one too. Talk to her and see what she says— after you've talked to Toni. If the guy's worth your time, he won't mind your getting input from other people. OK?"

Melissa nodded. "OK. You're right. I guess I knew that. I just needed to hear someone say it. And I can always trust you to tell me the truth."

"That's because I care about you."

"I know."

Brad smiled. "Anything else?"

Melissa shook her head and returned his smile. "No. I guess that's about it."

"Good." Brad rose from his chair. "Come on. I'll walk you out. But stick close to me, will you? If Jeanine's after me like you say she is, I might need some protection."

Laughing, they exited the office and made their way down the hall. Sure enough, Jeanine was waiting for them, her cheeks flushed a bright pink and her eyes following their every move.

~~~

It was Thursday evening and Toni had just finished putting the last of the dishes in the dishwasher when the phone rang. Grabbing the receiver from the kitchen wall phone, she sat down at the table. "Hello?"

"Toni? Is that you, my dear?"

Toni smiled. "April! How nice to hear from you. How are you?"

"I'm fine. And you? And Abe and Melissa?"

"We're all doing great. Abe and I just got back from a long weekend in San Diego. It was wonderful. It's my turn for kitchen duty, so he's watching TV, and Melissa's in her room doing homework—geometry, I think. She's really struggling with that subject."

April laughed. "I can certainly relate to that. Math was never my strong point. But I'm sure she'll get through it. I remember how my Julie struggled when she was taking that class. . . ."

The elderly lady's voice trailed off, and Toni knew she was thinking of her granddaughter who had died less than two years earlier. It had been a tragic situation. The young girl had run off with a man named Carlo, a member of the baby-selling ring that had been responsible for Julie's death, as well as Toni's father's when he got too close to finding out what had happened to the missing girl. The mutual tragedy, along with the ensuing trials, had thrown April Lippincott and the Matthews family together, and they had become fast friends.

But they hadn't seen each other since Abe and Toni's wedding the previous spring. Toni decided she'd better change the subject before April
got too caught up in thinking about Julie. And she certainly knew how
easily that could happen. She still found herself slipping into periods
of depression when something reminded her of her father.

"So how's the weather in Colorado? Is it turning cold yet?"

"It certainly is, my dear. In fact, we're expecting our first snowfall
tonight."

"Wow, that soon? Sounds to me like you need to break away and
come out and enjoy some of our Indian summer. It's been beautiful
here."

"Actually, that's why I called. I wondered if I might come for a
short visit. My daughter and her husband are going on an extended
vacation, and I just don't think I can deal with being here alone right
now. Would you mind terribly?"

"Mind? April, we'd love it. You know you're always welcome here—
anytime. You're family now, remember?"

Toni could hear the smile in April's voice. "Yes, I remember.
Walking you down the aisle at your wedding was one of the great
privileges of my life."

"And mine. So when are you coming?"

"Oh, well, I don't have my ticket yet, but I can call and make reservations in the morning and then call you back. Would that be all
right?"

"Absolutely. Just let us know when and we'll be at the airport to
pick you up." Toni paused. "We've missed you."

"And I've missed all of you. I'll be looking forward to our visit, my
dear."

By the time she hung up, Toni was smiling. It would be wonderful
once again to see the wise, gentle lady from Colorado, the one with

the faith of a lion and the heart of a lamb. She knew Abe and Melissa would be as happy about the visit as she, and she somehow sensed that it was God's timing, as April's visits had been in the past. She only wondered what purpose God had in sending April to them at this particular time.

CHAPTER 5

Melissa's shoulders drooped and her step lagged as she stared at her feet and exited the hated geometry class. She was almost certain she'd failed the pop quiz, and she wondered why she even bothered to try. *It's impossible,* she thought. *I'll never understand this stuff! Everyone else seems to get it except me.*

"Bad class?"

She jumped when she heard the voice in front of her, but she knew immediately who it was. As Melissa raised her head, she was greeted by Eric's now familiar smile, and she marveled that he could so quickly elicit a return smile from her, particularly after her latest geometry disaster.

"How did you know?" she asked.

"Well, let's see. I could try telling you I'm psychic, but I don't think you'd buy it. So I guess I'll just tell you the truth. You walked out of there like you had cement bags tied to your feet—and one around your neck too. A dead giveaway, you know."

She sighed. "You're right. We had a pop quiz."

"Uh-oh. Should I ask how you did?"

Melissa shook her head. "Please don't."

Eric took her hand. It was the first time he had done anything like that, and Melissa, though surprised, was glad. She only hoped that her hand wouldn't start sweating and her face turn red. She also found herself thinking of Brad's advice to her earlier that week. She still hadn't talked to Toni about Eric, and she knew she couldn't put it off much longer.

"Look at the bright side," she heard Eric say. "At least it's the last class of the day, and it's Friday besides. No more school till Monday."

"I'm sure glad of that."

"Me too. In fact, I was just thinking about going somewhere to get a soda or something. Want to come with me?"

"Oh, I don't know. I . . ." Staring into his brown eyes, she tried to think of a plausible excuse, even while her heart was screaming at her to go. "I should probably get home."

Eric shrugged. "So I'll take you, right after we have our soda. It's not like we'll be gone long or anything. Come on. How can it hurt? We can even go over some of your geometry problems if you want."

Melissa opened her mouth to offer one last feeble protest but felt what little was left of her resolve melting within her. "OK," she said, nodding. "Why not? Maybe that's just what I need."

Eric's smile widened. "I've been wanting to take you for a ride in my car anyway, so this will be perfect. Come on. Let's grab our books and get out of here."

~~~

The early October sunlight was fading as Toni leaned back in the porch swing and sighed, realizing suddenly how close they were getting to the long, dark days of the Pacific Northwest winter. Soon they would be turning the clocks back, and it would be getting dark even sooner. The sunlit evenings of summer would be but a memory, and the reminder hit her as it always did this time of year—as a loss, evoking a feeling of sadness that she had never been able to identify or understand.

It had been that way for as long as she could remember, even before she lost her mother when she was twelve years old. Each year about this time the feeling returned, and each year she wondered why, because once winter arrived she really didn't mind it that much. As a result she had long since come to the conclusion that it really wasn't the anticipation of dreary winter days that evoked this inexplicable sadness within her but rather the passing of something warm and beautiful and full of life. A summer lived could not be relived, and as silly as that sounded, it somehow made her sad. It also made her that much more aware of the fact that this life would not last forever and that it was not all there was. She was grateful that God had given her such a wonderful husband, and she was confident that she couldn't possibly be any happier than she was right now—at least, not here on earth. But someday all that would pass away, and because of her close relationship with God, she knew beyond a shadow of a doubt that what lay ahead was so much better.

Maybe that's what this is all about, she mused, gazing out at the familiar backyard from her comfortable perch. *This vague sense of nostalgia and loss. Maybe, with the passing of summer, I'm just feeling a little bit homesick for heaven. Is that it, Father? Am I experiencing at least a hint of what Adam and Eve felt when they were banned from the garden, sent out from that beautiful place of never-ending summer, full of eternal life and fellowship with you? Am I homesick for heaven—and for you, Father?* She smiled. It did make a lot of sense, especially when she realized that the passing of winter to spring also evoked strong feelings within her, a renewed sense of hope and a promise of new life.

She heard Abe's car pull into the driveway, and she waited. She knew it wouldn't be long until he came out to join her. It was their favorite spot on nice evenings, and since they were all going out for dinner later, she didn't even have to rush inside to cook. She wondered if Melissa would want to bring Carrie along. The two girls had been inseparable since grammar school, and even the shooting that had placed Carrie in a wheelchair hadn't slowed down their relationship. In fact, Toni was sure that's where Melissa was right now. She thought about giving her a call to remind her about their dinner plans but thought better of it. Melissa had been as enthusiastic as she and Abe about their evening out when they discussed it that morning at breakfast. There was no way she was going to be late.

"Hey, gorgeous!" Abe's greeting preceded his appearance on the porch by a few seconds. Toni started to get up to greet him, but he shook his head. "Stay where you are," he said. "You look beautiful sitting there—comfortable too. I've been looking forward to joining you all afternoon."

She smiled and patted the empty cushion next to her. "And I've been looking forward to having you here beside me."

He sat down and put his arm around her shoulders, then kissed her. "So how does it feel to be a lady of leisure for a change?"

Toni laughed. "I come home two hours ahead of you, and suddenly I'm a lady of leisure? Actually, though, I have to admit, it's been nice. I didn't do one constructive thing. Just sat out here and relaxed and enjoyed what could easily be one of our last nice afternoons for a while."

"That's true. I just hope the good weather holds for April's visit. Must be awful to live in a place where snow starts so early and goes on for so long. I don't think I could handle Colorado for any length of time. I know we have lots of rain here, but at least we don't have to shovel it."

Toni laughed again. "You sound just like Dad. He used to say that all the time."

Abe smiled. "It's good to hear you talk about your dad without so much sadness in your voice."

Toni paused. "Sometimes I do OK, but other times . . ."

Abe kissed her again. "I know, sweetheart, believe me. I still miss my own parents, and it's been years. And my Uncle Sol . . ." He shook his head. "That's still pretty fresh, I'm afraid. And the way he died—somehow that makes it so much worse."

"He gave his life to save you."

"I know. And I love him for it, believe me. But if he just hadn't let himself get involved in that crime ring in the first place, he'd still be alive today. Maybe your father would too—and Julie."

They paused for a moment, as Abe nudged the swing back and forth with the toe of his shoe, causing the ancient swing to squeak. As she did every time she heard it, Toni thought that one of them should oil it, but she knew they wouldn't, because as soon as they got up and went into the house, they would forget about it until the next time they sat out here.

"So," she said, purposely changing the subject, "did you get much done after I left the office?"

Abe seemed to break out of his reverie and turned toward her. "On the Landry case? Not really. I thought sure I'd come up with some little clue by now, something to at least indicate that the guy was actually here when he called his mother two years ago. But so far, nothing. Makes me wonder if he really was in River View or just told her that. Maybe he was just passing through town and decided to stop and call her on the way. Although his brother seemed to think, from what his mother said, that he was living here. Not sure why he thought that, just a 'gut feeling,' he said. I'm going to meet with him on Monday and see if I can pull anything else out of him, something he may have forgotten or . . ." He paused. "Do you want to sit in on the meeting? Maybe you can pick up on something I'd miss."

Toni shrugged. "Sure, if you want me to. I haven't even met this guy yet, so why not? It's worth a try, I suppose. What's he like?"

"Not much different from what I've told you already. Middle-aged, slightly overweight, thinning brown hair. Sort of surly, maybe even a little secretive. Not really the kind of guy you'd expect to be scouring the earth for his long-lost brother, but you never know." Abe smiled down at her. "To tell you the truth, right now I really don't care much about old George Landry, or his missing brother. I'd rather hear about you. I thought you'd come home and get some writing done on your book."

"I meant to. That was my intention anyway. But I came out here to sit down for a few minutes, and . . . well, the rest is history. Guess I'd better get a lot more disciplined if I'm going to do anything serious with my writing."

"I wish you would. I'm eager to read the next chapter."

Toni smiled. "You really like it so far?"

"Like it? I love it. You've got me hanging on a hook, and I don't think it's right to spend your spare time daydreaming instead of writing the next installment. I want to see what happens next."

"So do I." Toni giggled when Abe raised his eyebrows questioningly. "To tell you the truth," she explained, "I'm not sure what's going to happen next. That's why I was out here—trying to figure that out. But I guess I got a bit sidetracked."

"Well, no more sidetracking, OK? Come on, when can I read the next chapter? Set yourself a deadline."

"OK, you're right. How does one week from today sound?"

"It doesn't sound as good as tonight, but I guess that's not going to happen, is it?"

"Absolutely not. In fact, we should go in and get changed soon. We do have a dinner date, you know."

"I know. I didn't forget. So where's Melissa?"

Toni frowned as she glanced at her watch in what little was left of the day's light. "I imagine she's at Carrie's, although she usually calls or comes home before this. I think maybe I'll go in and give her a call. Maybe she'd like to bring Carrie along, and we could just pick them up on the way."

"Sounds good to me. I can't remember when I last got to take three beautiful women out for dinner."

Toni stood up, then leaned over and kissed him on the forehead. "And don't even try to remember, detective, because I don't want to hear about it."

She could hear Abe chuckle as she walked into the house and went to use the phone on the kitchen wall. Punching in the numbers for Carrie's home, she wondered if she should wear a dress or slacks. She imagined the temperature would drop considerably in the next couple of hours, so slacks sounded more practical.

"Hello?" It was Carrie's voice that greeted her, and Toni smiled.

"Hi, Carrie. It's Toni. How are you?"

"I'm fine, thanks. And you?"

Was it her imagination, or did Carrie sound a bit standoffish, not at all like her normal, bubbly self? "I'm fine too. I just called to remind

Melissa about our dinner date tonight. Would you like to come along?"

Carrie's pause before answering was too long. Something was wrong.

"Dinner? Tonight? Um, I . . . I can't," she said finally. "I have a lot of homework, and . . ."

"But it's Friday," Toni reminded her. "Surely you can break away long enough for a nice dinner. We love having you with us, you know that. I'm surprised Melissa hasn't already asked you. Can I talk with her for a moment?"

Carrie hesitated again. "She's not here."

The alarm bells began to ring in Toni's head. "What do you mean, she isn't there? Didn't she go home with you after school?"

"I'm afraid not."

"Well, then, have you seen her? Do you know where she is?"

"I saw her at school today."

"And after school?"

Another pause. "Toni, the last time I saw Melissa she was getting into the car with Eric Fullbright."

Toni's heart skipped a beat, and she gripped the receiver tighter. "Eric Fullbright? Who's that?"

The surprise in Carrie's voice sounded genuine. "You don't know who Eric Fullbright is? Melissa hasn't told you?"

"Told me what? Carrie, what are you talking about? Who is Eric Fullbright, and why is Melissa with him?"

"Eric is a new student at school. A senior. He and his family moved here recently from Nebraska. He and Melissa have been, well, spending a lot of time together lately. But today is the first time I ever saw her get into the car with him. I thought she would have talked to you about him by now."

Toni closed her eyes and took a deep breath. "Melissa hasn't said a word to me about any of this. But obviously she has to you. What do you think about it, Carrie? What's this Eric like? And why would she keep her relationship with him a secret from me?"

"Actually, she hasn't talked to me about him either. I kept hoping she would, but I really don't know Eric, Toni. He seems OK, but I just don't know."

Toni took a deep breath. She was going to have to deal with this quickly. "Thank you, Carrie. I'll check into it." She hung up the phone and sat down at the table, resting her head on her hands. This was just too much like that fateful afternoon slightly more than one year earlier when Melissa hadn't come home as expected. But then she had been kidnapped. This time, it seemed, she had gone willingly.

～～～

Melissa was nervous. She should have gone home long ago, or at least called. But she and Eric had picked up some sodas and driven to a nearby park and found a secluded spot under a tree where they had settled down for several hours. Eric had promised they wouldn't stay long, but they had started talking about geometry, school in general, their lives, their likes and dislikes, their dreams, and the next thing Melissa knew, the sun was setting, and the day had gotten away from them.

"I really need to get home," she'd insisted, wishing one of them had a cell phone. The last thing she wanted was to worry Toni and Abe; she only hoped they still assumed she was at Carrie's. Maybe she could get home before they found out otherwise. As they drove the ten or so miles to her house, she promised herself that the first thing she would do when she arrived was sit down with Toni and tell her about Eric.

Less than a block from home, Melissa worked up her courage and asked, "Can you drop me off here? I live on the next street, but . . ." When Eric seemed puzzled, she hurried to explain. "I know I should invite you in, but I haven't said anything to Toni about you yet, and I need to tell her right away—tonight. I think it would be best if I do that alone."

Eric nodded. "Whatever you say. I don't want to get you in any trouble."

Melissa smiled gratefully as he pulled to the curb. "Thanks. I knew you'd understand." But before she could grab her books and reach for the door, Eric put his arm around her shoulder and pulled her close. His kiss was gentle and warm, and she could hear her heart pounding in her ears, even as she returned his kiss and wished it would never end.

And then he released her and pulled back. "I want to see you again," he said, his voice husky as he gazed into her eyes. "Soon. Like tomorrow maybe?"

"I . . ." Melissa swallowed. She wanted to see him again too—tomorrow, and the next day, and the next. But she had to talk to Toni first. "Can you call me in the morning, and we'll talk about it then?"

"OK. Till morning." He kissed her again, then reached across and opened the door for her. His nearness made her lightheaded, and she was still breathing hard when she got out of the car and watched him drive away before turning and heading toward home. Only then did she remember the dinner date she'd made with Abe and Toni that morning at breakfast.

CHAPTER 6

If Melissa thought her heart was racing when Eric kissed her, it only got worse when she walked in the front door and saw Toni, with Abe standing beside her in the entryway, his arm around her shoulders. When Melissa caught sight of the look of relief that washed over their faces when they saw her, she knew she was too late. Obviously they had already found out she hadn't been with Carrie; what else they knew, she could only guess.

"I . . . I'm sorry I'm late," she said, trying to sound nonchalant. "I should have called, but—"

"But what?" Toni demanded, seemingly having regained her composure. "Eric didn't have a cell phone? You couldn't stop at a phone booth somewhere? Melissa, we were worried. We were just about to go out looking for you."

Her last shred of hope for being the one to break the news about Eric to Toni evaporated before her eyes. Her sister and brother-in-law had somehow discovered that she'd spent the afternoon with Eric Fullbright. For the first time she could remember, Melissa regretted being in a family full of detectives.

Before she could respond, Abe intervened. "Let's all go sit in the living room and talk about this calmly. Standing here in the entryway arguing isn't going to solve anything."

Melissa could see Toni's resistance melt as she gave in and allowed her husband to steer her toward the living room couch, with Melissa trailing behind, scolding herself along the way. Why hadn't she thought to call? Why hadn't she taken Brad's advice and talked to Toni about Eric before now? This was not at all the way she'd hoped to introduce the topic of Eric Fullbright into their family, but it looked as if she had waited too long and she now had no choice in the matter. The cat was out of the bag, as her dad used to say, and she was just going to have to deal with it.

As Abe and Toni sat down on the couch, Melissa perched carefully on the recliner across from them. She felt she needed some distance from them right now, though she desperately wanted to throw her arms around them and tell them how sorry she was for worrying them, and assure them it would never happen again. She also wanted to tell them how wonderful Eric was, and how much they were going to like him— but she wasn't too sure they would accept that at the moment.

After a brief, uncomfortable silence, Toni spoke. "So? Are you going to tell us where you've been and what you've been up to? And who is this Eric Fullbright you were with? Why haven't you told us about him before this? Carrie says you've been spending a lot of time together lately. Why didn't you say something? We're a family, Melissa. We don't keep secrets from one another. What's going on?"

Abe laid his hand on Toni's arm. "Slow down, sweetheart. Give her a chance to explain."

Melissa breathed a silent prayer of thanks for Abe, even as she asked God how and where to start. "I met Eric at school—not long ago, really. He just moved here from Nebraska with his family. He's a senior, and . . ." She stopped herself. She'd been about to say he had a nice car, but she thought better of it. "He's a straight-A student, and he's good at geometry, and he offered to help me, and—"

Toni interrupted her. "Are you saying you were out with him today studying geometry somewhere? If so, where did you go? Were you studying in his car? His house? The library?"

Melissa swallowed. She wished she could say they had been doing homework, but she wasn't about to add a lie to this already awkward situation. "No," she said, shaking her head slightly. "We weren't studying, although he has offered to help me. Actually, I failed a pop quiz in geometry today—at least, I think I did—and he picked me up right after class, and I was feeling so bad, and he offered to take me for a soda, and . . ." She stopped and took a deep breath. She knew that she and Eric hadn't done anything wrong, and yet she felt so guilty. Was it because she had made Toni and Abe worry unnecessarily? Yes, that had to be the reason. She certainly hadn't meant to. If only she'd talked to Toni the way Brad had told her to.

"I'm really sorry," she said. "I didn't mean to upset you or worry you. I didn't think that—"

"Exactly." Toni interrupted her again. "You didn't think, except about yourself. Did you even remember that we had a date to go out for dinner tonight? Didn't it occur to you that we would be concerned when you didn't come home, especially once we'd called Carrie's and found out you weren't there? The only reason we know about Eric was because Carrie assumed you'd already talked to us about him, so she told us she'd seen you getting into his car after school." Toni shook her head. "Melissa, this just isn't like you. You always call when you're going to be late. You know how I worry, especially after what happened last year."

Melissa nodded. Her voice was hushed as she dropped her eyes. "I know. I thought of that too—just now. I'm truly sorry. I didn't mean to . . ."

Abe cleared his throat. "We know you didn't mean to worry us, Melissa. You're normally a thoughtful and considerate person. Maybe that's why we're so concerned about this Eric Fullbright. No one seems to know much of anything about him, other than the fact that he's new in town, he's older than you, and he has a car. With your behavior being so out of character, we can't help but wonder if he's a bad influence on you."

Melissa's head snapped up. "Oh, no," she said. "Really. He's not a bad influence at all. He's a very nice person, a good student, and you'd like him if you just gave him a chance. I know you would. And I wanted to tell you about him, but . . ."

"But you didn't," Toni said. "Why?"

Melissa shrugged. "I'm . . . not sure. I guess I didn't know at first how I felt, so I didn't want to talk to anyone about it. But then I went to see Brad, and he told me I should talk to you right away."

Toni raised her eyebrows. "You told Brad, but you didn't tell us?"

"I hadn't really planned to tell him. It just sort of happened. And he said I should tell you, but . . ."

"But you didn't. Well, I'm glad he at least gave you good advice, although it would have been nice if you'd taken it. More importantly, I wish you'd talked to us instead of him. According to Carrie, you haven't even confided in her about your relationship with Eric, and that only adds to our concern. You two have always been so close, and you've always talked about everything—until now."

Melissa closed her eyes and took a deep breath. She was feeling more and more guilty by the minute, and yet she really didn't think she should. This was all so confusing. The only thing she was certain of right now was that she wanted to see Eric again. She was already looking forward to his phone call tomorrow. But what would she tell him? Would Toni and Abe agree to let her go out with him?

She took another deep breath and opened her eyes, forcing herself to look straight at them. She might as well just say it and get it over with. "Eric is going to call me in the morning. He wants me to go somewhere with him tomorrow."

Abe and Toni looked at each other, then back at Melissa, before Abe asked, "Where does he want you to go?"

"I . . . don't know. We didn't really decide on a place. We just want to go somewhere—together."

For a moment no one spoke. Finally Toni stood up. "I think it's too soon for that," she said, her voice steady and determined. "Abe and I need to discuss this; we'll talk to you later. And whatever we decide, you're not going anywhere with this boy until we've had a chance to get to know him. Is that understood?"

Melissa opened her mouth. She wanted to tell Toni that she really didn't care what she or Abe said; she was going to see Eric, and that was that. But she couldn't. Too many years of love and respect prevented her, and so she nodded in agreement. It was going to be a long night, and she had no idea what she was going to tell Eric when he called in the morning. Remembering the feel of his lips on hers, she got up and walked slowly to her room. Dinner was the furthest thing from her mind.

~~~

Melissa had stayed up late, writing in her journal and trying to sort through her thoughts and make some sense of her feelings. It hadn't helped much, and she had tossed and turned for hours after turning off her light. Finally, after a restless sleep filled with disjointed dreams, mostly about Eric, she had managed to force down some juice and toast when Toni called her to breakfast. But when neither Abe nor Toni had brought up the subject of Eric or her desire to see him again, she had retreated to her room to await his call. She was determined to be the one to answer the phone, so she reread her journal entries from the night before and then lay on her bed, staring at the ceiling, listening to the clock tick on the bed stand beside her. Had he said what time he would call? She didn't think so, but she was sure it would be soon. And when he did, what would she say? What would she tell him when he asked her what time he could pick her up or where she wanted to go? The confusion that had swirled around her since she'd first met Eric continued to grow—and yet, so did the excitement. The mention of his name made her heart pound in her ears. And his kiss . . .

Melissa had to admit, she'd never been kissed before—not like that, anyway. A couple of boys had given her a peck on the lips over the last year or so, but it had meant nothing to her, and she hadn't cared if they ever did it again. With Eric, it was different—so different. She couldn't wait for him to kiss her again, to feel his arms around her, or his hand holding hers.

Was this what love was all about? Could it be that she and Eric were in love, that he was the one who would become her husband someday? In some ways she felt foolish even thinking about it, since she wouldn't be sixteen for two more weeks. And yet Toni and Brad had already been a steady couple when they were still in high school. A lot of students were paired off, and many seemed to be in love. Why not she and Eric? He certainly made her feel like she was in love. And if she was, she had to admit, she liked it—a lot.

Except for what it was doing to her relationships at home. That part she didn't like at all. But it really wasn't Eric's fault, she reminded herself. If it was anyone's fault, it was hers. She should have told Toni and Abe right away. She should have brought Eric home to meet them, and they would have seen what a great guy he is. They would have approved of him, she was sure. But now she had to find a way to convince them to give him a chance.

She jumped when the phone rang, pouncing on it before it had time to ring a second time.

"Hello?"

"Melissa?"

She swallowed, trying to calm her heart. How was it possible that just his voice could have such a strong effect on her? Maybe she was right. Maybe she really was in love with Eric Fullbright.

"Eric," she said. "I was waiting for your call."

"I'm glad. I wanted to call earlier, but I was afraid I'd wake somebody up."

She smiled at his thoughtfulness. Abe and Toni would be impressed, she was sure. "Thanks. That was nice of you. But we've all been up for hours."

"Me too. It's beautiful outside. Have you noticed? A perfect day for a ride in the country. I was thinking about going to the park for a picnic. What do you think? I can pick you up anytime you say."

Melissa's heart sank. There was nothing she'd like better, but she knew she couldn't—not until after she'd talked to Toni and Abe. But what if they said no? Then what? How could she tell Eric that she couldn't go out with him? How could she bear it if she weren't allowed to see him at all? And what would he think of her if she told him her older sister and brother-in-law had forbidden her to date him? He was a senior, after all, and she was only a junior. Maybe he'd find an older, more mature girl to go out with him, one whose family didn't treat her like a child. The thought started her heart racing again, and she refused to consider the possibility.

"I'd like that," she said, "but I'm not sure what we have planned today. Can I talk to my sister and then let you know?"

"Sure. I'll call you in a couple of hours. How's that?"

Melissa nodded. A couple of hours. That didn't give her much time to convince Toni and Abe to allow her to go out with him. But she was going to have to try. "OK. I'll talk to you then."

Eric hesitated before he spoke. "I miss you. I thought about you all night."

"Me too," she answered, her voice barely above a whisper. It was all she could trust herself to say.

"I'm glad. Talk to you in a couple of hours."

She hung up the phone and wondered if she dared to ask God for the right words to convince Toni and Abe to let her go out with Eric. In the end she breathed a quick prayer for a miracle, then got up off her bed and went out to present her case.

～～～

The sun seemed thinner and paler as it began its slide down the mid-afternoon sky. It was obvious that summer was over, but at least it wasn't raining, and for that Toni was grateful. She wanted so much for April's visit to be a pleasant one.

Abe had stayed after church for a men's ministry meeting, and Melissa had gone home with the Bosworths. Toni had left right after the service, picked up a sandwich to eat on the way, and driven straight to the airport to pick up April, whose plane was due in at three-thirty. Now, as she waited alone for the shuttle that would take her from the parking lot to the terminal, she couldn't help but hope that Melissa and Carrie were finally having a long overdue heart-to-heart about Eric Fullbright.

What a weekend it had been so far. After Friday night's fiasco with Melissa's having been out with Eric, Toni and Abe had decided against going out to eat, settling instead for tuna sandwiches, and had then stayed up talking late into the night. Toni was all for banning any further contact between Melissa and Eric, period. Abe, on the other hand, had encouraged her to at least meet the kid and give him a chance. Toni knew he was right, but she had resisted his arguments and ignored the subject when she saw Melissa at breakfast on Saturday. But then, an hour or so later, Melissa had come out of her room after a phone conversation with Eric and practically begged her and Abe to let her go out with him. They had finally come to a compromise: Melissa would not go anywhere with Eric this weekend, but she could invite him over for dinner that night so they could all get to know him. Then they would decide.

Toni smiled. Looking back on last night's visit with Eric Fullbright, she wasn't sure who had been more nervous, she or Melissa. It was obvious that Melissa was a wreck, her eyes darting from Eric to Toni to Abe and back again, trying to read everyone's reaction to everything that was said or done. And, she admitted to herself, she hadn't been much better. She had studied Eric as if he were some sort of science experiment, trying to dissect him and find something that would justify her objections to Melissa's having a relationship with him. Unfortunately, she didn't find anything—nothing concrete anyway. He seemed nice enough, but she still had her reservations. And when she'd invited him to attend church with them the next morning, his answer of "Thanks, but I don't do church" hadn't helped his cause one bit.

The shuttle arrived and she climbed onboard, chewing her lip as she spotted an empty space and plunked down between an elderly gentleman reading a newspaper and a teenager sporting a nose ring. *How appropriate*, she thought. *Here I am, stuck in the middle between two different generations. I'm not exactly a senior citizen by any means, but I'm no teenager anymore either. I'm only twelve years older than Melissa, but right now it seems like a lot more. But Abe's right. We've got to handle this with lots of patience and prayer. It would be so easy just to tell her to forget Eric. He's older than she is, and he doesn't even go to church. What could they possibly have in common? Why couldn't she go out with some nice Christian boy? But no, she has to pick some heathen.*

She stopped herself. That wasn't fair. Just because he didn't "do church" didn't make him a heathen—although the chances that he was a true believer were just about slim to none, of that she was certain. But then Abe wasn't a believer when she met him, and look how that turned out. Still, she reminded herself defensively, she had refused to get seriously involved with him until he received Jesus as his Savior. Melissa, on the other hand, was rushing headlong into a relationship with someone who might never have any interest in God whatsoever.

She sighed. One step at a time. That's what she had promised Abe, and that's the way they would deal with this situation. In fairness Eric had been polite and seemed intelligent and willing to talk about himself and his family. Maybe they could get the two families together sometime and see what the rest of the Fullbright clan was like. She couldn't help but smile again as she thought of the case of nerves a gathering like that would set off.

The driver announced her stop, and Toni got up and exited the shuttle, suddenly more eager than ever to welcome April Lippincott back into their home and their lives. If ever she needed the benefit of an older woman's advice, it was now.

CHAPTER 7

Carrie had missed Melissa, and she was glad she had agreed to come over after church, but she still felt as if they weren't really connecting. It was the first time in all the years they'd known each other that she could remember feeling that way, and she didn't like it one bit.

It was also one of the first times she could remember Melissa's opting to retreat to the bedroom rather than sit outside on such a nice day. Things weren't right, it was obvious, but Carrie just wasn't sure how to broach the subject, though she had wanted to ever since the first time she had seen Melissa and Eric together. The more she tried to think of a diplomatic approach to get the conversation going, the more she thought she should just jump right in with both feet and get it over with. But before she could make up her mind one way or the other, Melissa solved the problem for her.

"I guess I really messed up by keeping this Eric thing to myself, didn't I?"

Carrie raised her eyebrows, surprised that her friend had finally blurted out what had apparently been on both their minds all day. Praying silently for wisdom, she said, "I suppose it created some unnecessary problems."

Melissa nodded, her voice hushed as she spoke. "I know. I never meant for things to turn out the way they did, honest. I even talked to Brad about it last week, and he told me to talk to Toni right away. But I didn't. I waited too long, and she found out." She fixed her green eyes on Carrie. "But I want you to know that I don't blame you for telling her. I know you had no choice. I should have called Toni or gone home earlier." Her words drifted off, then a hopeful smile began to curve her lips. "But we did have Eric over for dinner last night. I think it went OK."

Carrie returned her smile. "That's good. I hope you're right. Abe and Toni didn't say anything after Eric left?"

"Not really. Just that we'd talk about it more later. Whatever that means." She sighed, and her eyes turned serious. "I really like him, Carrie. A lot." Her voice dropped a notch. "I think I might even be . . . in love with him."

Her words twisted Carrie's heart. She and Melissa had always been as close as any two best friends could possibly be. She had been at Melissa's side throughout the loss of her father and then the emotional period following her kidnapping and the subsequent trials. In return Melissa had helped her through the long weeks and months following the shooting that had put her in a wheelchair. And for years they had shared every dream and desire and heartache, spent countless hours at each other's homes, laughed together, cried together. She thought she knew Melissa as well as anyone could, but until now she hadn't realized just how immature her friend really was. And suddenly she wondered if Melissa was in for her biggest heartache yet.

~~~

Jinx loved Sundays, especially when the weather was nice. It was the one day every week that he had free, and he relished it. It didn't bother him that many of the other prisoners had visitors while he sat alone on a bench in the yard. The rest of them could count the days, even the hours and minutes, until their next visit. Not Jinx. A visit was the last thing he wanted. If he ever had a visitor, he'd know he was in big trouble.

He smiled and tilted his head back, basking in the afternoon sunshine. He'd grown accustomed to the Pacific Northwest weather over the last couple of years, and he knew there weren't going to be many more days like this one for several months. But that was all right with him. Weather didn't make much difference to a guy who was counting the days toward something a lot bigger than a Sunday afternoon visit. It didn't matter to him if the sun shone, if it rained, hailed, snowed, or flooded. As long as he played his cards right, kept his nose clean, and had just a little bit of luck, he'd be out in less than two years. After all, he had no previous record. And he hadn't been in one bit of trouble since he set foot in this place. So there was no reason to think he wouldn't get an early parole. Then he'd be free to carry out the rest of his plan.

He smiled, his eyes closed as he soaked up the rays. It was a brilliant plan, he told himself. Risky—but brilliant. It had taken him a while to come up with it and a little longer to work up the courage to carry it out. But he'd done it, and no one knew but him. It was perfect. And it would be worth the wait. Worth the sacrifice. Worth all it had cost him to get to this point. He wasn't about to let anything get him off-track now. And when he'd finished waiting, he'd be able to spend the rest of his life with his face to the sun, and nobody would be able to do anything about it.

Jinx chuckled. No wonder he loved Sundays. Dreaming about what would someday be his was almost as good as being there.

$\sim\sim\sim$

Across the yard three other inmates watched him, even as they made plans of their own. He was an odd one, they agreed. Never mixed with anybody. Didn't argue or cause trouble but didn't run from it either. Just avoided it as much as possible. He had earned a grudging respect from many of the prisoners, though few really liked him.

More than once they'd discussed his name and wondered how he'd come by it. Jinx. Who'd want a name like that? Seems like you'd just be looking for something bad to happen. And in a place like this, bad things happened a lot.

In fact, they knew well that they were planning something right now that could turn out really bad if anybody found out about it. And that's why they were being so careful to make sure nobody did. But they were going to have to include Jinx in the plan whether they liked it or not—and whether he liked it or not. They needed him if it was going to work, and that was that. But how much would they have to tell him to string him along? How could they best avail themselves of his help while still insuring his silence? Could they bring him in willingly, or would it take some "friendly persuasion"? After all, there was only one of him and three of them.

And that was the topic of the day as they huddled in their corner of the yard and watched Jinx from a distance. If this thing was going to happen the way they'd planned it, they couldn't afford to make any mistakes. It had to come off without a hitch—and right on time. As far as they could see, the plan was perfect. All they needed now were the hostages.

~~~

The sunlight was fading fast as Toni exited the freeway and headed toward her home. April's plane had been late, and Toni had ended up with a lot more waiting time at the airport than she had anticipated. And that meant more thinking time.

Over and over she had rehearsed the situation with Melissa and Eric, asking herself if there was something she could have done to handle things better, or even to have prevented it in the first place. But the only thing she had come up with was that her little sister was growing up, and Toni was just going to have to start facing and dealing with that reality.

Having served as surrogate mother to Melissa since their mother died almost fourteen years earlier, it was not going to be an easy transition. In Toni's mind Melissa would always be a little girl in need of her protection. Although she realized that wouldn't always be true, she didn't think Melissa was at that point yet. All she could hope and pray for now was the wisdom to deal with the situation without alienating the impressionable teenager entirely.

A smile played on her lips. *Thank you, Father,* she prayed silently, gratefully aware of the dear lady sitting next to her. *Once again you've sent April at just the right time.*

"You look happy," April commented. "Or amused. What's on your mind, my dear?"

Toni glanced at her passenger, surprised. "I thought you'd dozed off. The last time I checked, your eyes were closed."

"They were. And I did—a little. It's been a long day, and I am a bit tired. But I'm eager to see Melissa and Abe too. I've missed all of you more than I ever imagined I could."

"I'm glad," Toni commented, turning her eyes back to the road in front of her. "We've missed you too. As I've told you before, you're family now. And we're so glad you're here."

April laid her hand on Toni's arm. Her voice was gentle, probing. "You say that as if you need me to be here."

Toni smiled again. "I never could hide anything from you, could I?"

"And why should you? If we're truly family, then we have no secrets."

Toni sighed and shook her head slightly. "God sent you to us right now, April. I really believe that. I don't have my parents to turn to for wise advice. And I should warn you that I intend to avail myself of all the wisdom and advice you have to offer."

April's laugh was light and easy. "Well, my dear, I'll certainly give you what advice I've got, but I can't guarantee how wise it will be. But I'm sure God knows what to do, so we'll trust that he will guide us, as he always does when we seek him."

Toni nodded. April had a way of simplifying things by narrowing them down to the bottom line: God. What does God say about the problem? What would he have you do in this situation? How would he handle it? What does his Word have to say about it? Have you prayed? Have you listened? Have you sought wise counsel? Have you obeyed?

"It's Melissa," she said. "She has a boyfriend."

"Oh, my. Not that I'm surprised, mind you. Melissa is a beautiful young girl, and I remember at your wedding how all the young men from church were falling all over themselves to impress her—though she scarcely seemed to notice. Is it one of those boys that's finally caught her eye?"

"I'm afraid not." Toni sighed again, glancing once more at April, noticing even in that brief glance the look of compassion and concern in the elderly lady's pale blue eyes. "It's a boy from school," Toni explained. "A senior named Eric Fullbright. He and his family moved here from Nebraska during the summer, and apparently they met soon after school started. They've been spending quite a bit of time together, but Abe and I didn't find out about it until Friday."

"Hmm. And from the sound of your voice, you didn't find out about it directly from Melissa."

Toni pulled to a stop at the final light before turning onto her street. This time she looked directly at her friend. "You're right. We found out when she was late coming home and we called Carrie's house, assuming she was there. Carrie thought we already knew about Eric, so she told us that she had last seen Melissa getting into his car after school."

April Lippincott raised her eyebrows. "He has a car? Well. So what's he like? Have you met him yet?"

The driver of the car behind them honked impatiently, and Toni discovered the light had changed. She accelerated slowly as she answered. "My first inclination, when Melissa finally walked in Friday evening, was to forbid her to ever see him again. But Abe convinced me we needed to talk it over first, maybe even get to know Eric, since Melissa was so adamant about wanting to continue seeing him. So we had him over for dinner on Saturday."

"And?"

"And he was nice enough, I suppose. Very good-looking, of course."

"Of course."

"He was polite. Obviously intelligent. But . . ."

"Ah. That's what I was waiting for."

Toni drove down the street toward her home as the last of the sun's rays died away. "But he's not a Christian. At least, I don't think he is. I mean, I don't see how he could be. He said he doesn't 'do church.' I know that doesn't necessarily prove he's an unbeliever, but . . ."

"But. That word keeps coming up, doesn't it? You're definitely not comfortable with Melissa's continuing to see this young man, are you?"

Toni pulled into the driveway and parked the car. "No, I'm not," she said, turning in her seat to look at April. "And I know I met Abe before he was a Christian, but . . ."

"But you didn't allow yourself to become seriously involved with him until he was," April added quickly. "And Melissa is still a child."

"Exactly. And she's been through so much in the past couple of years."

"You all have, my dear. And none of it has been easy. But—and here's the important 'but'—God has been faithful. Through it all he has guided you every step of the way, and he's certainly not going to let you down now."

Toni nodded. "I know you're right. It's just that it seems like such a huge responsibility, raising a teenager. I knew we'd have to deal with this sort of thing sooner or later, but I guess I hoped it would be later."

"Everyone who has ever raised a teenager has hoped that," April reminded her. "So what does Abe think about all this? And Carrie? Have you talked with her?"

"Abe is much more patient than I am, more rational. I'm trying to keep my emotions out of the way, but it's not easy. I'm glad I have Abe to lean on."

"I'm glad too, my dear. God sent him to you for just that reason—to lean on and to listen to. He's a good man."

"I know. But right now we're both just a little bit baffled about what to do next. As for Carrie, I've only spoken with her briefly, but my impression is that she's concerned too. I think Melissa has pretty much left her out of the loop on this."

"That's not like Melissa at all. Those two girls have always shared everything together."

"I know. And that's one of my main concerns. Melissa just isn't acting like herself. I think maybe this Eric Fullbright is already having far too much influence on her. Thankfully, though, Melissa spent the afternoon with Carrie today. She's home by now, I'm sure, awaiting your arrival. But I'm hoping she and Carrie had a chance to talk about this Eric thing while she was there."

"I'm sure they did," April said. "Melissa is a sweet girl, and so is Carrie. But Carrie seems mature beyond her years. I'm sure she'll continue to exert a positive influence over Melissa."

"I hope you're right." Toni hesitated, suddenly remembering something. "In fact, right before school started they were talking about going into prison ministry together some day—when they're older, of course. I guess it all started after Carrie wrote those letters to Tom Blevins, the young man who shot her and put her in the wheelchair. Her letters of forgiveness had quite an effect on Tom, and he eventually accepted Jesus as his Savior. Soon after that Melissa was finally able to write a letter to Bruce Jensen. You remember him, don't you? The doctor who was responsible for my father's death and was involved with Melissa's kidnapping? Anyway, as hard as it was for her, Melissa told Dr. Jensen that she forgave him, and she told him of God's love for him. She's never had any response from the letter, but it was a huge step for her to be able to write it."

"I think that's wonderful. And that's exactly what I mean about Carrie's being a positive influence on Melissa. Give it time, my dear. Be patient, pray, and wait for God's answer. In the meantime, maybe that prison ministry isn't such a far-fetched idea. I remember your mentioning something about it last spring, right after you and Abe were married. And the thought crossed my mind even then that the two of you might end up doing something like that someday yourself. Have you ever considered such a possibility?"

Toni was amazed. The idea had rolled around in her mind several times in the last few months, but she had never really mentioned it to anyone. But God knew, of course. And now April was bringing it up. Was God trying to tell her something? Was it possible that he was calling her into prison ministry?

She shook her head. If God wanted her to get involved in something like that, he was going to have to be a lot more direct. There were just too many other things to deal with at the moment. For now they needed to get inside before Abe and Melissa came out looking for them. There would be plenty of time over the next few weeks for Toni and April to pray and talk together and to try to discover where God might be leading them all.

CHAPTER 8

Toni suppressed a yawn. They had all been up fairly late the night before, catching up with April after several months of not seeing one another. Then, even after going to bed, Toni hadn't slept well, and this meeting with George Landry seemed to be dragging on forever. Peeking at her watch, she realized it wasn't even nine-thirty yet, so obviously the meeting hadn't lasted more than fifteen minutes or so. It just seemed longer, she supposed, because the man spoke in such an unemotional monotone, almost as if he were trying to control his feelings as he spoke. She wondered briefly if that was exactly what he was doing, then dismissed the idea as a suspicious over-reaction. Sometimes she took her private detective's job much too seriously. She had better just pay attention to what the man was saying rather than worry about his level of sincerity in saying it. After all, it was for her benefit that he was repeating what he had already explained to Abe.

"Like I told your husband, ma'am, my brother, Jimmy—James—was the youngest; I'm the oldest. We have a sister named Mindy, who's right in the middle. With James bein' our baby brother and all, we're both naturally protective of him. We've been real worried ever since he disappeared a few years ago, but it wasn't until just before our mama passed away that we found out she'd had a phone call from him right here in River View. The call was more than two years ago, and I sure wish she'd told us sooner, but for some reason she didn't. James has always had trouble keepin' jobs, and he bounces around a lot. Maybe he'd fallen on hard times again when he called, and she just didn't want us to know. It's too bad she didn't tell us, though, 'cause we might've been able to help him somehow."

The man was saying all the right words, but something just didn't ring true for Toni. Maybe it was that annoying, droning drawl—or maybe it was the lack of emotion she saw in his narrow brown eyes. His hands bothered her too. He clasped them tightly in his lap, as if trying to keep them in control, right along with his voice. Whether George Landry's story was legitimate or not, Toni decided, she just didn't like the man.

She glanced at Abe, but he wasn't watching Mr. Landry. His eyes were fixed on her, and she knew he was anxious to get her impression of their newest client. She realized she should at least give the man the benefit of the doubt, and she certainly intended to try. After all, he claimed he was attempting to find his younger brother to let him know of their mother's passing and to distribute to him his share of a small inheritance. And yet she just couldn't shake the feeling that there was more to his story than he was telling.

Things aren't always as they seem. Hadn't she learned and relearned the truth of that statement over the last couple of years while investigating her father's death, as well as the high school shooting that had left one teacher dead and several students and faculty members injured? She could almost imagine her father telling her to look beneath the surface, to listen for what the man *didn't* say.

Mr. Landry's monotone continued. "Mindy and I are real torn up about our mama's death, as you can imagine, ma'am. All we want is to find our little brother, make sure he's all right, let him know what's goin' on, and get his money to him—which, knowin' him like I do, he can really use. Right now River View is our only lead, and you and your husband are our best hope."

The overweight man blinked as he spoke, and Toni found herself focusing on his eyes rather than his words. The more she stared at him, the more often he blinked or dropped his gaze. His forehead glistened with tiny beads of perspiration. Toni surmised that Mr. George Landry didn't like her anymore than she liked him. So why was he here? Matthews and Matthews wasn't the only detective agency in the region. Why had he picked them?

Stop it, Toni. You're just overtired. You spent too much time lying awake last night, thinking about Melissa and Eric—and about what April said concerning a possible prison ministry. None of that has anything to do with Mr. Landry, so just pay attention and do your job. Maybe you can be more objective about all this when you're not so tired.

Part of her believed that; the other part still eyed the man suspiciously and wondered about his real motives. She was anxious for him to leave so she and Abe could discuss the Landry case by themselves.

~~~

Toni didn't realize how tense she had been throughout the meeting until the man was finally gone and she felt her shoulders and neck relax. It had been a while since anyone had affected her so adversely, and she wasn't sure what to make of it.

Abe was sitting behind his desk—the desk that had once belonged to Toni's father, Paul Matthews—and she sat across from him, watching him watch her. Something told her he had his own misgivings about the case. A third chair sat glaringly empty beside her. She was relieved that their client was no longer sitting there.

Abe leaned forward in his chair as he spoke. "So what do you think, sweetheart? Is our Mr. Landry being straight with us?"

Toni hesitated. Why would the man lie to them? What could he possibly have to gain in hiring them to find his younger brother? And even if he did stand to gain something, so what? His motives really weren't their business. All he wanted them to do was locate James Landry. A simple request, one they could accomplish—or not. Many missing persons' cases were never solved, regardless of the time and effort invested. Some people just don't want to be found. Others— well, there were lots of reasons that some people disappeared forever. And locating missing loved ones is one of the most common reasons clients hire private detectives. Maybe she should stop trying to ana- lyze Mr. Landry and his story and just get busy trying to find his brother.

"I don't know," she said, shrugging her shoulders. "His story sounds straightforward enough, I suppose. But . . ."

"But you think there's more to it."

Toni nodded. "Yes. Although I'm not sure it really matters."

"I was thinking the same thing. Maybe we should just find out what we can about James Landry, if anything, pass along the information to his brother, collect our fee, and let it go at that."

Toni nodded again. "I think you're right. And if we come across anything suspicious along the way . . ."

"Exactly. We can decide what to do at that point."

"Agreed." Toni felt relieved to have the matter settled. After all, there were other matters—both private and professional—that demanded their attention right now. First on her list was what to do about Eric Fullbright. Now that they'd had him over for dinner, it was just a matter of time—and probably not much time, at that—until he once again invited Melissa out on a date. It was obvious they weren't going to be able to put off their decision much longer.

~~~

Ever since Melissa's visit the previous week, Brad hadn't been able to stop thinking about what she had said regarding Jeanine Simmons. Was the firm's new receptionist really interested in him, or did he just want to believe that to feed his starving ego? He couldn't deny that he had noticed the attractive, petite redhead, but he had worked hard to convince himself that he simply wasn't interested. Even though everyone kept telling him he needed to get over Toni and get on with his life, he was convinced he wasn't ready. But Melissa's comments had nudged him into at least considering the possibility of dating someone new. Now he wondered if Jeanine might be just that someone else he needed to resurrect his love life.

Sitting behind his desk, he glanced at his watch. It was almost noon. Would he be out of line to invite her to lunch? A lot of people frowned on dating coworkers. He wasn't even sure how the firm's other two partners, one of them being his father, felt about it since the topic had never come up. *Then again,* he thought, taking a deep breath and rising from his chair, *there's only one way to find out.*

His resolve wavered as soon as he approached Jeanine's desk and saw three people sitting in the waiting room. He wasn't about to present his invitation in front of an audience. Maybe he should go back to his office and buzz her on the intercom. Then again, that might be too impersonal; she might even interpret it as a business lunch. Worse yet, she might feel obligated to say yes because he was one of her employers.

When Jeanine looked up at him and smiled, he opened his mouth to speak, but he had no idea what to say. Instead he nodded to her and walked past her desk and on out the front door, opting for an early lunch by himself. What was he doing, he wondered, putting stock in a teenager's opinion? Melissa was so caught up in her own romantic daydreams these days that she had probably read something into Jeanine's manner that simply wasn't there. Brad was relieved that he hadn't followed through on his impulse and made a complete fool of himself.

After all, he argued silently, *being alone isn't all that bad. In fact, I think I'm getting used to it. And it sure is a lot safer.*

~~~

April was surprised when the doorbell rang in the middle of the afternoon. It was Monday and both Toni and Abe had said they would be at the office most of the day. Melissa, of course, was at school, so Mrs. Lippincott couldn't imagine who had dropped by. She had just come out of her room after taking a brief nap and was finally feeling rested from her trip the day before, as well as from their gabfest in the evening after her arrival. It had been so good to see everyone again, and their reunion had given her a second wind, so they had stayed up talking for several hours after dinner.

But it had finally caught up with her this morning. She had slept a little longer than usual, then gotten up and had something to eat before going back to bed and falling asleep again. *But why not?* she asked herself. *I'm an old woman and I can take a nap if I feel like it. Besides, I'll be refreshed when everyone gets home this evening.*

Stepping into the entryway she reached out and pulled open the front door. There in front of her stood a woman who looked to be close to her own age. She also looked familiar. April frowned, trying to remember.

"I'm Sophie," the woman said, holding out her hand. "And you are April Lippincott, are you not? I remember you from the wedding."

Of course! That's where they had met. How could she have forgotten? Sophie Jacobson, Abe's aunt. What a wonderful surprise.

April smiled and took Sophie's hand in greeting. "Sophie Jacobson. Of course. How are you? Please, come in."

Sophie stepped inside. "I hope I'm not disturbing you. I spoke with Avraham yesterday, and he told me you were coming to visit. I thought I might catch you if I dropped by this afternoon. Do you mind?"

"Absolutely not. I'm delighted. I've always hoped we would have a chance to get to know each other better. Please, come into the kitchen. I was just about to brew myself some tea. May I fix you some?"

"I'd like that, Mrs. Lippincott," Sophie answered, following her into the kitchen. "Thank you."

"Oh, please, call me April. And may I call you Sophie?"

Sophie nodded her agreement as April indicated a chair at the table. "Please, sit down. I'll have that tea ready in a jiffy. Do you take cream or sugar?"

Sophie smiled. "Is there any other way to drink tea?"

April laughed. "Not in my opinion." She put the water on to boil and brought cups to the table, then sat down across from Sophie, studying her all the while.

"I'm puzzled," she said. "And frank too, I'm afraid. So I must ask: Did you come specifically to talk with me?"

Sophie hesitated. "I suppose I did. It was a bit of an impulse visit, you see. When I was talking to Avraham yesterday, he said something about Melissa's birthday coming up next week, and I started thinking. What do you buy for a sixteen-year-old girl that you don't know well, even though she's family? I was going to call Avraham back and ask him, but I thought better of it. He probably wouldn't know either. And I suppose I could have asked Toni, but . . . then I remembered that you were going to be here. I know I should have called first, but I was out driving when I thought of it—in fact, I was more than halfway here when it occurred to me and, well, here I am."

"That's all right," April assured her. "I'm so glad you decided to come by. I hate drinking tea alone."

Sophie smiled again. "You're kind. I know you've spent a lot of time with Melissa, and you had a granddaughter about the same age."

Her voice trailed off, and she looked uncomfortable. April reached across the table and patted her hand. "It's all right to talk about my granddaughter. I may not be over her death, but I certainly have accepted it by now. Yes, Julie was just about Melissa's age when she was . . . when she died. We were close, and I miss her very much. But I think maybe it's good for me to talk about her—once in a while, at least."

Sophie's smile was tender. "I understand. I've lost loved ones too— my husband, my sister, and most recently, my only brother." She sighed, and April thought she saw a hint of tears in her brown eyes.

"We never really get over it, do we? But it does get easier with time, I suppose."

When April nodded, Sophie went on. "I never had children of my own, you see—only my nephew, Avraham, who has been like a son to me. But daughters or granddaughters? I have no experience at all—although I am praying for a grandniece or nephew soon, yes?"

April grinned. "Yes. I am praying the same way."

"Good. Meantime, I need your advice about Melissa's birthday. Sixteen is such a special age. It seems she is no longer a child, and yet she is. Does that make sense? What do you get for a girl that age?"

"I'm not sure," April answered truthfully. "In fact, I've been wondering myself. I suppose I could talk to Toni, or maybe even Melissa, if I do it carefully enough, and get some ideas. Then maybe you and I could go shopping together. Would that be all right?"

Sophie Jacobson's face lit up. "That would be wonderful. Yes, I would like that very much. Maybe we could even have lunch." Her smile faded slightly. "Of course, I only eat kosher, and I don't know the restaurants in River View."

"That's not a problem," April answered. "I'm sure we can find somewhere in this town to get a kosher lunch. And if not, we'll just make one ourselves—right here in this kitchen. Or else we'll drive on up to your place. I've never seen your town, and I would love to do that while I'm here. That way you can show me around, and then choose wherever and whatever you want to eat."

The teakettle began to whistle, and April rose from her seat. Before she could walk away, Sophie stopped her. "You are a good woman," she said. "A righteous *goy*—excuse me—a righteous Gentile. Thank you, April."

April smiled. She couldn't help but wonder if there was more to Sophie's visit than simply wanting help picking out a gift for Melissa.

If so, she would let Avraham's aunt broach the subject in her own way and time. "You are welcome, Sophie. And I think we're going to become good friends. I've always believed in divine appointments, and there's no doubt in my mind that this is one of them. In God's time, we may even know why."

CHAPTER 9

The Texan was fuming. It was bad enough having to deal with that pretty-boy detective, but his snobby wife—now she was something else. He'd felt her looking down her nose at him the entire time he'd been in their office. If it wasn't for the Matthews and Matthews reputation of finding things even the cops had overlooked, he would have walked out of there and never looked back. But he needed them if he was going to find that worthless brother of his and settle the score once and for all. So he'd sat in his chair and talked to Toni Matthews as if he really cared what she thought. And he knew she thought plenty.

It was *what* she was thinking that bothered him most. He hoped he'd convinced her—both of them—that all he wanted was to find his long-lost brother and deliver the bad news of their mother's death, as well as his share of a pittance of an inheritance. And, of course, a pittance was all there was. That part, at least, was true. But it was true only because little Jimmy boy had long since absconded with the family treasures, and a pittance was all that was left for their mother to pass on.

George hoped they believed what he'd told them—but he didn't really think so. He was almost sure they suspected there was more to the story, but he also hoped they would be satisfied with what information he'd given them and just go out and find Jimmy. Still it was obvious he was going to have to keep a close eye on them. A return trip to Texas was out of the question. He would just have to make do in this rinky-dink town until the Matthews and Matthews team either discovered something about Jimmy or gave up trying.

The knock on the door made him jump. He glanced at his watch. Nearly four o'clock. He was sure it wasn't the maid because she'd already been there to clean up. It had to be his contact.

He walked to the door and peered out the peephole. It was him, all right. He opened the door carefully.

"It's about time," he said gruffly, darting a furtive glance up and down the dark motel corridor before grabbing the wiry little man by his dirty shirt and pulling him inside. "I thought you forgot me."

"Oh, no, Mr. George. I wouldn't forget you." The man's bloodshot eyes were wide and frightened yet hopeful. "I promised you I'd bring it, and here I am, just like I said."

George grunted. He was glad he hadn't revealed his last name to this worthless slimeball, but he wondered if even giving him his first name had been a mistake. He couldn't afford to be tied in with the likes of this junkie.

"Let me see the stuff," he said.

The man pulled a package from his pants pocket and held it out with trembling hands. "Here you go, Mr. George. Just like I said. It's good stuff—the best."

"Humph. We'll see about that." He opened the package and dabbed the powder with his finger, then touched it to his tongue. Not bad, considering the source, and undoubtedly worth the amount he'd promised the guy. Besides, it would help him get through his boring stay in River View. What else was there to do in this town while he waited?

He dug in his pocket and pulled out a small wad of bills. Peeling off what he owed him, he thrust the money into the man's eager hand. "Now go on. Get out of here. But don't forget—I'll be wanting more in a couple of days. Understand?"

"Oh, yes sir, Mr. George," the man answered, backing toward the door. "I understand. And I won't forget. A couple of days. I'll be back, Mr. George. You'll see."

"You'd better be, or I'll come looking for you," George warned, then closed and locked the door behind the man and plopped down in his chair in front of the TV. He sure was glad he wasn't some worthless junkie like the one that just left. No sir, not George Landry. He was a respectable user—strictly for pleasure. And cocaine wasn't like heroine or some other lowlife drug. He could quit anytime he wanted. But right now, quitting was the last thing on his mind.

≈≈≈

Carrie and Melissa were doing homework in Melissa's room when the phone rang. Melissa grabbed it quickly, certain it was Eric. Her heart beating wildly, she glanced self-consciously at Carrie as she put the receiver to her ear. Carrie didn't even look up.

But it wasn't Eric—just an after-dinner telemarketer. Melissa hung up the phone with mixed emotions. She was disappointed that it hadn't been Eric but relieved and hopeful that maybe he wouldn't call until after Carrie left, which should be soon. Immediately she felt guilty for wishing her friend would go home.

"Wrong number?" Carrie asked, her head still bent over her books and her not quite shoulder-length dark hair falling forward to cover her face.

"Telemarketer."

"Hmm. I hate that. They always call in the evening. Very annoying."

Melissa didn't really have an opinion about telemarketers one way or the other. She cared only about hearing Eric's voice and seeing him again. He had met her at school first thing this morning and walked her to every class, holding her hand as he escorted her around the campus. Melissa had felt so proud as her friends looked on. It was becoming common knowledge that they were an item, and it certainly didn't hurt Melissa's status to be seen with such a good-looking senior. But every time she saw Carrie, wheeling her way from class to class alone, guilt stabbed her heart. She didn't want to hurt her best friend or ignore her, but she had missed Eric so much on Sunday that she just couldn't wait to see him again when school started Monday morning. Besides, she had spent the previous afternoon at the Bosworths' home, and she had also invited Carrie for dinner tonight so she could see April Lippincott once again. And now the two girls were studying together. It wasn't as if she were abandoning Carrie or anything.

So why did she feel as if she had betrayed her best friend? After all, they had talked about her relationship with Eric, and she had explained to Carrie how she felt about him. She seemed to understand—at least, Melissa hoped she did. What more could she do?

Carrie looked up and yawned. "I think I'd better take Abe up on his offer to drive me home. I'm getting sleepy."

"I'll ride with you," Melissa offered.

Carrie glanced at the phone, then smiled at her friend. "No need. You just stay here and . . . finish your homework. I'll catch you at school tomorrow."

Relieved that Carrie hadn't taken her up on her offer to accompany her, Melissa sat on her bed after her friend left and willed the phone to ring. When nearly fifteen minutes had passed without a call, she picked up the receiver and dialed Eric's home. After all, things were different now, she reasoned, even as her heart hammered and her hands trembled. Girls called guys all the time. It was no big deal. She just wanted to hear his voice, to hear him tell her how much he missed her and couldn't wait to see her again. But there was no answer. She hung up when she heard the answering machine click on.

≈≈≈

It was Tuesday morning, and the rains had come. Kelly Schillo sighed. *Perfect*, she thought. *Four preschoolers and I can't even send them outside to the backyard to play.*

Only one of the little ones actually belonged to Kelly. Madison was almost four, the youngest of Doug and Kelly Schillo's three children. The older two, Monte and Marianne, were in elementary school, and Kelly looked forward to the day when Madison would join them. With all three kids in school, she would finally have a few hours each day to do whatever she wished—read, paint, clean house undisturbed, maybe even get a part-time job. . . . It sounded wonderful. With the three siblings spaced two years apart, it had been a long time since

Kelly had enjoyed much time to herself—except when it was one of the other three moms' turn to keep the children.

The four mothers were neighbors, living within a couple blocks of one another. They had met when Kelly had taken Marianne to her first day of kindergarten. The other moms were also there, bringing their kindergartners to class while holding on to younger children at the same time. As the women became acquainted and found out how closely they lived to one another and that each of them had one preschooler left at home, they decided to create a sort of co-op, taking turns keeping the four children one morning a week and thus providing a few hours of relative freedom for the others.

Today it was Kelly's turn. The weather had been so nice up until yesterday, and she had planned to take the kids on an outing to a nearby park. But the steady dripping she had heard when she first awoke that morning had ended that idea.

It wasn't too bad yet, she had to admit. So far the children had settled for watching cartoons and eating a fruit snack while she cleaned up the kitchen and put the dishes in the dishwasher. But it wouldn't be long until the fussing started, and then she would have to come up with some sort of activity to keep them entertained.

Still, it was only for a few hours, she reminded herself. Kindergarten would be out by noon, moms would meet to collect and distribute kids, and she could come home with Marianne and Madison and put them down for a nap. *I just might join them*, she thought, smiling. *I'll still have a couple of hours before Monte gets home from school, and plenty of time before Doug gets here. He said he had a late meeting this afternoon, and I'll just fix something simple for dinner. Soup, maybe. That would be perfect for this weather.*

"Mommy, Cory hit me."

It was Madison, pulling on Kelly's pant leg. The dishes weren't even quite done, and already the fussing was starting. Kelly sighed and smiled down at her youngest, dried her hands on a dish towel, and said, "Let's get some crayons and paper and color some nice pictures. Would you like that?"

Madison grinned, her blue eyes sparkling and her blonde curls bobbing. "Can I make a picture for Daddy? Can he take it to work and put it in his office?"

Kelly smiled. It was amazing how much her youngest child resembled the Schillo side of the family. And Madison adored her father. Kelly had once heard her bragging to her three preschool friends about how her daddy "took care of lots of bad guys." *A simplistic description of a prison warden's job,* Kelly had thought at the time, *but fairly accurate as well.* Kelly just prayed, as she did many times each day, that God would take care of Doug while he was at work taking care of the bad guys.

≈≈≈

Abe and Toni had taken advantage of the brief rain break just before noon and left the office for a short walk, although Abe had brought an umbrella along just in case. As many years as Toni had spent in the Pacific Northwest, she still never ceased to be amazed at how fresh and clean everything smelled after a good rain, especially the first good rain of the season. And she never ceased to remember her dad's commenting on the same thing.

"There's nothing like a good rain to clear the air," he'd say. "Don't know why anybody would want to live somewhere where it didn't rain a lot—and often. That's one of the reasons your mother and I picked this place, you know. The rain."

Toni smiled at the memory. She knew she would never stop missing the man who had been her first hero, but at least she could think of him now without feeling she was about to break down in tears. And besides, she thought, looking up at Abe, God had given her another hero.

Abe, still walking, turned his head and looked down at her. "Hmm. You're looking at me and smiling. Should I be flattered or worried?"

She shrugged playfully. "Maybe you'll just have to wait and find out."

"Uh-oh. Now I'm nervous."

They stopped beside a wrought iron bench in front of a deli. The bench was underneath an awning and relatively dry. Abe took off his trench coat and spread it across the seat. "Care to sit for a minute?" he asked. "Maybe we could talk about just what it is that's making you smile."

Toni laughed and sat down beside him. "You really are paranoid, aren't you, detective? Not to mention a little egotistical. What makes you think I was smiling about you anyway? Maybe I was thinking about something else entirely."

"But you were looking at me."

"I like to look at you."

Abe's dark eyes joined his lips in a broad grin. "Now *that* I like to hear." He kissed her and then leaned back. "So are you going to tell me?"

Toni feigned ignorance. "Tell you what?"

Abe shook his head and shrugged but didn't answer.

"You mean, that's it? You're going to give up that easily? I thought maybe you'd beg or plead or bargain a little, and then I could break down."

"Nah." Abe's eyes were closed now, and his head was tilted back. "I'm really not that interested."

"Oh, I get it. You think I'll tell you if you pretend you don't want to know."

"Who said I was pretending?"

"You're impossible, you know that?"

Abe grinned. "I work at it."

"Well, then, I'll tell you. I was thinking about my dad, how he loved the air after a rain, and how he was my first hero, but now God has given me a new hero." She paused and laid her hand on his arm. "You."

Abe's eyes opened and he turned to look at her. "OK, you win. I give up. There's no way I could resist a line like that." He kissed her again and smiled. "I love you, Mrs. Matthews."

"I love you too."

They sat silently for a moment before Abe said, "So you're really OK with this George Landry thing, right? I mean, are you ready to jump into the case and start trying to track down his brother, James?"

Toni shrugged. "Sure. Why not? We might as well. What have we got to lose? After all, the guy came all the way from Texas to find him—for whatever reasons, who knows, but it must be important to him. He is awfully secretive, though, isn't he? Did you ever find out where he was staying?"

Abe pointed to his left. "In that old motel down the street. Not that he told me. I just happened to see his rental car turning into the parking lot the other day. Not too many silver Caddies with rental car plates running around River View, so it wasn't hard to figure out it was him. Must be boring sitting there waiting, day after day. You'd think he'd head back to Texas and wait for a call from us. But at this point he seems determined to stick around."

"I can't imagine why. But, as they say, it's a free country. He can stay if he wants to, I suppose."

"I guess you're right." Abe took a deep breath and stood up. "Well, maybe we'd better get back to the office and get to work. What do you think?"

Toni got up from her seat. "Do we have a choice?"

"Not if we want to pay the bills."

"So it's hi-ho, hi-ho, back to work we go."

Abe laughed and put his arm around her as they headed down the street. They hadn't even noticed the wiry little man with the dirty shirt, standing in the open doorway of the deli, sipping a cup of coffee and listening to their every word.

CHAPTER 10

It had been a long day, and Doug Schillo was ready to go home. Just one more meeting and he could leave.

He glanced at his desk calendar. Mark Johnson. Doug had never met the man, but he had been one of his biggest fans for years. For as long as Doug could remember, he had loved the game of football and had even hoped to play professionally one day. But when he developed asthma during his early college years, he knew it was out of the question.

Not that he would have made it anyway, he reminded himself. It was one thing to be a gridiron star in high school, another to be good enough to make it to the pros. Still, he had continued his quarter-backing from the sofa, watching every game he could and following the careers of some of his favorite players. Mark Johnson had been one of those players.

So many of today's professional athletes are stuck on themselves, Doug mused. Not Mark. This guy seems to have his head together and both feet on the ground. Throughout Mark's fifteen-year career he had consistently played as well off the field as on. Never any rumors of misconduct, or splashy headlines about mismanagement of money or success—just a stable family man with good morals.

And that's why Doug was meeting with him today. When Doug had first received the letter from Mark requesting an appointment to discuss a possible ministry weekend at the prison, Doug had been excited about meeting one of his sports heroes face-to-face. But he had also been impressed with Mark's track record of successful prison ministry in the past five years since his retirement from football. It was obvious they shared not only a love for the game but a love for God as well. Tired as he was, Doug found himself reenergized at the idea of their upcoming meeting.

Doug's eyes wandered from his desk calendar to his favorite family picture, right next to his phone—the picture they had taken just a few months earlier. Kelly sat beside him, her brown hair falling softly to her shoulders, her dark eyes shining. He wondered how it was that each time he looked at her she seemed more beautiful. They had been married for almost twelve years, and he was sure he was more in love with her now than on the day she had become his bride.

To his left and just slightly behind him, with his hand resting on Doug's shoulder, stood Monte, their only son and firstborn child, now seven years old. Monte looked just like his mother, with straight chestnut brown hair and large, liquid eyes. But the similarities between mother and son stopped at their looks. Kelly was outgoing and vivacious, the life of every party. Monte was more like Doug. The feelings were there, but he had a hard time showing or expressing them. Still waters run deep, Kelly always said, and the saying certainly applied to both father and son.

Doug smiled as he looked at his daughters, the older one sitting on his lap, the younger on her mother's. Marianne had just started kindergarten and was always so proud to show off her "schoolwork" when Doug got home. Her coloring was also dark, like her mother and brother, and she definitely had her mother's life-of-the-party personality. Madison, on the other hand, was the only one of their three children who resembled Doug and his side of the family. Her short blonde curls had a mind of their own, and no matter how hard Kelly tried to comb them into place, they sprang right back in whatever direction they wanted to go. Madison didn't seem to care, though, as she was too busy enjoying life. The almost-four-year-old with the sparkling blue eyes had fun no matter what she was doing.

Thank you, God, Doug prayed silently. *You've blessed me with such a wonderful family.*

The knock on the door startled him. He looked up to see his secretary, Elena, peeking in at him.

"Your four o' clock is here," she said, obviously trying to remain calm and unimpressed. But the shine in her eyes gave her away.

Doug smiled. "Send him in," he said, standing to greet his longtime hero. It would be interesting to see where this meeting would take them.

~~~

The small man with the grubby clothes was hiding in the alleyway. And he was nervous. He always hated this part—waiting to get the stuff. This was when things could go wrong. It had happened before, many times. The one thing Ernie did not want to do was another stint behind bars. The last time had almost killed him. He wasn't sure he could survive if he had to go back. He was small, and he was scared. The other inmates spotted that right away. He never had a chance.

He was sweating now, even though the weather was cool and damp. He needed his stuff real bad. Where was Louie? It would be dark soon. He said he'd come before dark. Why wasn't he here? Had something happened? Should he just turn and run before it was too late?

Ernie tried to swallow, but his mouth was too dry. He was starting to shake, not only because he needed a fix but also because he didn't know what he would tell Mr. George if he couldn't bring him what he'd promised. The man had said he'd come looking for him if he didn't come back. And Ernie had a feeling that Mr. George could be just about as mean as some of the guys in prison.

Mr. George . . . Ernie squinted as he tried to remember. What was it those two had said about the guy from Texas? That he stayed at the old motel and he drove a silver Caddie. That's right. Now he remembered. It had to be him. A Cadillac. A Texas accent. Yep, it had to be him.

But there was something else, something about his name.

Ernie smiled. George Landry. That was it. Mr. George's last name was Landry. And he had a brother named James that he wanted to find real bad.

The little man couldn't put it all together yet, but he somehow sensed that this information might come in handy someday. Meanwhile, he just wanted Louie to show up with his stuff. Where was he anyway?

He was just about to sneak back down to the end of the alley and peek around the corner when he heard a noise. He tensed, ready to run if it was anybody other than the man he expected, a man he knew only as Louie. Ernie had been buying from Louie for a few weeks now, so he was beginning to feel fairly confident that he was safe doing business with him. His last contact had been arrested, and Ernie was sure glad when he'd found a new supplier.

When the man rounded the corner, Ernie relaxed. Louie was late, but at least he had come.

"Did you bring it?" Ernie asked. "Do you have my stuff?"

Louie smirked. "Sure I do, Ern. I've got your stuff. You didn't think I'd let you down, did you?"

Ernie shook his head. "Oh, no, Louie. I knew you wouldn't let me down. You're a good guy, Louie. A real good guy."

"That's right. And don't forget it, slimeball." Louie reached into his pocket and pulled out two tiny packages. "One for you," he said, still holding them in his hand, "and one for your friend."

When Ernie reached for them, Louie snatched them away. "Where's the money? You know you don't touch the stuff till I get my money."

"Oh, sure, Louie. Sure." Ernie dug in his pocket and pulled out a wad of bills. Selling to Mr. George sure made it easier to pay for his own stuff. "Here you go, Louie. You can count it."

Louie grabbed the money from Ernie's hand. "I will," he assured him, doing so before handing him the two bags. Then he turned to leave.

"Hey, don't I get to taste it first?" Ernie asked, immediately regretting his question when Louie turned back, his dark eyes smoldering.

"You don't trust me, Ern? Is that what you're trying to say?"

Ernie shook his head real fast this time. "Oh, no, Louie. That's not it at all. I trust you. You bet I do. You're a good guy, Louie. A real good guy."

Louie nodded once and turned again. By the time he was out of sight, Ernie was feeling a lot better. His fear was dissipating as anticipation of euphoria took its place. Tucking the bags into his pocket, he began to make his way down the alley, planning to make a stop and take care of himself before heading to the motel to deliver the second bag to Mr. George. But just as he was about to step out of the alley into the street, he was grabbed by two men with guns and slammed up against the wall. He opened his mouth to scream for help, but before he could utter a sound, one of the men was reading him his rights. As the darkness of night descended on the back allies of River View, Ernie sobbed and began to shake. He was going back to prison, and he was sure he'd never make it out alive.

~~~

April was pleased that she and Sophie were spending the day together. She had offered to rent or borrow a car and drive up to Olympia so they could do their shopping there, but Sophie had insisted on coming back to River View instead. She also said she'd found out about a great little lunch spot on the outskirts of town that offered a kosher menu, so their plans were made. Now she was just waiting for her new friend's arrival.

The two women had spent several hours together on Monday, just two days earlier, getting to know each other as they discussed their families, their lives, their likes and dislikes, and even their faith. April had been careful to avoid such inflammatory words as *convert* and *Christianity,* sticking with terms more acceptable and understandable to a devout Jew, such as *the God of Israel, the Word of God,* and even *Messiah.* She wasn't kidding herself that they agreed on the complete meaning and application of those terms, but at least they didn't slam the door shut to further discussion.

Help me, Lord, April prayed, as she waited for Sophie to arrive. *Give me wisdom to speak the right words and restraint so I won't speak the wrong ones. This woman is precious to you, Father, and therefore precious to me. Use me to draw her to your heart, Lord.*

The rain had let up earlier that morning, though it was still overcast and could start again at any time. April was glad for at least a temporary respite while Sophie was on the road. Once they were off shopping for Melissa's birthday gift, the weather wouldn't really matter so much.

Melissa. You are such a dear girl. In a few days you'll be sixteen. What do I buy you for such a special birthday? What would you like? April sighed as she wondered what her granddaughter, Julie, would have wanted for her sixteenth birthday had she not been killed just before that date.

She shook her head. No, she would not let herself get caught up in missing Julie again. Right now she needed to concentrate on Melissa.

April had asked Toni for some birthday gift ideas, but nothing she suggested had sounded right. And when April had tried to pull some information from Melissa without letting the girl know her reasons, she'd gotten nowhere. It seemed the teenager was too caught up in daydreams about her new boyfriend to be able to focus on much else.

I suppose that's natural, she reminded herself, as her thoughts drifted to her late husband. *I can still remember when I was that age. I had already met my dear Lawrence, and I knew he was the one. There would have been no persuading me otherwise. Thankfully, my parents didn't try. They always thought we were a perfect match. And, of course, we were, weren't we, my love? We had a wonderful life together.* She sighed again. *I still miss you, dearest, even after all these years.*

April jumped at the sound of the doorbell. Getting up from the couch, she hurried to the front door and opened it to see a smiling Sophie Jacobson waiting for her.

"Welcome," April said, opening her arms and drawing the woman inside. "Did you have a good drive down?"

"Very nice, thank you," Sophie answered, returning April's embrace. "It was drizzling when I got up this morning, but it stopped just before I left and didn't rain a drop all the way down here."

"Wonderful. I'd been praying you'd have a safe trip."

Sophie didn't answer.

"Can I take your coat? I can make some tea," April offered. "Or do you want to get going right away?"

Sophie shrugged, and her smile returned. "I'm ready if you are. Are the others already gone?"

April nodded. "Yes. Melissa's gone to school, and Toni and Abe had to leave for the office early. But they all said they would plan on seeing you for dinner this evening. Toni promised to fix something you can eat. Will you stay?"

"I wouldn't miss it. That's kind of all of you. Toni really is good about accommodating my dietary restrictions."

"You've grown fond of her, haven't you?"

Sophie's hesitation was brief. "Yes. I was naturally disappointed at first. I always dreamed Avraham would marry a nice Jewish girl. But dreams don't always come true, do they? And so we must accept what comes. And if Avraham had to marry a *goy*, then I'm glad it was Toni. She's really a lovely girl."

"I agree completely," said April, grabbing her coat from the entryway closet. "Well, then, shall we go? We have our work cut out for us today—finding the perfect birthday gift for a sixteen-year-old."

April pulled the door shut behind her, and the two elderly women walked arm in arm toward Sophie's car, chattering all the way.

～～～

The second worst thing about being in jail was the smell. The first, of course, was the danger from the other inmates. Ernie was surrounded by both, and he was terrified. But he was also beginning to experience some serious withdrawals since he hadn't had time to shoot up before he was busted and thrown into the back of the police car. For now, at least, that was his biggest regret.

But at least he'd made it through the night. His cellmate seemed to be sleeping off a drunk, so he hadn't bothered him much. That was one good thing.

And there was something else. A big thing, really—at least, for Ernie. Always before when he'd been arrested, he'd never had anyone to call. But this time when he was offered his one phone call, he knew exactly what to do. He had called the motel and asked for George Landry. Sure enough, Mr. George had answered. He'd been angry when he first heard Ernie's voice, and he'd hollered at him about not bringing him his stuff and wanting to know how he'd found out his last name. But once Ernie had explained how he'd overheard those two people talking about him and saying that he was from Texas and was looking for his lost brother, and then how he'd been arrested right after making his buy, Mr. George seemed to settle down. To tell the truth, he'd been almost nice to Ernie after that and had even promised to try to find a way to get him out of jail. That hadn't happened yet, but it was the closest Ernie had ever come to having someone bail him out. And he was really hoping that Mr. George would come through for him before his withdrawals got any worse and before they stuck anyone else in the cell with him. He could handle a sleeping drunk, but he wasn't up to dealing with much else.

But it wasn't long before Ernie learned that his worst fears were about to be realized. It wasn't even lunchtime yet, and suddenly he heard a commotion. The noise was headed his way.

As Ernie sat, shaking on his upper bunk, trying to be as invisible as possible, the cell door was yanked open, and a huge mountain of a man was thrust inside. Close to seven feet tall, with arms twice the size of Ernie's legs, the man with the shaved head and tattoos covering every visible inch of his skin roared his anger at the guards who had brought him to Ernie's cell. Even after the guards had gone, the man continued to rattle the bars and breathe threats of murder and revenge against everyone even remotely connected to the legal or judicial system. Ernie could only hope that if he continued to huddle silently against the wall in the corner of his bunk, the man's fury would abate before he turned around and began checking out his new surroundings.

To some degree that was the case. At least the man was no longer screaming and raging when he finally let go of the bars and turned to look at the rest of the cell. He spotted the drunk first and walked over to nudge him. "Hey," he growled, "get up from there. That's my bunk."

When the sleeping inmate didn't move, the interloper simply threw him off the bed and onto the floor, then kicked him toward the corner. The drunk responded with a groan but continued sleeping.

Ernie began to hope that his newest roommate would just lie down and go to sleep without even noticing him. But just before flopping down on the bottom bunk, the giant peeked over the top mattress and spotted Ernie cowering in the corner. The smile that spread across his face reminded Ernie of a cat that has just discovered a live mouse caught in a trap. And that's exactly what he felt like.

"Well, well, what have we here? Looks like the pigs gave me two playmates this time. I just might have to thank them for their thoughtfulness."

"I . . ." Ernie tried to think of something more to say, but he only swallowed and began to cry. He had so hoped that Mr. George would get him out on time. But now he knew better.

"You what?" the man demanded, reaching across the bed and grabbing Ernie by the shirt, then pulling him toward himself. "You what? Did you want to say something, little man?"

Ernie shook his head no, horrified to realize that he had just wet himself. The man was holding his face only inches from his own, and the smell of sweat and tobacco, though familiar to Ernie, suddenly made him nauseous. He gulped, determined not to vomit on the man, as he knew he would be killed on the spot.

After a moment Ernie's captor began to laugh, then released his hold and pushed him back onto the bed. "Don't worry, little man. I'm not going to hurt you—yet. But if you're still here tonight when the lights go out, you're mine. Got it?"

Ernie got it. He knew exactly what the man meant. He'd spent a lot of years behind bars, so it wouldn't be the first time. But something told him that this time he wouldn't live to tell about it, even if he had someone to tell.

The giant was still laughing as he lay down on the bottom bunk. "Hey, little man," he called. "Better get some rest while you can. This just might be your last day on earth." He laughed again. "After all, I got nothin' to lose. They'll be sending me away for a lot of years this time, so what's one more mark on my record?"

Ernie tried to concentrate on breathing deeply as he slowly crawled under the scratchy blanket on his bunk, pulling the cover up to his chin. Even his insides felt icy cold, and he wondered if that was what it would be like when he died. Or was there really a hell, a place of never-ending fire, where he would burn for eternity? If there was, he knew he would end up there. But could it really be any worse than his life had been for the last twenty years?

Hell or not, maybe it was better this way, he decided. Maybe he would just stay right there on his bunk and wait for the night to arrive so the giant could kill him. Maybe it was better than hoping that Mr. George might come for him or that some other miracle might occur and he would get out of this place alive. Because it just wasn't going to happen.

"Hey, little man. What are you doing up there? Praying?" The giant's laughter resumed. "'Cause it's gonna take a lot more than prayer to get you out of this one. You know that, don't you?"

Ernie didn't answer. He knew the man was right, but he figured that anything he said would just further aggravate his tormentor.

Suddenly the man bounced from his bed and was in Ernie's face again. "Hey, I'm talking to you, creep. I don't like being ignored."

Ernie felt his heart racing, and sweat began to pour from his body. "I . . ."

"Is that all you can say? 'I, I, I.' Pathetic. You can't even finish a sentence. You'd think they'd give me someone with a little more guts for a cellmate—or at least a better vocabulary." He smiled again, and the evil Ernie saw mirrored in the depths of the man's eyes sent lightning bolts of fear shooting through his body. "But then, who knows? Maybe our other roomy will wake up, and I'll have two of you for the price of one." His smile faded and his eyes went cold. "Listen, puke-bag, when I feel like talking, you talk. And when I don't feel like talking, you shut your mouth and keep it shut. Got it?"

Ernie nodded.

"And right now I feel like talking. So talk. Tell me what you're here for. What'd you do, steal a box of cookies from a Girl Scout?" He laughed again, then waited as Ernie tried to make his mouth work.

"I . . . My name is Ernie Benson. I . . . got busted for drugs . . . last night."

The giant didn't move. His eyes were still fixed on his prey, so Ernie continued to talk.

"I'm . . . waiting for my friend to . . . get me out."

The man raised his eyebrow. "Oh, yeah? You got a friend, huh? And he's coming to get you out of here."

Ernie nodded again. "Yes. Mr. George . . . George Landry. He's . . . from Texas. He's here in River View looking for his brother, James. He even hired some people to help him, and—"

The man's arm shot out, and once again he grabbed Ernie by the shirt and pulled him up from the bed. "I don't care what your friend's name is, you sniveling little wimp. 'Cause he's not gonna get here in time to save your worthless carcass, you hear me? You're mine, and that's that. Now lay down and shut up. I'll tell you when you can talk again."

With tears dripping from his eyes and down into his ears and onto his thin pillow, Ernie lay as still and quiet as he could, hoping the man would kill him quickly and not cause him too much pain in the process.

And then he heard a voice—another voice. It was a guard, calling his name. "Benson. Get up off that bunk and get over here," he ordered. "I don't know why, but for some reason somebody's bailed you out. Let's go."

As the reality of the guard's words began to sink in, Ernie heard the giant cursing his loss. He felt sorry for his drunken cellmate and could only hope that he too would be released before the sun went down.

But even if he wasn't, Ernie reminded himself, the drunk really wasn't his concern. If the guy died in that jail cell, that was his problem. Mr. George had come through for him, and that's all that mattered.

He jumped down from his bunk and hurried to the cell door. It looked like he was going to live after all.

CHAPTER 11

The restaurant was crowded, but Sophie and April were able to get seated in just under ten minutes. Sophie was relieved that it hadn't taken longer, as she hadn't wanted to say anything and spoil April's shopping, but she was getting hungry. She knew she should have eaten something before leaving her house that morning, and she had planned to. But instead she had sat down at the breakfast table and started reading the *Tenakh*, and the next thing she knew, it was time to leave.

As they waited for the waitress to bring their menus, Sophie reflected on the morning's Scriptures. She had been reading from *Iyov*, or Job, the great man of patience who had been tested by Adonai. It was the twenty-fourth verse of chapter 33 that had caught her attention, as God said, "Redeem him from going down to the pit; I have found a ransom."

There it was again, that same word—*ransom*. For years she had been reading the Holy Scriptures, but never had she noticed how often that word appeared. Now it seemed to jump out at her from almost every page. It appeared to be a recurring theme, and Sophie was beginning to think it might be the key to unraveling her many questions about *Yeshua*. But she wasn't ready to voice her questions and suspicions to anyone else, including April Lippincott—at least, not yet.

The waitress appeared, carrying a couple of menus and two glasses of water. "Thank you," April said, smiling up at the young woman. Sophie nodded at her and took a menu, hoping her information about this being a kosher restaurant had been accurate. She was greatly relieved to open to the front page and see some of her favorite dishes listed, particularly lox. Her mouth watered just thinking of it.

"Everything looks wonderful, doesn't it?" April asked, still studying the menu.

Sophie looked at her and smiled. "Yes, it does. And I know exactly what I'm going to order."

April looked up and raised her eyebrows questioningly.

"Lox," Sophie answered. "And bagels, of course. I know they're fresh because I smelled them baking when we walked in."

"I was thinking the same thing," April said, returning her smile. "The smell is irresistible. But I have to tell you, I've never tried *lox*."

Sophie laughed. "Well, then, today you are in for a big treat. You will have lox with me, yes?"

April shrugged. "Why not? When in Rome, as they say. But I think I'd like a little greenery on the side."

The waitress, who was still standing there, observing and listening, smiled. "I think that can be arranged." She wrote down their orders, gathered their menus, and walked away toward the kitchen.

"So," April said, "what do you think? Are we going to find anything? We certainly haven't done too well so far."

"We'll find something," Sophie assured her. "The day is young. And I, for one, do my best work on a full stomach."

April laughed. "I'm with you." She leaned forward and spoke almost conspiratorially. "I must admit, I was getting a bit hungry."

"So was I. I just didn't want to say anything since it was my own fault for not eating breakfast before I left."

"I wish I could say that was my excuse. But I'm afraid I ate breakfast, and I'm still hungry. Must be this Pacific Northwest air. I seem to be hungry all the time."

"That's good," Sophie said, smiling, "because lox and bagels should be eaten on an empty stomach to be fully appreciated."

April laughed again, and her pale blue eyes twinkled. "Are you trying to tell me that I'll like them only because I'm starving?"

"No," Sophie assured her, still smiling. "Not at all. They're wonderful. They were my dear husband's favorite, and Avraham loves them as well."

"Well, that's good enough for me," April said. "We'll eat and fortify ourselves for some serious shopping this afternoon. I for one do not intend to go home until we have accomplished our mission."

"Agreed. Somewhere out there is the perfect birthday gift for Melissa, and we're going to find it."

"Amen," said April.

"*Omayn*," agreed Sophie, and grinned.

~~~

Melissa wished this moment could go on forever, as she sat beside Eric in the front seat of his black-and-silver El Camino in the school parking lot. Classes had let out an hour early that day so they had a little extra time to spend together before she had to say good-bye and head for home. She had promised Abe and Toni she would not go anywhere with Eric until they had discussed the situation, which they had assured her they would do after school on Friday, and she had honored her promise. But it had not been easy.

Now, with his arm around her shoulders, she leaned against his chest, eyes closed, listening to the radio as it played a love song that she felt sure had been written just for the two of them. Eric occasionally kissed the top of her head, but for the most part they sat silently, lost in thought and enjoying their brief time together.

Melissa couldn't help but hope—and pray—that her sixteenth birthday would have some bearing on Abe and Toni's decision. After all, it wasn't like she was too young to date. Many of her friends had been dating since their first year of high school. For Melissa it had never really been an issue because, until now, she simply hadn't met anyone she was interested in enough to even consider dating. But Eric . . . well, Eric was definitely different. It wasn't just his good looks—although that certainly didn't hurt—but deep inside Melissa was convinced that God had purposed for them to be together. If not, why would she feel this way? And if it was God's will, then how could Toni or Abe stand in their way?

Eric shifted in his seat and then lifted her chin with his finger until she was looking into his eyes. He smiled, kissed her, and then asked, "So what do you want for your birthday? Have you thought about it?"

Melissa had thought about it a lot, and she knew exactly what she wanted. "To be able to go out with you," she answered. "That's what I'm praying for. I don't care if I get anything else."

Eric's dark eyes went soft. "That's sweet. But I really want to get you something special. I know you're having a birthday dinner with your family on Sunday, but I want to take you out to dinner too, maybe on the coast somewhere. Do you think there's a chance your sister and her husband will let us do that? Like Friday or Saturday night maybe?"

Melissa sighed. "I don't know. I hope so, I really do. And they promised we could talk about it on Friday afternoon. Just two more days, and then we'll know. I don't see why they'd have any problem with it though. After all, I am going to be sixteen on Monday."

Eric smiled again. "Sweet sixteen. Beautiful, too. I'm a lucky guy." He looked down at her and winked. "And I sure am glad I listened to my dad and fixed up this old muscle car instead of buying one of those newer foreign jobs. They all have bucket seats, but my El Camino has this nice bench seat so we can sit real close. Good planning, don't you think?"

Melissa nodded, and her heart sang with the music pouring forth from the radio. Being in love was the most incredible feeling in the world. How could anything that felt like this possibly be wrong? When Eric kissed her again, she closed her eyes and returned his kiss with an intensity that made her heart hurt.

～～～

Toni and Abe sat across from each other at the breakfast table on Thursday morning. Their first appointment wasn't until nine, so they were enjoying a few quiet moments together before jumping into a busy day. Melissa had already gone to school, and April was still sleeping. As Toni sipped her orange juice, Abe scanned the front page of the paper.

"Anything new and exciting this morning?" Toni asked.

Abe didn't answer.

"Hellooo."

Abe looked up. "Huh? Did you say something?"

Toni feigned indignance. "I most certainly did, Mr. Matthews. Don't tell me we've been married so long that you're starting to ignore me already."

Abe smiled. "Never. And if I ever do, shoot me, will you? Because anyone who could ignore someone as beautiful and fascinating as you is already dead anyway."

Toni laughed. "Oh, you're quick, detective. Really quick."

"Thank you. Can I read my paper now?"

"Not a chance. If I'm so beautiful and fascinating, talk to me."

"About what?"

"I don't know. The weather. World affairs. Whatever."

"How about Melissa and Eric?"

Toni hesitated, then sighed. "I know. We have to get this settled, don't we?"

Abe nodded. "The sooner the better. Didn't you promise her we'd give her our answer by tomorrow afternoon?"

"I'm afraid I did. And I've prayed about it, I really have. I just wish I had a clear answer, one way or the other. Overall, I'm not too thrilled about it."

"No parent, and that includes big sisters, ever is when this situation comes up. But you had to know it would happen sooner or later. In case you haven't noticed, Melissa is an attractive young lady. It was just a matter of time until some guy came along and swept her off her feet."

"I suppose. I just wish I felt better about the whole thing. We hardly know this guy."

"So we start spending more time with him. Get to know him better."

Toni nodded. "I guess that's the only way. Do you think we should invite him over for Melissa's birthday dinner on Sunday?"

Before Abe could answer, April appeared in the doorway. "Good morning," she said, walking to the refrigerator and helping herself to a glass of juice. "Forgive me, but I couldn't help overhearing. You must be talking about Eric."

"Who else?" Toni asked. "And don't worry about overhearing. You're just in time. We could use your wise advice."

April smiled and took a seat across from Toni, next to Abe. "Regarding?"

"Regarding getting to know Eric better," Toni answered. "I was just asking Abe what he thought about having Eric over for Melissa's birthday dinner on Sunday."

April turned to Abe. "And what do you think?"

"I think it's a good idea. It worked out OK on Saturday when we had him over. Why not try it again?"

"For what it's worth," April said, looking from Abe to Toni, "I agree. In fact, if you really want my advice, which you say you do, then I'd invite his parents too—his entire family, for that matter. Carrie's coming, isn't she? Why not make it a real party? After all, a girl turns sixteen only once."

Abe and Toni looked at each other, then back at April. "Well, why not?" said Toni, shrugging her shoulders. "What have we got to lose? And I think you're right. Seeing him with his family might give us a better idea of who he really is. I just wonder what Melissa will think of it."

"Melissa will be fine," April assured them. "As long as Eric is included, she won't care about anything else."

"That's for sure," said Abe. "But what do we tell her when we talk to her tomorrow? She wants an answer from us about dating the guy. We can't put her off forever."

Toni opened her mouth to speak, then thought better of it, and looked to April once again. "Any more words of wisdom, oh, venerated mentor?"

April smiled. "If it were strictly up to me, girls wouldn't be allowed to date anyone until they're at least twenty. Of course, that's easy for me to say at my age. But I must admit that I was already dating my Lawrence when I was Melissa's age. And thinking back, I wonder how I might have reacted if my parents had forbidden us to see each other." She paused, looking from one to the other before continuing. "You may not want to hear this, but since you asked for my advice, I'm going to give it. Melissa is a good girl. She's honest and respectful, and she's been raised with strong moral values. You need to honor and trust that. At the same time she is a bit immature emotionally, so you don't want to give her too much leeway. Maybe you could allow her to see Eric but with some strong boundaries on the relationship."

Abe raised his eyebrows. "Such as?"

April paused a moment before answering. "Such as, keeping reasonable curfews, including others on their dates when possible, and restricting the amount of time together when they're completely alone. I believe Melissa will respect whatever guidelines you set."

Toni wasn't convinced. "But will Eric?"

"If he doesn't," April answered, "you'll know that soon enough. And that will force you to reevaluate your decision about their seeing each other. Besides, if Eric doesn't respect your guidelines, then I don't think Melissa could respect him for very long either. And that just might be the end of their relationship."

"I hope you're right," Toni said, shaking her head slowly. "But can we trust Melissa with this much responsibility?"

"My dear," said April, reaching across the table to cover Toni's hand with her own, "even if you can't trust Melissa, you know you can trust the Father. He cares for her even more than we do."

Toni had to admit the elderly woman with the silver hair and innocent blue eyes had nailed her to the wall with that one. "All right," she said, looking at Abe, who nodded his head once in agreement, "we asked for your advice, you gave it, and we'll take it. We'll sit down with Melissa tomorrow afternoon and tell her what we've decided. And then we'll continue to pray—a lot."

"What better way to handle this or any situation?" April asked. "Now, to change the subject, did I tell you what Sophie and I came up with for Melissa's birthday? It took us the better part of the day yesterday, but we finally figured it out."

"What is it?" Toni asked, eager to hear what they'd decided since she and Abe still hadn't bought her anything.

"We got to thinking about how much she loves to write in her journal," April explained. "Since I've known her, she's carried it almost everywhere with her. I know she always talks about being an actress someday, but Sophie and I wondered if she might just follow in your shoes and aspire to become a writer instead. Who knows? But meanwhile we decided she needed something that she could use, not only for writing her journal but to help her with her schoolwork as well. So we thought maybe she should have a computer. Nothing fancy, just something basic. We priced them, and they're really not too bad if we go in on it together. But we wanted to ask you two first and get your opinion."

Toni was stunned. Why hadn't she and Abe thought of this? It was so obvious. Melissa had even mentioned how much easier it would be to do some of her homework if she had a computer at home. Toni glanced at her husband. She could tell by his eyes that they were thinking the exact same thing.

"April, that's perfect," Toni said. "Don't you think so, Abe?"

"Absolutely. I just don't know why it didn't occur to us to get that for her ourselves."

"So why don't we?" Toni asked. "I mean, why don't we all go in together and get it for her? Would you mind, April? Do you think Sophie would care if we all went in on it as a family gift?"

April's eyes sparkled. "I think that's a wonderful idea. Maybe together we could get her a nicer setup. And I'm sure Sophie will agree wholeheartedly. We wanted to talk to you about it at dinner last night, but of course Melissa was here so we couldn't. But I'll call Sophie right now and tell her, if that's all right with the two of you."

"Go right ahead," said Abe. "And be sure to thank her for being half of the team that came up with the perfect solution to this birthday present dilemma."

When April had gone back to her room to make the call, Abe looked at Toni. "I just thought of something," he said. "When April was talking about Melissa and her journal, she mentioned the possibility of her becoming a writer someday. Not that I mind having two writers in the family, but it reminded me that you made me a promise last week."

"I did?"

"Yes, you did. You promised you'd have another chapter for me to read by tomorrow."

Toni smiled. "I bet you thought I forgot."

"Did you?"

"Almost," she admitted. "But I spent the better part of yesterday afternoon working on it."

"So that's why you went home early yesterday."

"That's it. And with just a few more tweaks, which I plan to take care of today, you'll have your chapter tomorrow, as promised."

"A woman of her word. I like that."

"Well, this woman of her word had better finish getting ready for work. Give me fifteen minutes."

"You got it. Now does that mean I can finally get back to reading my paper?"

"I suppose so, detective. Just let me know if you find anything interesting since I won't have time to read it myself."

Abe chuckled as she got up from the table and carried her glass to the sink. She was about to leave the room when he said, "Another death in River View. We sure have had our share lately."

"What?" Toni hurried to stand behind him and peer over his shoulder. "What do you mean? What happened? And why are you reading the obituaries?"

"I'm not. This is just a back-page news item—nothing big. Just some druggie that died of an overdose. They found him in an alley last night. You know that area down by the river in the old part of town. They have a lot of problems with drugs down there."

"That's true. It is a bad section of town. What a waste of life. Who was he? Or was it a she?"

"A guy. Had a record a mile long—all drug related. In fact, he just got arrested the other day and was let out on bail yesterday. Says here his name was Ernie Benson. Ring a bell?"

Toni shook her head. "Never heard of him. Sad, though."

Abe nodded his agreement, and Toni went to her room to finish getting ready for work.

CHAPTER 12

Toni had left work early on Friday for two reasons. First, she wanted to do some last-minute touch-ups on the chapter she would show to Abe later that night. Second, she needed a little time to prepare for their discussion with Melissa regarding the boundaries of her relationship with Eric. The first goal had been relatively easily achieved; she was having a bit more trouble with the second, and time was running out.

She glanced at her watch when she heard Abe's car pull into the driveway. Three-thirty. Melissa would be home any minute. Toni sighed and set out some glasses for iced tea. The early fall weather, which had been relatively cool for the past few days, had warmed again and promised a sunny weekend. She was grateful for that, as they'd hoped for sunshine so they could have a barbecue for Melissa's birthday dinner on Sunday. But she still had an alternate plan for an inside meal, just in case. Growing up in the Pacific Northwest, Toni knew all too well how quickly the weather could change.

The weather, of course, was the least of her worries when it came to Melissa. Toni wished she could come up with something that would convince her younger sister to stop seeing Eric altogether, but she had finally reached the conclusion that it simply wasn't going to happen. *All right, God. I've prayed and prayed, and prayed some more. So I guess I'd better just let it go now and believe that you're going to help us work out the details of this situation.*

"Hey, beautiful." Abe put his arms around Toni's waist and kissed the back of her neck as he walked up behind her. She was still standing in front of the kitchen counter, contemplating the three empty glasses. If only Mrs. Lippincott had agreed to join them for this discussion, she was sure things would go much more smoothly. But April had declined their invitation, insisting that it was better for the three of them to talk alone. She said she would be spending the day at her former church, helping to finalize plans for the upcoming harvest party at the end of the month, and then she would be home in time for dinner.

Toni turned to Abe, and he pulled her close. "Stop worrying," he said, gazing down at her with his dark, expressive eyes.

She smiled. "You know me too well, detective."

Abe kissed her. "And the more I know you, the more I love you. But worrying doesn't help or change anything, you know that."

Toni nodded. "I know it—in my head. I just wish I could convince my heart."

Before Abe could respond, the front door opened and they heard Melissa's voice. "I'm home," she called. "Where is everybody?"

"In here," Toni answered.

As Melissa walked into the kitchen, Toni dropped ice into the glasses and set them on the kitchen table. "Iced tea?" she asked.

"Sure," Melissa said, taking a seat. "Sounds good."

Toni couldn't help but wonder if her sister's voice sounded a bit unnatural, as if she wanted to appear confident and unconcerned about the upcoming discussion. Toni, of course, knew better.

She poured the tea, and then sat down beside Abe, across from Melissa.

"So how was school?" Abe asked. Toni wondered if he, too, was trying too hard to act as if this were no more than an everyday conversation.

Melissa shrugged. "Fine. Not too much homework for a change."

Abe smiled. "I'm sure you appreciate that—especially on your birthday weekend."

"I sure do. I'm looking forward to Sunday. But I was just wondering . . ." She paused, and Toni was sure Melissa's next question would be about more than just idle curiosity. "Who's coming, anyway?"

Toni smiled. She'd been right. Melissa definitely had an agenda. "Well, there are the three of us, of course. And April. Carrie's coming, too, and more than likely, her parents. And Aunt Sophie said she'd come." She took a deep breath and went on. "We wondered if you'd like to invite Eric—and his family."

Melissa's green eyes went wide. With surprise? Dismay? Toni couldn't be sure.

"I . . . Eric's family? You mean, like, his parents?"

"Sure," Toni answered. "And brothers and sisters, too, if he has any."

Melissa's tone was hesitant, even guarded. "He has two brothers, but they're older. They're both married and live back in Nebraska."

"Well, then," Abe said, "just his parents. We'd really like to meet them."

Melissa's eyes darted back and forth between them, until a look of resignation settled on her face. "This is the only way I'm going to be able to see him, isn't it? You want to meet his family first."

Toni nodded. "Of course we do. And I would think they'd like to meet us as well. Then, depending on how everything goes, we'll talk about some guidelines as far as the two of you seeing each other in the future."

Melissa's face lit up. "Does that mean I can go out with him? You're going to let me date Eric?"

Abe laid a restraining hand on Toni's arm before he spoke. "It means that if all goes well on Sunday, we'll talk again when the party's over about your dating Eric."

Toni whispered a prayer of thanks for Abe's perfect timing. She had been about to say something less diplomatic in answer to Melissa's question. Once again Abe had sensed what she was thinking and had intervened just in time.

"But . . ." Melissa was frowning now. "What if Eric's parents can't come?"

"Why don't you ask them," Abe suggested, "and let's see what they say? Fair enough?"

It was obvious Melissa was considering her options and realizing there weren't many. "OK," she agreed, her smile tentative. "I'll go call him right now. I just hope it isn't too awkward. I've never even met them myself."

"All the more reason to have them over," Abe said.

Melissa nodded and got up from the table, her tea untouched as she walked toward the kitchen door. Suddenly she turned and came back and kissed each of them on the cheek. "Thanks," she said, then turned again and hurried off to her room.

"And thank you," Toni said, looking up at her husband. "You jumped in at just the right time—as usual."

He smiled. "Like I said, I'm getting to know you better every day, and every day I love you more. It's going to be OK, sweetheart. You'll see."

Toni nodded, knowing he was right but wondering at the same time how it would all play out.

<p style="text-align:center">~~~</p>

Later that evening, as she lay in bed with her head resting on Abe's shoulder, Toni was still wondering the same thing. Even if the birthday party went smoothly, what would happen after that? Would Melissa and Eric become a permanent item? Was it possible that she would be meeting her sister's future in-laws in a couple of days?

"You're worrying again," Abe murmured.

Toni sighed. "You're right—again. Maybe this getting-to-know-me-better-every-day stuff isn't so great. I can't get away with anything anymore."

Abe chuckled, then kissed the top of her head. "Look, all we've committed to so far is having a few people over for a barbecue on Sunday. That's it. No big deal. I think we can handle it."

"Oh, sure. But what about after that? What if we don't like Eric's parents? Then what? Or worse, what if we do? Then we have absolutely no reason at all not to allow Melissa to date him, other than just saying no—which, I might add, I haven't ruled out entirely."

Abe slipped his arm out from under Toni's head and rose up on his elbow. "I thought you resigned from that job," he said, his face serious as he looked down at her.

Toni was puzzled. "What do you mean? What job?"

Abe's dark eyes began to sparkle. "You know, master of the universe—the one who holds everything together and runs the whole show. I thought you'd resigned and relegated that job to God. Did you decide to take it back because he wasn't doing very well at it?"

Toni did her best to give him an indignant glare, but she knew it was unconvincing because of the smile that she just couldn't keep from turning up the corners of her mouth. "All right," she said, granting the smile full reign. "You got me again. I give up. You win. No more worrying about what's going to happen on Sunday. From now on I'll stick to one day at a time. Will that make you happy, oh, wise one?"

Abe grinned, and Toni's heart melted as he leaned down to kiss her. "I'm already happy," he whispered, his lips close to her ear. "But I'll tell you something that will make me even happier, and it's not what you think."

Toni arched her eyebrows. "You are just full of surprises, aren't you, detective? OK, what is it that you want from me now? An oath signed in blood? An ice cream sundae?"

Abe pulled back and looked down at Toni as if her words had triggered an up-till-now un-thought-of idea. "An ice cream sundae?" he said. "Could I get one of those, right here, right now, in bed?"

"Not a chance. An oath signed in blood, maybe. An ice cream sundae in bed? Never happen."

Abe looked crushed. "I should have known it was too good to be true." His sigh was exaggerated. "OK, then, I guess I'll have to settle for my original idea."

"Which was?"

"Reading your next chapter. You did finish it, didn't you?"

Toni smiled. "Yes, I did. And I just happen to have it right here in the nightstand." She sat up and reached over to pull open the drawer, then handed him the next nineteen pages of her masterpiece.

"There you go," she said. "And remember, my ego is very fragile."

Abe chuckled again, then lay back on his pillow to read. "I'll remember," he said. "Just like I'll remember that I promised to love you—for better or worse."

Toni smacked him playfully on the arm, then lay down next to him to await his verdict. She never felt more vulnerable than when her husband read her work. How would she ever survive if her writing actually made it to print and she knew it was being critiqued by strangers who felt no compunction to love her for better or worse or even to be gracious in their response? Then she reminded herself that, once again, she was borrowing trouble. Better to stick with today and let tomorrow take care of itself. Besides, at this point, getting into print was no more than a distant dream.

~~~

Sunday had dawned clear and crisp, and Melissa had been a nervous wreck from the time she'd first opened her eyes. She hadn't been able to concentrate on one word the pastor spoke at church that morning, and now she was pacing, waiting for the guests to start arriving, and checking and rechecking her image in the mirror.

My last day as a fifteen-year-old, she thought, looking at her reflection. *Tomorrow it'll be official. I'll finally be sixteen. I always thought the big thing about this birthday would be getting my driver's license. Now I don't even care about that. I'd rather just ride in Eric's car and let him drive. That's what I really care about—being with him. Oh, please, God, let it all work out.*

She glanced at her sandals. Were they too casual for her dress? Or was her dress too much for an outside party? The green matched her eyes and complemented her auburn hair, but maybe she should change into something more casual. She wanted so much to look just right for Eric, and especially for his parents. She still couldn't decide whether she was glad they were coming. It was flattering to know they felt it was important enough to be here but nerve-racking to know they'd be watching her every move—and that Abe and Toni would be watching theirs.

Who am I kidding? It's me they'll all be watching. And to think I always dreamed of being an actress. Now that the spotlight is shining right on me, I don't like it at all. This should be the best day of my life, but I can't wait till it's over.

The doorbell rang then, and she knew it was too late to worry about changing clothes. She would just have to make do with what she was wearing and hope it didn't look too out of place when she compared it to everyone else's attire. Why hadn't she thought to call Carrie and see what she was wearing? *Because you were too busy thinking about Eric,* she chided herself. *You forgot anyone else was even coming.*

She jumped when she heard the knock on her bedroom door. "Melissa," Toni called, "you have company."

Taking a deep breath and one last look in the mirror, Melissa went to the door and pulled it open. Toni smiled when she saw her. "You look beautiful," she said. Melissa wanted to believe her, but she knew she wouldn't until she heard it from Eric.

"Carrie and her parents are here," Toni said. "Why don't you take them out back? Abe's already out there, getting the grill ready, and I'm going to help April with some last-minute things in the kitchen."

Melissa nodded. "Sure," she said, and walked to the living room to greet her guests.

Carrie sat in her wheelchair between Mr. and Mrs. Bosworth, who stood on either side of their daughter. Mr. Bosworth's eyes lit up the minute Melissa walked into the room.

"Wow!" he exclaimed. "You look fantastic, Melissa. What did you do, go and grow up on us all at once?"

Melissa felt her face grow hot, but she appreciated the compliment. She knew Carrie's father didn't give them easily.

"Thank you," she said, checking out Carrie's slacks and sweater ensemble. "I just hope I'm not overdressed."

"Not at all," Mrs. Bosworth assured her. "My husband is right. You look absolutely fantastic." She handed her a wrapped gift. "Happy birthday, Melissa."

Melissa took the gift and gave them each a hug and a thank you, then offered to take them out to the backyard. Once they were outside, Abe spotted them and hurried over to help Mr. Bosworth maneuver Carrie and her wheelchair from the porch to the yard, where she could then get around on her own. Melissa placed her recently received gift on the smaller of the two picnic tables, next to a large box that was signed, "with love from Abe, Toni, Aunt Sophie, and April." Melissa had been eyeing it since they'd first set it out and couldn't begin to imagine what was inside.

"So what do you think is in there?" Carrie asked, wheeling herself up beside Melissa.

"I wish I knew. I've been wondering about it all day."

"I see Abe's aunt signed the gift card. Does that mean she's coming?"

Melissa nodded. "She should be here any minute."

"That's great. I'm so glad she and Abe are getting along again. So who else is coming? Or is this it?"

Melissa swallowed. "Eric and his parents."

Carrie raised her eyebrows. "Really? His parents too?"

Melissa nodded again. "I'm a nervous wreck. I'll be so glad when this is over."

"You're kidding. This is your sixteenth birthday party. You should be looking forward to it, not dreading it."

"I know. But a lot hinges on how things go with Eric and his parents today."

"What do you mean?"

"As far as Toni and Abe letting me go out with him. I—"

Her explanation was interrupted as Eric and his parents stepped out onto the back porch, along with Sophie, who Melissa assumed had arrived at approximately the same time. Melissa's heart soared when she saw Eric smiling at her, the sunlight gleaming on his dark hair, his shirt and pants impeccably pressed and matched. He had dressed up for her, and she was suddenly glad she had decided to wear a dress.

"You'd better go say hello," Carrie said. "They're waiting for you."

Melissa prayed her smile looked natural as she made her way across the lawn. As she stopped in front of her most recently arrived guests, the look in Eric's eyes flooded her heart with longing, and she wished the two of them could celebrate her birthday alone, away from everyone else, where she could relax in his arms and let him kiss her and tell her all the things she wanted to hear. But for now she would have to give her best performance and hope that the outcome was all she'd dreamed it would be.

~~~

The breeze ruffled Brad's hair as he sat alone on the park bench with his eyes closed, thinking that there were few things as beautiful

as an autumn afternoon. True, the sun faded earlier and didn't shine
as brightly as it did in the summer, but that's what made it so sweet,
he thought.

Bittersweet, he corrected himself. *Like the fading memories of a
once-warm relationship.* He shook his head. *I've got to stop thinking
about Toni. She's another man's wife now. I have no right. . . .*

And when he was honest with himself, he had to admit that it
really didn't hurt as it once had. He still missed her and sometimes
wondered if he always would, but even the fading autumn sunshine
held a promise of spring. Was it possible that God had someone else
for him, someone other than Toni with whom to share his love and
his life? Was it even possible that the loneliness he felt was more of a
longing to find someone new than an ache to return to the past? He
certainly hoped so, because he'd long since come to the conclusion
that getting mired in the past was a sure way to sabotage the future.

Brad breathed deeply. Everything smelled so fresh. And he especially loved the sounds of the park on a Sunday afternoon—children
laughing and playing, ducks quacking and geese honking, the noise of
traffic in the distance. He had come here after church, feeling sorry for
himself because he had overheard Carrie's family, who had been sitting in the pew in front of him, making plans to go to Melissa's birthday party. *Sixteen. My little sis is going to be sixteen tomorrow. I thought
by now she'd be my sister-in-law. Instead, I'm not even included in their
birthday celebration.*

*No! Enough. This pity party has got to end. Please, God, help me to
get past this. Help me to move on, to see that there really is a future for
me without Toni. Show me, Lord.*

"Is this seat taken?"

Brad flinched and opened his eyes, squinting against the mid-
afternoon rays. The petite form standing in front of him was topped

with red hair that shone in the sun like a halo. Her brown eyes were soft, her smile tentative. Jeanine. What in the world was she doing here?

"May I join you?" she asked.

Brad smiled. What could it hurt? It wasn't as if they were going out on a date or anything.

He patted the seat beside him. "Be my guest," he said. As she settled in next to him, he noticed the sun seemed to warm a few degrees.

CHAPTER 13

By the time Brad walked Jeanine home, the sun had set and Brad had long since stopped trying to convince himself that he was simply spending an enjoyable, serendipitous afternoon with his employee. The truth was, he liked Jeanine—a lot. And he intended to see her again.

First, of course, he would let his father know what was going on. As one of the two senior partners at the firm where Brad had worked for the past few years since completing law school, his father had a right to know that his son, the junior partner, was dating their receptionist—or, at least, hoped to do so. And judging from the time he and Jeanine had spent together that afternoon, Brad was relatively sure she would accept when he formally asked her out, which he intended to do immediately after talking with his father.

For the first time in many, many months, Brad Anderson found himself humming as he headed for home. It was a good feeling. It had been far too long since he'd walked with such a spring in his step and an expectancy in his heart. He smiled as he rounded the corner toward home. In fact, he was still smiling when he let himself into his apartment and closed the door behind him.

∾∾∾

Melissa had never been so happy about waking up on a Monday morning, and it had almost nothing to do with the fact that it was her birthday. All she wanted was to get to school and see Eric. The birthday dinner had gone as well as could be expected, and Abe and Toni had talked with her afterward and told her she could see Eric on a limited basis. They preferred that she and Eric include others on their dates whenever possible, they expected curfews to be met without exception, and they wanted to know exactly where the two would be whenever they did go somewhere together. Melissa had readily agreed, thrilled that at last she and Eric were going to be able to date. She had told him about it on the phone before falling asleep the night before, but now she just wanted to see him in person.

She had covered all but the last two blocks on her way to school when Eric pulled up in his El Camino. "Hey, beautiful," he called out, reaching across the front seat to open the passenger door, "does this new blessing on our relationship include rides to and from school in my car?"

Melissa giggled and hurried to climb in. She hadn't even pulled the door shut behind her or set her books down on the seat before Eric gathered her into his arms and pulled her close for a kiss. "I missed you," he said, his voice husky. "It was terrible being so close to you all afternoon yesterday and not being able to hold you. You looked so beautiful in that green dress. I couldn't keep my eyes off of you."

"I know what you mean," Melissa agreed, melting at the sight of his warm brown eyes gazing down at her. "I thought the day would never end."

"Happy birthday," Eric whispered. "I couldn't wait to give you a birthday kiss." And then he kissed her again . . . and again.

Melissa's head was swimming. "We have to go to school," she murmured, wishing they didn't, wishing they could go somewhere alone together for the entire day. She couldn't imagine a better birthday present than that.

"We have a few minutes yet," Eric said between kisses. "And then we'll pick up where we left off after school. No more driving home alone while you walk off in the other direction. From now on you have your own personal taxi service to and from school—every day."

Melissa was so caught up in Eric's kisses that she couldn't even answer. Finally he pulled away and looked down at her. "We really better get going," he said. "I don't want to risk being late to our first class. The last thing we need now is for you to get in trouble with your sister." He turned away and put the car back in gear, then looked over his shoulder and pulled out into the street.

"That's for sure," Melissa said. "But what about your parents? We were so busy talking about Abe and Toni on the phone last night that you didn't even tell me what they said. What happened after you left our house? What did they say? Do you think they liked me? Could you tell?"

Eric glanced at her and grinned. "How could they not like you? You're beautiful and sweet and smart." He looked back at the road. "Of course they liked you. And before long they'll love you. You'll see."

Melissa smiled and leaned her head on Eric's shoulder. "I hope you're right," she said as they pulled into the already crowded school parking lot. "They seemed really nice."

"They are—for parents." He slipped into a vacant parking space and turned off the engine, then looked down at her again. "Just kidding. They really are great, and I'm lucky to have them. I know how much you miss your own parents."

Melissa did her best to ignore the lump in her throat. She nodded. "I do miss them, you're right—my dad especially. I really don't remember my mom. As I told you, I was only two when she died."

Eric took her hand and pressed it to his lips. "I know. And I understand that's why you're so close to your sister. So we'd better do our best to keep her and her husband happy, right? Come on; let's get going. Classes start in fifteen minutes."

Melissa gathered up her books, but Eric took them from her when they got out of the car. As they walked hand in hand across the campus, Melissa noticed a couple of her friends watching them, and she beamed with pride. Nearly everyone now knew they were a couple, and Melissa loved the new level of admiration and recognition that gave her. But not nearly as much as she loved Eric, she reminded herself, happily squeezing his hand.

"So," Eric said, "what do you think of that new computer your family got you? Where are you going to put it?"

"In my room, I think. Probably on my desk. I'll have to clear everything else off to make it fit, but it'll be worth it."

"Do you want me to come over and help you set it up?"

Melissa's eyes opened wide. "Would you? I don't have a clue how to start. Toni and Abe said they'd give it a try next weekend, but they're not too experienced at that sort of thing. I don't think they'd mind if you came over and helped. I'll ask them about it after school today."

"Good. Meantime, you never did tell me what you want from me for your birthday."

"What do you mean? You gave me a gift yesterday—a beautiful new journal and a stationery set, remember?"

Eric smiled. "That was from my parents. Sure, I told them what to get you, but Mom picked it out and signed all our names to the card. You didn't think that was all I was going to give you, did you?"

"Eric, you don't have to get me anything else, honest. I love the stationery and the journal. That's more than enough."

"Well, I'm getting you something else, whether you give me a hint or not. But I'm going to wait and give it to you at your birthday dinner."

Melissa frowned. "My birthday dinner? We just had that yesterday."

"That was the family birthday dinner. I'm talking about *our* birthday dinner—just you and me. I already told you I wanted to do that, remember? Do you think you can talk Toni and Abe into letting me take you out to eat this coming weekend? I know it'll be a little late for your birthday, but I want it to be really special."

"I think so. I'll give it my best try anyway." She smiled. "I would really love that. It would make my sixteenth birthday absolutely perfect."

They stopped in front of Melissa's classroom. "That's exactly what I want to give you—the perfect birthday." He kissed her. "I'll pick you up after class. Think about me till then."

"I always do," she said, as Carrie rolled past her going to her own class. The three of them nodded in greeting, then Eric kissed Melissa again and was gone.

~~~

George Landry was glad that Ernie was dead. He had been nothing but a pain, a problem waiting to happen. And when the little creep had learned his last name, not to mention the information about his brother and where they were from, that was the final straw. He had to go. And it had been so easy to make it look like an accident. A homeless junkie overdosing on heroin. The cops would never bother to follow up on that one.

The downside was that George had lost his contact. But he had managed to get Louie's name from Ernie before he died. Then a few discreet questions of the right people in the right places and George had tracked down his new contact. After some initial haggling Louie had agreed to keep George supplied while he was in town, but George had learned that Louie wasn't nearly as easily intimidated as Ernie. He was paying Louie a premium for what he'd practically been stealing from Ernie, but it was worth it. He didn't see any other way to endure his stay in this nowhere town, especially hanging around in his motel room day after day. It didn't get much more boring than that. He'd even begun to think that he was going to have to ask Louie for an additional form of entertainment—a young lady to keep him company while he waited for those two Matthews creeps to do his dirty work for him, since he certainly hadn't been able to discover anything on his own.

He smiled at the thought. Yes, a steady supply of cocaine and female companionship could definitely make his stay in River View a lot more endurable, maybe even enjoyable. He would have to get hold of Louie before this day had drawn to a close.

~~~

Brad leaned back in his leather chair behind his desk and waited. Monday had been a busy day, and he was glad it was almost over—for more reasons than one. Though he had fielded his share of clients over the past several hours, his mind had been elsewhere. He had managed to squeeze in a quick lunch with his dad earlier, telling him of the situation with Jeanine. Rather than expressing concern over his son's dating an employee, the senior Mr. Anderson had encouraged him to pursue the relationship and see what came of it.

"It's about time you got past the breakup with Toni," he had said. "I know it was hard on you, especially after all the years you two spent together. It was hard on your mother and me, too, believe me. We loved her like our own daughter, you know that. But there comes a time when you just have to let go and move on. I'm glad to see you're finally ready to do that. And Jeanine seems like a nice enough girl."

"She is," Brad had assured him. "We spent several hours together yesterday, getting to know each other and talking about ourselves— our pasts, our dreams for the future, things like that. I think we have a lot in common."

Mr. Anderson raised his eyebrows. "Such as?"

"Such as, a love for the law, for one thing. Jeanine has always dreamed of going to law school someday. She just didn't have the money. That's why she wanted to at least work in a law firm for now, even if it was just as a receptionist. She's intelligent, and she picks things up quickly."

"I've noticed that. And she mentioned her dream of going to law school when I interviewed her for the job." He smiled and winked. "She's not bad looking either. Of course, you probably didn't even notice that."

Brad grinned. "It would be impossible not to notice. She's beautiful, no doubt about it."

Mr. Anderson's smile faded, and he'd hesitated before speaking again. "And spiritually? What do you know about that area of her life?"

"That's the best part of all. She's a longtime member at Community Heights. Not much different from our own church, from what I understand. Her faith is important to her, Dad. She even told me how happy she was when she found out that you and I are believers."

His father nodded his approval. "Then I say go for it, son. What have you got to lose?"

And going for it was exactly what he planned to do. He had passed by Jeanine's desk several times throughout the day, and each time she had looked up at him expectantly, her brown eyes inviting. But it had never seemed the right time. He had decided to wait until the last client had come and gone, when he was sure the waiting room would be empty, before saying a word. And now, as he sat behind his desk and glanced at his watch, he concluded that he had waited long enough. All the clients were gone for the day. He knew Jeanine usually stayed for an hour or so after the last client left, so this was his chance.

Taking a deep breath, he rose from his chair and walked purposefully out of his office and down to the receptionist's area. He was surprised to see Jeanine's chair empty but decided she was probably in the restroom. Then he noticed that her desk was cleared off and her jacket no longer hung on the back of her chair. She had left early, and Brad had missed her.

Chastising himself for being too slow, Brad returned to his office, gathered up his things, and made his way out of the building and out to the parking lot. He was just about to put his key into the front door of his car when he saw her, sitting alone in her dark blue Toyota Camry. It was already dark and he couldn't be sure, but it looked as if her head was bent down. He decided she probably hadn't seen him. Determined to talk with her, he hurried to her car and, when she still didn't look up, knocked on the window.

Jeanine flinched and raised her head, appearing startled at first, and then pleased, as a smile crept across her face. She lowered her window and spoke. "Brad. I'm sorry. I didn't notice you standing there. I was praying." She smiled. "I hope that doesn't sound too overly spiritual, but I usually do that before going anywhere."

Brad was impressed. "It doesn't sound overly spiritual at all. I admire you for being so faithful."

Jeanine looked relieved. "I was just about to leave for home."

"So I noticed. Don't you usually stay a little later?"

She nodded, the highlights in her red hair gleaming softly in the streetlight. "Normally, yes. But I have to get home early today. My mother is coming over for dinner tonight. We try to get together at least once a week, especially since my dad died."

Brad nodded. Her devotion to her mother didn't surprise him. "That's nice," he said. "But bad timing on my part, I guess. I was hoping to invite you out to dinner myself tonight, but it looks like I'm too late."

Jeanine smiled. "For tonight, yes. But I don't spend every evening with my mother."

"Does that mean you'll go out with me some other time? Like tomorrow?"

"Tomorrow would be perfect. I'd love to, Brad."

For a moment they didn't speak. Then Brad cleared his throat, wondering if his excitement was as evident on his face as he imagined it to be. But he decided he didn't care. He wasn't going to play games with this woman. He wanted to see her, and it was OK if she knew that. "Then it's a date," he said. "Tomorrow."

Jeanine nodded. "Tomorrow." She started her car and raised her window. Just before backing out, she waved and smiled, and Brad felt his heart leap. It was all he could do not to throw his briefcase in the air and let out a victory shout. But he felt that at least a little restraint was in order, so he limited his response to a return wave before walking back to his own car and climbing inside.

"Thank you, God," he whispered, closing the door and fumbling with his keys. "Thank you for giving me hope again. Whether Jeanine is the one for me or not, it feels so good just to be happy, to have something to look forward to." He smiled and started the car, once again humming as he headed for home.

CHAPTER 14

The days were getting shorter, as Washingtonians were apt to say. Brad smiled, relishing the feel of the warm water pouring over his head, relaxing his muscles and soothing his nerves. The hours in each day stayed the same, of course, but he knew what people meant by the saying. In June it didn't get dark until nearly ten o'clock, but the daylight was long gone in December by four in the afternoon. With the end of October looming, they were fast approaching the "short" days of winter. Northwesterners tended to dread those days, anticipating long hours cooped up inside and week after week without sunshine.

Tonight, though, Brad really didn't mind, even though he'd had to turn on his headlights before getting home from work that evening. It was Tuesday, and he had a dinner date with Jeanine. In fact, as soon as he finished getting showered and dressed, he would climb back into his car and head straight over to her apartment to pick her up. And unless she had another suggestion, he knew exactly where he would take her. He had a favorite restaurant up in the mountains, an eatery as famous for its romantic ambience as for its excellent food. He had taken Toni there many times over the years and after their breakup had wondered if he would ever be able to set foot in the place again. Now, with the memory of Jeanine's warm smile and inviting brown eyes gazing up at him, he felt confident that he was ready to give romance another try.

By the time he was out of the shower and toweled dry, he found himself humming again. *This is getting to be a habit*, he thought, grinning at his reflection in the mirror. He splashed on a little extra aftershave and went to the bedroom closet to find just the right shirt and slacks. The evening was cool, with the usual hint of rain in the air, so he grabbed a pullover sweater as well. He was sure the restaurant would have their fireplace blazing by the time they arrived, and he could almost imagine the soft glow of Jeanine's red hair in the firelight. He wondered what she would wear. He wondered what they would talk about. He wondered if she was looking forward to their date as much as he. And he wondered why he hadn't initiated their relationship sooner.

Still humming, he finished dressing and pocketed his keys as he headed for the front door. Short days or long days, it made no difference to him. It was going to be a good evening, of that he was sure. And right now that was all that mattered.

~~~

Toni could hardly believe it was Wednesday already. The days were flying by, and soon it would be November. The next thing she knew the holidays would be upon them again. How was that possible? Had it truly been almost a year since that horrible school shooting that had left Carrie in a wheelchair? Almost a year since Abe had proposed to her in the snow and placed an engagement ring on her finger?

She gazed at her left hand, the cluster of diamonds shining in the overhead light. She felt so honored to wear the ring that had once been Abe's mother's and grandmother's. She only wished she could have known them.

Toni sighed and tried to pull herself back from her daydreams. She had, after all, come into the office early so she could catch up on the paperwork that nearly covered her desk. She had been there more than an hour now and had scarcely made a dent. She glanced at her watch. Abe should be there any minute. He had said he was going to stop by the library on his way in that morning so he could look at some old newspapers from the time when George Landry's brother had made his call to his mother, claiming to be in River View. Abe hoped to find some clue about the missing man somewhere in the paper's back pages. Toni hoped he was right because they certainly hadn't come up with anything else to prove that James Landry was ever in River View for any length of time. They also were trying to obtain copies of Mrs. Landry's phone records from that time period, hoping to at least show that he had actually made the call she claimed to have received.

Toni began to sort through the papers piled in front of her, determined to pay the bills and finish the correspondence before the day was over. She hadn't gotten far when she came across a piece of what she termed junk mail and was about to toss it into the wastepaper basket when she noticed the postmark was from a small town in Nebraska. It wasn't the Fullbrights' hometown, but she was sure it was a town fairly near there, and it didn't take long before she was thinking again—this time about Eric and Melissa.

She had to admit that Eric and his parents seemed nice enough, and having them at Melissa's birthday dinner on Sunday had turned out all right. In fact, after everyone had gone home, she and Abe had told Melissa that they were going to allow her to date Eric, so long as she kept their relationship safely within certain boundaries. Melissa had readily agreed, and by Monday night she was begging them for permission to go out to dinner with Eric—alone—on Friday. She explained that he wanted to take her somewhere special for a late birthday celebration of their own, and though Toni was anything but comfortable with it, she and Abe had consented, with the provision that they not go out of town and that Melissa would be in by eleven.

Toni shook her head and ran her fingers through her short blonde curls, trying to convince herself that they had made the right decision. After all, she had been dating Brad when she was Melissa's age. But, she reminded herself, their families had known each other forever, and they shared the same values. Though the Fullbrights were nice people, they did not attend church or profess any religious beliefs whatsoever. Toni couldn't help but wonder if Melissa was strong enough in her faith not to allow herself to be influenced by Eric or his parents.

To be fair, Eric seemed to be more open to Melissa's faith than was his family. He had, in fact, told Melissa that he would attend church with her sometime if she really wanted him to. It was something, Toni conceded, although it still would have been much easier if Melissa had just fallen for some nice young man from church.

But then, you never did promise that life would be easy, did you, Lord? Toni prayed silently. *All right, she's in your hands—again. No more playing master of the universe. But please, Father, if there's something Abe or I need to know or do regarding this relationship, something besides the boundaries we've already placed on it, please show us. We want to trust you, but we also want to be responsible as her guardians.*

Digging back into her pile of papers, she had just begun to make entries into the accounts payable book when the phone rang.

"Matthews and Matthews," she answered absently. "May I help you?"

"Is this Toni Matthews?"

The voice on the other end of the line was hesitant, and . . . what? Accented? Yes, that's what it was—a definite drawl.

"Yes, this is Toni Matthews. How may I help you?"

"My name is Mindy. Mindy Jordan. I'm George and Jimmy Landry's sister."

Toni dropped her pen and sat up straighter. She and Abe had tried calling Mindy Jordan several times but had never succeeded in reaching her, nor had she called back in response to their phone messages—until now.

"Mrs. Jordan. Thank you so much for returning our call. We've been hoping to speak with you."

"I'm sorry," she mumbled. "I would've called sooner, but I didn't realize y'all were tryin' to reach me."

Toni was puzzled. "You didn't get our phone messages?"

"No. I . . ." Toni could hear the woman take a deep breath, then let it out slowly. "No. I don't live there anymore—at home, I mean. Y'all called my house, right?"

"Yes. The number your brother George gave us. What do you mean, you don't live there anymore?"

"My husband, Harley, he . . . I mean, we . . . separated. A couple of months ago. I been stayin' at my mama's house, goin' through some of her stuff, clearin' things out. I guess we're gonna have to sell this place. Sure hate to, though. So many memories here."

Toni nodded. She understood only too well what Mindy meant about memories. It had been a year and a half since her father's death, and the memories still tore at her heart. What she didn't understand was why George Landry had given them Mindy's home number if she no longer lived there. He obviously knew about the separation and that Mindy was staying at their mother's home, and he must have realized that she and Abe would want to talk to Mindy. Had he purposely tried to keep them from speaking with her?

"I'm puzzled," Toni said. "If you didn't get our messages, how did you know to call us? Did your brother give you our number?"

"Oh, no," Mindy answered quickly, and Toni was sure she heard fear in her voice. "George doesn't know I'm callin' y'all. He wouldn't like it if he did. Y'all gotta promise me not to tell him, please."

Toni frowned. She didn't like being forced into a situation where she had to make a promise she might not be able to keep. "I'll certainly try not to," she said. "But why wouldn't he want you to talk to us? After all, he hired us to help him find your brother. To do that we need all the information about him that we can get, which obviously includes speaking with other family members."

"I think that's why he wouldn't want me to talk to y'all. See, George and Jimmy, they never got along real well, if you know what I mean—even when we were kids. George was always real jealous of Jimmy 'cause he was the baby—Mama's pet, I guess. George didn't like that much. In fact, when Jimmy first disappeared, George said he was glad he was gone and hoped he never came back. But when Mama died, I don't know, somethin' changed. I can't figure out what it was, but I heard him and Harley talkin' one day—somethin' about Jimmy and money. When I asked 'em, they said they was talkin' about tryin' to find Jimmy and give him his share of the inheritance. But that didn't make too much sense to me 'cause—well, there wasn't much, you know what I mean? We all thought there'd be a lot more, but, I don't know, Mama must've spent it, or—anyway, like I said, there wasn't much. And what little there was, I didn't think George would want to bother lookin' for Jimmy to give it to him."

Toni was more confused than ever. There was obviously a lot more to George Landry and his missing-brother story than he had told them—which they had suspected all along, of course—but the holes in the story looked as if they just might be bigger than they had imagined.

"You still haven't told me why you called," Toni said. "How did you even know how to reach us?"

"I found a newspaper in the back bedroom of Mama's house—the room where George was stayin' while Mama was sick. It was from River View, and it had a story in it about some of the cases y'all had solved, even when the police weren't able to. I got to thinkin'—after hearin' George and Harley talkin' and then George takin' off and all—I thought maybe he might've hired y'all to try to find Jimmy. But I still can't understand why. I thought maybe he might've told y'all his reasons."

Toni hesitated. She didn't want to divulge any more than she should about the reasons George had given them for wanting his brother found; after all, George was their client. Then again, he really hadn't told them much at all.

"To tell you the truth," Toni said, "the only thing your brother told us was that he wanted us to help him find James so he could give him his share of the inheritance. He said that before your mother died she told him she'd had a phone call from James soon after he'd disappeared and that he'd been in River View at the time. It seemed to be George's only lead, so we agreed to take his case. But I have to admit, we haven't come up with anything yet."

"I see. Well, if y'all find him—Jimmy, I mean—is there any way y'all can call me here first? Before y'all tell George? I'll be glad to give y'all the phone number here, but please, don't tell George I called. Please."

Toni didn't like this at all. She wished Abe would walk in the door and tell her what to do. George Landry was their client. He was the one who had hired them, not Mindy Jordan. And yet something inside—a detective's hunch, her father used to call it—told her it was Mindy she could trust, and not George.

"All right," she said, knowing she was taking a big chance by agreeing to keep Mindy informed of anything they might discover, even before telling their client of their findings. "But you have to promise that you'll call me back if you find out anything else—if you hear from Jimmy or even from George. Will you do that?"

The fear was back in her voice. "All right. I will, but . . ." The woman took another deep breath. "Please, Mrs. Matthews. Please, whatever y'all do, don't tell George I called. Or Harley. If y'all ever call here and he answers, don't tell him anything. Please?"

Toni agreed and took down Mindy's number. She had no sooner hung up the phone than the door opened and Abe walked in.

"Hey there, beautiful," he said, walking toward her and bending down to give her a kiss. "What's up?"

She arched her eyebrows and nodded at the chair on the other side of her desk. "Sit down and I'll tell you," she said. "It's about George Landry—and his siblings."

~~~

It was Thursday night and the giant, more commonly known as Spider, had gone through three cellmates since the one he called "little man" had been bailed out. The first one had been so drunk he wasn't any fun at all—no challenge whatsoever. Spider never did enjoy beating up someone who didn't at least try to fight back. He did it, though—especially when he was bored. And he'd been bored ever since they'd transferred him to that cell. He supposed they'd put him there because the jail was so full. Otherwise they would have put him in a cell by himself, like they usually did. He had a reputation for mutilating cellmates, and he was proud of it. After all, he'd worked hard to earn it. But once in a while things got so crowded that they took a chance and put him in with the other inmates. This had been one of those times.

The drunk had left the next day—not for home but for the infirmary. The next two hadn't put up much of a fight either, and both had been bailed out within twenty-four hours. Now Spider was bored again. He'd been removed from the cell that morning and placed in one by himself—this time just for overnight because tomorrow they would come and transport him to the state prison. He'd been sentenced to twelve years, and now he was waiting, biding his time, wishing he could have one more playmate before they took him away. He still regretted that the little man had gotten away from him before he'd had a chance to rearrange his face, and he'd spent a lot of time thinking about the little creep. He remembered everything the pathetic guy had said about his so-called friend—George Landry from Texas, who'd come to River View to hire somebody to help him find his brother, James. Spider didn't know George Landry, and he didn't care one bit about his reasons for being in town. But he hated him nonetheless. The man had robbed him of a playmate before he'd even had a chance to get to know him. Spider didn't forget things like that, and he always found a way to get even.

He lay back on his bunk, staring at the ceiling, resigned to the fact that there would be no more playmates before he got transported to prison in the morning. But, he reminded himself, there would be plenty of new playmates when he arrived at his destination. And it wasn't like he hadn't been there before. He already knew a lot of the inmates from his last five-year stay—some on good terms, some not. But Spider didn't care. He loved a good fight, and he knew he'd have to reestablish his rank in the pecking order when he got there, so bring 'em on. Spider was ready for anything they threw at him. Old Warden Schillo ran a tight ship—that much he knew from experience—but not tight enough to keep Spider in line. *There isn't a ship in the world that's that tight,* he thought, smirking to himself as he rolled over and closed his eyes. *Not tight enough for me.*

CHAPTER 15

Melissa had been so excited all day she'd scarcely heard a word any of her teachers had said. She had tried to concentrate enough to write down her homework assignments for the weekend, but that was about it. All her energies had been focused on her date with Eric that night.

And now it was time. He would be there any minute, and she had already changed clothes three times. She couldn't wear the same green dress she'd worn at the barbecue on Sunday, so that was out, even though it was her favorite. And slacks just wouldn't work. Even though Abe and Toni had restricted their date to somewhere in town rather than the long romantic drive to the coast she had hoped for, Eric had still assured her that they would go somewhere nice. So it had to be a dress.

After trying on and discarding a pink linen jacket and matching skirt because she was sure it would wrinkle the minute she sat down, she'd finally decided on a pale yellow dress with three-quarter-length sleeves and a scoop neck, which she accented with a single strand of pearls. She hoped it made her look mature and sophisticated, although she certainly didn't feel that way. Her nerves were on edge, and she was as jumpy as a ten-year-old waiting to go to Disneyland. *Then again,* she thought, grinning, *I've already been to Disneyland, and I know this is going to be a lot better than riding on the Matterhorn.*

As she sprayed on her favorite cologne and debated about pulling her hair up or wearing it long and loose, she heard the doorbell ring. He was here. OK, her hair would have to stay the way it was— hanging below her shoulders, just the way Eric said he liked it best.

Her heart thudding in her chest, she took a deep breath, spun around one last time in front of the full-length mirror, then opened her bedroom door and headed down the hall. By the time she reached the entryway, Eric was already inside talking with Abe. They both turned toward her as she walked in.

"Wow," Eric said, his brown eyes opening appreciatively. "You look fantastic."

"She sure does," Abe agreed.

Melissa smiled, feeling her cheeks flush as she took in Eric's perfectly matched sweater and slacks. "Thanks."

"So," Abe said, "where are you two headed all dressed up like that?"

Eric grinned. "It's a surprise. I've been planning it all week."

Abe raised his eyebrows, just as Toni walked in from the kitchen.

"Hello, Eric," she said. "Abe's right. You two certainly do look nice tonight. This dinner must be special."

"It is," Eric assured her. "Like I said, I've been planning it all week. It's sort of a late birthday present, I guess."

Toni nodded. "I see. And I assume Melissa told you that we don't want her going too far for this dinner."

"She sure did. Don't worry. We're eating in River View. And I'll have her home before curfew."

"Good," Abe said. "There are a lot of great restaurants right here in town. No need to go anywhere else."

"My sentiments exactly," Toni said. "So, Eric, would you like to come in and sit down for a minute? We could have some iced tea or soda."

Eric glanced at Melissa, who begged him with her eyes to say no. She couldn't bear to sit around for the next fifteen minutes or so making idle conversation. She just wanted to get out the front door and be on their way.

Eric smiled and looked at Toni. "I don't think so, thanks. We have reservations, and I don't want to be late."

Melissa was sure her sister looked disappointed, but she acted as if she hadn't noticed, reaching immediately into the entryway closet for her sweater. "I'm ready if you are," she said, smiling at Eric.

He helped her with her sweater, then they said their good-byes and promised again to be careful and to be in by eleven. Moments later they were shut away, alone, in Eric's car, heading away from the Matthews' house.

"I can't believe we finally made it," Melissa said. "I was so afraid we'd get stuck in there forever or that Toni would come up with some last-minute reason I couldn't go out with you. But here we are."

Eric looked over at her and smiled. "It's about time, isn't it? I thought this night would never get here. Did I tell you how beautiful you look?"

"Not really. Actually, you said I looked fantastic."

"That too."

She shivered as his eyes drank her in before turning back to the road. "I can't believe you're all mine," he said. "For tonight, anyway."

"Till eleven," she said. "Five hours. Doesn't seem like very long, does it?"

"Not long enough, that's for sure."

"What time are our reservations?"

"Not until seven. I thought we'd take a little ride first. I want to show you one of my favorite spots."

Within minutes they were parked on the hillside overlooking the lights of River View. Melissa had ridden by this spot many times but had never imagined how romantic it could be.

"Come sit next to me," Eric said as he reached over and unhooked her seat belt. She scooted to the middle of the bench seat and snuggled into his embrace. "See why I like this car so much?" Eric asked. "I want you close to me."

She looked up at him, and he kissed her. "I want to be close to you too," she whispered. "Always."

He kissed her again. "Happy birthday—again."

She smiled. "That's true. You've already given me my birthday kiss—lots of them, as a matter of fact."

"I'm going to give you a lot more before the night's over. And if everything goes the way I want it to, I'll still be sitting here kissing you when your next birthday rolls around. Meanwhile . . ." He reached into his pocket and pulled out a small package. "This is for you," he said, placing it in her hand.

Melissa's eyes opened wide. Eric had said he was going to buy her a birthday present, and apparently he had. Her hands trembling, she opened the box. Inside was a heart-shaped gold locket on a delicate chain. The initials *E* and *M* were engraved on the front of the locket, and inside was her picture next to his, both photos taken at her birthday dinner on Sunday.

Her eyes misted over and she looked up at him. "It's beautiful," she said, scarcely breathing. "I don't know what to say."

"You don't have to say anything. Just promise me you'll wear it and think of me."

"Always. Forever. I promise."

Eric took the locket out of the box and put it around Melissa's neck, lifting her hair to clasp the chain shut. Melissa couldn't have felt more loved if he'd given her an engagement ring.

As his lips touched hers again, Melissa thought she could never be happier. *Love is a wonderful thing,* she told herself. Then she wondered if it would be too soon to tell him how she felt. Maybe it would be better, she decided, if she waited and let him say it first, even though the locket told her, without words, how deeply he felt for her. She was sure now that he loved her, but she wanted to hear him say it. So she would wait, for a little while, anyway. Besides, she enjoyed his kisses so much, there was no sense interrupting them by talking. As Eric intertwined his fingers in her long hair and held her close, she knew she'd made the right decision about leaving her hair down. She decided if that's the way he liked it, then that's the way she would wear it—along with the locket—every single day.

Within minutes Eric's kisses had taken on a more urgent tone, and his caresses were becoming more and more intimate. Melissa wondered if she should say something to stop him, but he really hadn't crossed any lines—yet. So once again she decided to wait.

Suddenly he pulled back. "We'd better get going," he said, his voice hoarse. "I don't want us to be late for dinner. And if we don't stop right now, we will be."

Melissa nodded. Dinner sounded like a good idea at the moment—not because she was hungry but because she wanted to skip dinner entirely and stay right here in the car with him for the rest of the evening. And that scared her.

Sighing with relief, she slid back to her side of the car and buckled her seat belt, then clasped her hand around her locket as Eric fired up the engine and cracked a window. "Getting warm in here," he said, then backed out and pulled onto the road, headed toward town.

<div align="center">~~~</div>

It had been a long week, and Doug was glad it was over. They'd received some new prisoners that morning, and when he'd checked their names, he recognized one of them immediately. Gerald "Spider" Owens had been there before, and he was known to be a problem—all seven feet of him. Doug had made it a point to alert the guards in Spider's area immediately.

But now it was Friday night, and all he wanted to do was forget about work for a couple of days. Easier said then done, he knew, but he had to try just the same. It wasn't often that he and Kelly had an evening to themselves. Even when they tried to get all three kids to bed early so they could enjoy some alone time, it was only a matter of minutes before a little voice called out for a glass of water or help slaying an invisible monster. But tonight Kelly's mother had taken the three little ones home with her for an overnighter. Doug imagined that his mother-in-law would be more than ready for a break when she brought them home the next morning, but for now he was going to enjoy every minute of their short vacation from kids.

He looked over at his wife, sitting next to him with her dark hair glowing in the light from the fireplace. She had fixed his favorite meal, and they had eaten it right here in front of the fire, curled up together on the couch. It had been a perfect evening so far, and he was grateful to have one of the children's grandmas so close by. His own parents lived way back in Vermont and scarcely knew their grandchildren. But Kelly's mom, since her husband's untimely death ten years earlier, had devoted her life to her four children and ten grandchildren, all of whom lived within a twenty-mile radius. Monte, Marianne, and Madison adored her, as did their seven cousins.

Kelly looked up at him, her eyes soft. "I felt you watching me," she said.

"Why shouldn't I? You're beautiful, you know."

"No, I don't know. But I'm glad you think so."

He smiled. "Anybody that didn't think so would have to be blind."

She returned his smile. "I bet you say that to all the guys you work with."

Doug laughed. "Yeah, right. Every one of them—prisoners and officers included."

"You haven't talked much about work lately. How's everything going?"

"Busy, as always. Not much to say really. Nothing new or different. A few new faces now and then. Some leave, others come to take their place. That's about it."

"Have you and Mark Johnson settled on a weekend for the prison ministry yet?"

"Not an exact date, but we're looking at early to mid-December. We'll offer the inmates we can trust out of their cells a chance to come to one of the chapel services, which Mark and some of the others on his team will lead. You know he always brings great singers and speakers when he goes into the prisons, and the inmates seem to respond well, from what I've heard. The ministry has a great track record;

I'm glad they're coming. And, of course, they'll be bringing in some volunteers from churches in the area to act as one-on-one counselors with the inmates—not just the ones who come to the chapel but even some of the ones in lockdown who request individual meetings too. Mark's is one of the few ministries that operates that way."

Kelly nodded. "I'm sure it'll work out well, especially right before Christmas. People are always so much more open that time of year."

"True. But it's hard to believe we're even thinking in terms of Christmas again. Didn't we just do the holidays a few weeks ago?"

Kelly laughed. "Sure seems like it, doesn't it? But the kids don't think so. To them it's been forever since Christmas, and they can't wait till it comes again. The passing of time is relevant to our age, I suppose."

Doug put his arm around his wife and pulled her close. "And at our age it passes much too quickly. So let's take advantage of it while we can. The three musketeers will be back in the morning, remember?"

Her eyes sparkled. "I remember. So what do you have in mind until then, Warden?"

~~~

Spider made his way warily across the yard. The first time out was always a challenge. But then Spider thrived on challenges. He was ready for them, and he never backed down. His size, of course, precluded most of the inmates' taking him on. But there were always a few who were his size or bigger, and most challenges came from groups rather than individuals. But his reputation also eliminated a lot of potential problems. He was known for annihilating rather than just defeating. Most comers thought twice before taking him on.

Let 'em come, he thought. *I've been bored long enough. I could use a little excitement in my life—one way or the other.*

He certainly hadn't gotten the excitement he'd hoped for when he'd arrived the previous day. When he'd walked into his assigned cell, his cellmate was gone. Spider found out he was sick and wouldn't be back for at least a day or two. That had been a real disappointment. He was itching for some company.

Across the yard he saw three inmates huddled together, watching him. That wasn't unusual, since most all eyes—inmates' and correctional officers' included—were on him as he sauntered through the middle of them. But these three seemed especially intent on checking him out. And since no one else was making a move on him right now, he decided he'd be the one to start something. So he walked straight toward them.

Spider kept his eyes focused on theirs. He sneered when he saw the realization of his approach registering on their faces. It was obvious they wanted to turn and run, but prison protocol would never allow it. Cowards didn't last long behind the walls.

"You guys got somethin' you wanna say to me?" Spider asked, drawing up in front of them. He sized them up, watching their eyes blink and their jaws twitch as each waited for the other to answer. All three of them were at least a head shorter than he, and Spider figured the three of them put together only outweighed him by a hundred pounds or so. Not much of an advantage, as far as he was concerned. Unless they had a hidden weapon he didn't know about, he knew he could take them all easily.

He decided they must be thinking the same thing, since such a brazen challenge should have been met by now. But still they stood, obviously wondering how to maintain their image without taking on this ugly giant in front of them. Finally the tallest of the three spoke.

"I seen you before," he said, cocking his head in a typical tough-guy pose. "You done time here a few years ago, right?"

Spider laughed. "I done time in a lot of places. What's it to you?"

The guy shrugged. "Nothin'. Just thought I knew you, that's all."

Spider leaned down and spoke directly into the man's face. "It could be arranged," he said, then laughed and turned away. He had memorized their faces, and he would see them again. Sooner or later he'd find out what their interest was in him, but right now he wanted to get on with finding someone who could offer him a real challenge, someone who would establish him as a force to be reckoned with. Those three just didn't cut it.

Then he saw him. A big guy—almost as big as he and with nearly as many tattoos—was swaggering across the yard in his direction. Spider figured they were on a collision course, and it wouldn't be long now until his reputation as annihilator was reestablished in this facility.

He smiled. Things were looking up.

CHAPTER 16

It was Saturday night, and Abe and Toni had gone out for the evening, leaving April and Melissa to fend for themselves. At Melissa's eager suggestion, April had agreed to a home-delivered pizza, which they now sat eating at the kitchen table. April smiled sadly, as she watched the sixteen-year-old devour her third piece. *Just like Julie*, she thought. *She'd live on pizza and Chinese food if she could.*

Refusing to allow the thought to drag her into a melancholy mood, April got up from the table and walked to the refrigerator. "More iced tea?" she asked.

"No, thanks," Melissa answered. "I've got plenty."

April returned to the table with the pitcher and refilled her own glass, then sat down across from Melissa once again. "So," she said, "how was your date with Eric last night?"

Melissa looked up, her green eyes wide. She swallowed and wiped her hands on her napkin. "Good," she said. "Great, actually. We had a fantastic dinner at The Hideaway—you know, that really nice restaurant down by the river. We even had window seats. Eric thought of everything."

April smiled. "I'm sure he did. He seems like a thoughtful young man."

"He is," Melissa agreed, nodding. She lifted the locket that hung around her neck and held it out for April to admire. "He gave me this."

"It's beautiful," April said, leaning across the table for a closer look. "I've been admiring it all evening."

"It has our initials on the front."

"So I see."

Melissa opened the locket and showed her the pictures. "These were taken at my birthday dinner on Sunday."

April nodded. "They're lovely. This will always be quite special to you, won't it?"

"Are you kidding? I'm going to wear it forever."

April smiled. *Forever.* Such a romantic word at sixteen. "You two are getting along well then, I assume."

"Very well. We . . ." Melissa hesitated, and her face flushed slightly. "We're in love."

April raised her eyebrows, though she wasn't totally surprised by Melissa's pronouncement. She had no doubt the girl believed it to be true. And maybe, to some degree, it was.

"I see," she said, her voice soft as she prayed silently. Obviously Melissa had entrusted her with a precious secret, and she knew she dare not make light of it. Watching Melissa's face, it was clear the teenager was waiting anxiously for her reaction.

"And what does that mean, exactly?" she asked. "How does being in love affect your lives at this point?"

Melissa dropped her eyes for a moment. When she looked back up, her long dark lashes were wet. "Thank you," she said, "for not making fun of me or telling me I'm too young to be in love."

April reached across the table and patted Melissa's hand as she waited for her to continue.

"I'm still trying to figure out what it means," Melissa said. "And to tell you the truth, I have no idea how it affects my life. In a lot of ways, it's wonderful, I guess. But it's kinda scary too. Does that make sense?"

"Of course it does, my dear. Believe it or not, I remember what it feels like to be in love, and you're right. It is a bit scary. But it doesn't have to be."

Melissa frowned. "I don't understand."

"It's all about who's in charge," April explained. "You and Eric and your feelings . . . or God."

Melissa dropped her eyes again, as April waited. Slowly the girl lifted her head. "I know you're right," she said. "I think God's been trying to tell me the same thing. Part of me wants to hear him, and part of me doesn't."

"A natural reaction. We all resist yielding control to God, no matter what area of our lives we're dealing with. Everyone wants to be the master of his own destiny—and in many ways we are. God allows us to choose—right or wrong, life or death, heaven or hell. But ultimately it all comes down to the same thing: Will we go his way or ours? Will we trust him or ourselves? He cares about every area of our lives, you know, including—and maybe especially—our relationships."

Melissa nodded. "I've been thinking about that—a lot. What if Eric isn't the one God wants me to marry? Do you think that's why part of me really doesn't want to listen to God about my relationship with Eric—because I'm afraid he'll tell me he's not the one?"

"I would imagine so, my dear. As I said, it all comes down to trust. Will you trust God to know and do what's best for you, even if it doesn't include Eric? Or will you take things into your own hands and do it your way, regardless of the outcome?"

Melissa's eyes began to fill again. "Oh, April, what if God doesn't want me to be with Eric? I don't know if I could handle that. I truly do love him, you know."

April nodded. "I'm sure you do. And I have no easy answers for you. But I will tell you this. Whatever God has planned for you—whether it includes Eric or not—will ultimately cause you to be happier and more fulfilled than anything you could come up with on your own. Jeremiah 29:11 promises us that God's plans for us are for good and not for evil, to give us a future and a hope. He loves us more than we can ever imagine, Melissa." She paused. "And he loves Eric too."

The tears spilled over onto her cheeks then, as the teenager nodded. "I know," she whispered. "I've thought of that too. It isn't just about me, is it? Maybe God's plans for Eric don't include me either. That's kinda hard to accept, but I know it could be true." She shook her head. "I don't know, April. I don't know what to do or what to think. I can't just change the way I feel about Eric."

"God knows that, my dear. And he doesn't expect you to. But he does expect you to love him more. More than you love Eric, more than you love anyone. That's what Jesus meant when he said that in order to be his disciples we have to love him more than we love our own family members. In other words, he was talking about placing the importance of our closest relationships a notch below the importance of our relationship with him. He must always come first if we are to be his true followers." She hesitated before continuing. "You see, Melissa, if God isn't first on our priority list, he will end up being last. There is no middle ground in our relationship with God."

"But how do I do that? How do I make sure that I love him more than anything or anyone?"

"Spend time with him, daily. Never neglect it. Pray, study your Bible, meet with others who share your faith. That is the secret to walking in the footsteps of Jesus. Remember what the Bible says? Jesus did only those things he saw his Father do. He did nothing on his own. He was always going off to be alone with his Father, to pray and commune with him. And that's what we must do as well. In fact, it is the most important thing we ever do in this life—the only thing that really matters to God. If we seek him above all else, then, as Jesus promised, God will give us whatever else we need. Loving God more than anything or anyone else is our first calling. When we're obedient to that call, our other relationships will fall into place—including yours and Eric's."

Melissa sighed. "I know you're right. I just wish I could talk to Eric about it, but he doesn't believe like I do. I mean, he says he believes in God, but it's not the same."

April patted Melissa's hand again. "No, it's not," she said. "I'm sure Eric believes God exists—almost everyone does, to some extent—but that's not the same as having faith in God, or putting your trust in him, or believing in him for salvation." When Melissa didn't respond, April said, "We need to pray for Eric to come to that place of faith, my dear, whether God's plan is for the two of you to be together or not."

Melissa bowed her head and nodded, her auburn hair falling down over her face. "I know," she whispered. "Will you pray with me?"

April, her hand still resting on Melissa's, closed her eyes and thanked God silently before beginning to speak to him audibly.

≈≈≈

No matter how hard she tried, Toni just couldn't keep her mind from wandering. And it was so unlike her—particularly during the sermon. She always enjoyed Pastor Michael's teachings and even took notes as he spoke. Today, however, there seemed to be so many other issues crowding in on her.

The first, of course, was Melissa and Eric. Toni had been trying since Saturday morning to talk to her sister about her dinner date with Eric, but so far all she'd been able to get out of her was that the date was "fine" and the meal was "good." When Toni had asked about the locket, Melissa had said only that it was a late birthday gift from Eric. Toni supposed she would just have to accept the fact that Melissa was not going to give her any more information—at least not for now—but the secrecy made her uneasy. To some extent she was even jealous when she'd learned that April at least knew the name of the restaurant where the young couple had eaten. It seemed her little sister was more open with their elderly houseguest than she was with Toni, and that hurt. But at least Melissa was talking to someone, and for that Toni was grateful. God had indeed brought April back into their lives at just the right time.

And then there was Brad. Toni couldn't help but smile as she looked ahead a couple of rows and saw her former fiancé sitting next to his receptionist. Brad had seemed pleased when he introduced the attractive redhead to them before the service began, and Toni knew him well enough to realize that something serious was brewing. Jeanine normally attended another church, Brad had explained, but she had agreed to come with him today, and then he would visit her church the following week. Even Brad's parents were grinning when Brad and Jeanine walked in together.

Thank you, God, Toni prayed silently. *You know how hard it was for me to see Brad so hurt—and to know I was the cause of it. Please let this relationship with Jeanine work out for him—if it's of you, of course. If not, oh, please, Lord, don't let him be hurt again.*

She glanced over at Abe, who sat beside her, his eyes straight ahead on Pastor Michael. She knew that he, too, had been pleased to see Brad and Jeanine together—not that he wasn't secure in Toni's love, but she knew it must be a bit of a relief for him to know that his wife's former fiancé was finally moving on with his life.

One more time she tried to pull her attention back to the sermon, but one more time it drifted off on its own course. This time she was thinking of the announcement she had seen in the bulletin when they first came in. She pulled the bulletin from the pages of her Bible where she had placed it and read it again: "Exciting ministry opportunity coming in December. If you would like to be a part of the upcoming prison ministry weekend to be conducted in conjunction with Mark Johnson Ministries, please contact the church office to sign up for training sessions."

Toni closed her eyes, remembering April Lippincott's comment last spring about a possible prison ministry in the future. Was God truly calling her and Abe to this sort of work? If so, was this the door he was opening for them to get started?

She resolved to talk to Abe about it as soon as church was over. If he felt they should at least take the training classes and see where God led them from there, then she would agree. After all, what could it hurt to at least get their feet wet by spending a few evenings in training and then one weekend at the prison? It wasn't as if they would be making a lifetime commitment with no way out.

~~~

Sophie closed her eyes and breathed deeply of the damp after-noon air. The rain that had started the previous night had continued through the morning hours, but now the sun peeked through the clouds, warming her as she sat quietly on Abe and Toni's porch swing. Sophie hadn't really planned to drive back down to River View so soon. After all, it had been only one week since she had come for Melissa's birthday dinner. But something had been nagging at her ever since the close of *Shabbat*, the Jewish Sabbath, on the previous evening.

She had been sitting in her favorite chair in the living room as the sun went down, reading from the *Tanakh* as she often did, particularly during *Shabbat*, and once again she had come across a Scripture containing that now familiar word, *ransom*. Sophie had almost completed her reading of the prophet *Hoshea* when she came upon these words in the fourteenth verse of chapter 13: "Should I ransom them from the power of *Sh'ol*? Should I redeem them from death?"

Stunned, she had stopped, setting her dog-eared *Tanakh* on her lap as she prayed silently. *Ransom. Again with the ransom, Lord. What is it, Adonai? What is it you wish me to understand about that word?* But no answer had been forthcoming, except the beginning of a desire to return to the Matthews' home for another visit. And so she had called and quickly received an invitation for the next day. She had arrived soon after the family had returned from church—all except April, who had a prior commitment and would therefore not be joining them until later.

After a nice lunch Abe, Toni, and Melissa had insisted that Sophie go outside and relax in the swing, and she had readily complied, sud-denly realizing how tired she actually was after her morning drive and the full meal. And now, with the sun shining on her and her eyes closed, she felt herself growing drowsy. Maybe an afternoon nap wasn't such a bad idea.

She wasn't sure how long she'd been sitting that way when she heard Melissa's voice. "Do you mind if I join you, Aunt Sophie?"

Sophie opened her eyes and blinked a couple of times, then smiled. Melissa truly was a beautiful child. *Almost a woman*, she thought, correcting herself. *Sixteen. Ah, to be so young again.*

"I'm sorry if I woke you," Melissa said. "I thought you were just resting."

Sophie patted the cushion beside her. "Please, sit down. I'm not sure if I was sleeping or resting, but it doesn't really matter. Either way, I would much rather have a visit with you. Sit, sit."

Melissa lowered herself carefully into the seat beside Sophie, scarcely moving the swing in the process.

Sophie smiled at her. "So, Melissa, how are you doing, now that you're sixteen? And how is your young man—Eric, is it?"

Melissa nodded, even as her cheeks flushed. "Eric's fine, thank you."

"He's quite handsome, isn't he?"

"I think so," Melissa answered, returning her smile.

"And it's obvious he's taken with you," Sophie said. "Do I dare ask how serious it is between you?"

Melissa's flush deepened. "Very," she said. "Serious, I mean. I just hope . . ." Her voice trailed off.

"You just hope what? That he feels the same as you do?"

"Not that so much. I'm sure he does—at least, I think he does. But . . ."

"But what? Is there a problem?"

Melissa shrugged. "I don't know. Not a problem exactly. Just a difference in our faith."

Sophie raised her eyebrows. Now this was a problem she could relate to, though it was strange to hear about it from a *goy*, a Gentile. "He doesn't share your Christian faith?" She still had trouble saying the word *Christian* without feeling as if she were uttering a curse, but she was trying to get past that for Avraham's sake.

"Not really. I mean, he probably thinks he does. He says he believes in God—and I'm sure that's true. But . . ."

"Again with the *but*. What is it, Melissa? What difference is it that's coming between you and your young man?"

"It's just that his family doesn't believe. I mean, they don't go to church or anything. They never have, and Eric doesn't really know much about Christianity. And he doesn't go to church either."

Sophie nodded. "Yes, that could definitely be a problem. In my faith we have been forbidden to marry outside our religion—forbidden to intermarry with the *goyim*, the Gentiles." She lowered her voice a notch. "Sadly, it happens all the time. Avraham's mother, my dear sister, Rachel, married a *goy*—a nice *goy*, granted, but a *goy*, nonetheless." She was whispering now. "Avraham did the same, you know. Your sister, Toni—whom I love dearly, mind you—is also a *goy*. It's the reason I was so opposed to their relationship in the beginning. And then, of course, Avraham converted." She shook her head. Though she had accepted Toni and reconciled with her nephew, his defection was still too painful to think about, let alone discuss.

"I don't mean to be critical," Sophie continued. "Your faith is your faith, and I am not trying to proselytize. But it is a sad day when we marry outside our religion. You see, as in Avraham's case, one almost always defects. In Rachel's case, she married a man who claimed not to believe in God at all, and she soon stopped practicing her faith altogether. Soon her relationship with God was no longer important to her. And nothing grieves the heart of Adonai more. Nothing. But it's inevitable. One will pull the other across the line, sooner or later. For Avraham, of course, it was sooner. He converted before he ever married your sister. With my sister, she thought she would be strong and not desert her faith, but it was only a matter of time."

Melissa's expression was pained. "But why does it have to be that way, Aunt Sophie? Why can't each person just continue to practice his or her faith without influencing the other one?"

"Because, young lady, when two people marry, they become one. Adonai, the Lord, has appointed it so. Look it up. It's in the Scriptures—not just mine, but yours as well, from what I understand. Your *Yeshua* . . ." Her heart caught at the word, but she continued on. "Jesus, as you call him, taught that very thing, yes?"

Melissa nodded, her eyes wide.

"There is no closer human relationship than husband and wife," Sophie explained. "Only our relationship with God is more important than that—which, of course, is how it should be. My dear David and I shared everything together—everything. But when husband and wife don't agree on the most important aspect of life—that which is eternal, the spiritual dimension—there can be no true oneness. And so the two either divide, or one goes over to the other side. It's as simple as that."

"But that's OK, isn't it? I mean, as long as the one who doesn't believe comes over to the side of the one who does?"

Sophie sighed. "If it happens that way, yes. But sadly, that isn't always the case. And so you can see why it so grieves the heart of Adonai."

Melissa didn't answer but appeared to be digesting Sophie's words, even as she fingered the heart-shaped locket around her neck. *Is this why you brought me here today, oh Lord?* Sophie prayed silently. *Was it to speak those words to this young girl's heart? But she's a* goy, *Lord. Why would it matter to you, the God of Israel, whether this goy marries outside of her faith? Christianity is, after all, a false religion, a religion whose followers have at times persecuted and murdered our own people. Why would you care, Adonai? Why would you be concerned about her actions? And even if you are, why would you use me to warn her?*

Sophie sighed again, more deeply this time. The older she got, the more she realized how little she understood—about life, about God, about anything.

CHAPTER 17

I t's been a good weekend, hasn't it?" Abe asked, his arm across Toni's shoulders as they sat together on the couch in the semi-darkness, watching the dying embers in the fireplace. Although the day had been relatively warm for this time of year, the temperature had dropped quickly when the sun went down. In the early evening the five of them—Toni, Abe, Melissa, Sophie, and April, once she had returned from church—had sat in front of the cozy fire, talking and laughing and enjoying one another's company, not to mention some of Sophie's homemade strudel that she had brought along with her. Then Sophie had announced that she'd better start for home before it got too late, and Melissa had gone off to her room to study for an exam the next day. After only a few minutes, April, too, had excused herself and gone to her room, leaving Abe and Toni alone at last.

Toni looked up and smiled, her blue eyes melting Abe's heart once again. "Yes, it has," she agreed. "A wonderful weekend. But it's nice to finally have a little time to ourselves, isn't it?"

Abe kissed her upturned nose. "It sure is. And I think April left us alone on purpose, don't you?"

Toni nodded her agreement. "She's thoughtful that way."

"I'm just surprised Melissa didn't ask to have Eric over today—or to go somewhere with him. She hasn't seen him since their date on Friday evening, has she?"

"No, she hasn't. I thought that was a little strange, too, but it's certainly fine with me. Once a weekend is more than enough—although I'm sure they spent plenty of time talking on the phone."

"No doubt. Did you notice the locket she was wearing?"

Toni nodded again. "Yes, I did. She wasn't very talkative about it, though. Seems it was Eric's birthday gift to her. That's about all I could get out of her."

Abe frowned. "I also noticed it had their initials on it, and it looked like real gold. Must have cost him quite a bit. Where do you suppose he gets his money? I mean, he has a car, he takes Melissa out to dinner, buys her presents. I've never heard any mention of a job, have you?"

"No. And I've wondered about that myself. He's a nice enough boy, but if his parents are supplying him with that much spending money, it can't be helping him to develop much of a sense of responsibility, can it?"

Abe shook his head. "I've never been in favor of just handing kids cars or money—or anything else, for that matter. Apart from necessities they should have to earn it."

"Absolutely. That's why Melissa spends most of her summers doing babysitting—just like I did when I was her age—so she can buy any extras she might want. I even wondered if we were going overboard buying her that computer for her birthday. But then again, we did all go in on it together, and I'm sure she'll get a lot of use out of it for school. And by the way, she mentioned that Eric had offered to come over and help her set it up. I told her it would have to be when we're home—especially since it's going to be in her room."

"That's for sure. We don't want him getting into the habit of coming over here uninvited or unannounced—and never when we're not here. But I think Melissa understands that."

"She does. And I'm sure she'll honor it." Toni sighed. "It was a lot easier when she spent all her spare time with Carrie, wasn't it?"

Abe laughed. "It sure was. But I guess this was bound to happen sooner or later. We'll just have to keep close tabs on it—as much as we can, anyway."

"I just wish Melissa would be more open with us. It's like pulling teeth to get her to talk about Eric. I asked her about their date on Friday night and could barely get three words out of her. But it seems she talked to April about it."

Abe raised his eyebrows. "Really? Well, that's good. At least she's talking to one of us. And I noticed she was outside talking with Aunt Sophie this afternoon, too, although I have no idea what they were discussing."

Toni smiled. "Aunt Sophie is becoming more and more a part of this family, isn't she? Not that she wasn't already, of course, but . . . you know what I mean."

"I do. And I think it's a good thing for all of us. And she and April seem to be developing quite a friendship too."

"Isn't that great? If anyone can reach Aunt Sophie with the gospel, I would think it would be April. She's so wise and gentle."

"Just like Jesus said," Abe agreed with a smile. "'Wise as a serpent but gentle as a dove.' That's a good description of April, isn't it?"

Toni nodded. "She's walked with Jesus for many years, and she's been through a lot in her life. I value her friendship and advice."

"Exactly why we should be pleased that Melissa is talking to her about Eric, even if she isn't talking to us about it."

Toni leaned her head back against the couch. "You're right," she said, closing her eyes and smiling as Abe played with her blonde curls. "I love it when you do that," she murmured.

"I know. I do too."

"So," she said, her eyes still closed, "enough about everyone else. I've been meaning to ask you something."

"Ask away."

"Did you notice that blurb in the bulletin about the upcoming prison ministry? They're going to have training classes for anyone who wants to be a part of it."

"I read that. And I've been wondering about it too. Are you thinking that you'd like to get involved?"

"I think so. At least, I think it would be worth taking the classes, don't you?"

"Why not? We've talked about it before, and this just might be what God is using to draw us in."

"My thoughts exactly. Let's call the church office this week and sign up."

"Deal." Abe paused for a moment, then asked, "OK, since we're changing subjects here, what about your manuscript? Get anything else done on it lately?"

Toni opened her eyes. "A little," she said. "Not quite a chapter, which is why I haven't shown it to you yet. But by the end of this week, for sure."

Abe smiled. "I'll hold you to that."

"Good. I want you to. It's the incentive I need to keep going." She sighed. "Do you think anything will ever come of it? Will it ever get published?"

Abe kissed her. "I don't know. But I do know one thing. It will have a much better chance if you finish writing it."

Toni laughed. "With you as my taskmaster, do I have a choice?"

"No."

"That's what I thought. OK, slave driver, I'll get on it tomorrow afternoon, how's that?"

"Perfect. And now that we have that settled, I have one more thing on my mind."

Toni looked up at him and raised her eyebrows. "What's that, detective?"

Pulling her close to him, he kissed her again, slowly and passionately, and then whispered, "Let's go to bed and I'll show you."

∼∼∼

The motel room seemed to be getting smaller by the day. George wondered just how long he was going to be able to hold out. Even his supplies from Louie weren't enough anymore. The cocaine always helped, of course, but the women . . .

He shook his head. He should have known better. Louie ran a drug business, not an escort service. The woman he'd sent over the night before looked about as old as his mother just before she died, though George imagined the haggard prostitute hadn't been more than forty or so. But the drugs and lifestyle had definitely taken their toll.

That's when he'd decided that he'd find his next female companion himself. He looked in the mirror. He had showered and shaved and put on a fresh shirt. Combing what little was left of his hair, he wondered what his odds were of finding a willing companion at the nearby bar on a Sunday night. Then he shrugged. So what if he didn't? At least he'd be out of this room for a few hours. And a couple of good, stiff drinks wouldn't hurt at all. What did he have to lose? Maybe he'd even get lucky and hear something about that worthless brother of his.

But he had to be careful, he reminded himself. It was OK to ask a few questions, which he'd already done several times since arriving in this two-bit town, but he sure didn't want to say too much and risk having it get back to that detective team he'd hired. He was sure they didn't completely trust him as it was, and there was no sense confirming their suspicions.

Dabbing on an extra drop of aftershave, he grabbed his keys from the nightstand next to the bed and headed out the door. *A blonde would be nice*, he thought. *But a redhead'll work too.* He smiled. *Just so she's tall and leggy—and young. That's what I really like.*

~~~

Spider sat with the three inmates he'd seen on his first venture into the yard two days earlier. After nearly annihilating the man who had challenged him that day, his respect level in the institution had risen considerably. He could now hang out with just about anyone he wanted to. He had chosen these three because he sensed there was something going on with them that would be good for him to know. They'd seemed scared at first, then pleasantly surprised, though still a bit nervous, when he'd aligned himself with them. And so they sat together in the mid-morning sun during a brief work break on Monday.

But the more time Spider spent with these three losers, the more he wondered about the prisoner they called Jinx. He was the one who really interested him, and he'd already decided that he would take the first possible opportunity to get to know him. Of course, Spider hadn't told his three companions about his plan. He somehow sensed they wouldn't like it. But then, what did he care what they liked or didn't like? He didn't particularly like them, but here he was, wasting his time with them, hoping for an opening so he could find out what was on their minds. The more time he spent with them, the more sure he was that they were hiding something from him—something important.

He glanced at the smallest of the three, who always seemed to be watching him. The minute their eyes met, the man looked away. He was scared of him, Spider knew—as were most of the inmates. But the knowledge of this particular man's fear could be a good thing. Spider would just bide his time. Sooner or later he would learn what he wanted to know—and he would find a way to use it to his advantage.

∾∾∾

School was finally out, and Melissa was happy to be sitting in the front seat of Eric's car once again, nestled in his arms and savoring the feel of his kiss. She knew he wanted to go back to the parking spot up on the hill where he had given her the locket on Friday night, but she'd resisted. And she couldn't quite figure out why.

He had wanted to go back after dinner on Friday too, but she had convinced him that if they did, she might miss her curfew. Eric had reluctantly agreed, but she knew it was just a matter of time until she ran out of excuses for not going back there—or somewhere equally private. And the strange thing was that she desperately wanted to be alone with Eric.

Too desperately, she thought. And that's what was scaring her off. It was the reason she hadn't pushed to see him again over the weekend. She had needed some time to think about her feelings, about the advice she'd received from April and Aunt Sophie, and about where her relationship with Eric might be headed. At least here in the school parking lot she knew that nothing would happen beyond a few hugs and kisses. But alone? Her heart ached with longing, even as her mind raced with the frightening implications.

What's going on with me, Lord? she prayed silently. *I can't remember when I've ever felt so confused. It's not that I want to do anything wrong, but I love him so much. I just can't think about anything else. All I want is to be with him. And that scares me, God. It really does.*

"What are you thinking about?" Eric asked, lifting her head to look at him.

Her racing heart pumped even faster as she gazed into his warm brown eyes. She thought sometimes that she could get lost in them— just let them swallow her up and carry her away.

She shook her head. "Nothing, really," she said. "Just you . . . me. Us."

Eric raised his eyebrows. "Nothing? Is that what you think of our relationship?"

Melissa was horrified. "Oh, no," she said quickly. "Not at all. It's everything to me. But I just get scared sometimes."

Eric looked puzzled. "Scared? Of what? Me?"

Melissa shook her head, desperate to make him understand. "No, not you. Just us. The way you make me feel."

Eric kissed her gently. "How do I make you feel, Melissa? Tell me."

What should she say? She loved him, she was sure of it. But she had never really said the words out loud—except to Carrie and April, of course. Should she tell Eric? Would he laugh at her? Or would he tell her he loved her too? Oh, she hoped so, but if he did, then what?

"Talk to me, Melissa," Eric urged, his voice as warm and soft as his eyes. "Tell me how you feel about me. Please."

Melissa's heart felt as if it would explode out of her chest. She took a deep breath. "I love you," she said, her voice so soft she wasn't sure if she had actually spoken the words or just thought them. But then she saw his face, and she knew she had finally said it.

"Oh, Melissa." He pulled her closer, pressing his lips against hers again and again. "I love you too. I love you so much . . . and I want you—"

His declarations of love were suddenly interrupted by a pounding on his window. Eric and Melissa jerked upright and turned toward the noise. It was Mr. Fletcher, the boys' PE teacher. Melissa felt her face going red as Eric rolled down the window.

"Hello, Mr. Fletcher," he said. "We were just—"

"I know what you were 'just' doing," Mr. Fletcher said. "I was young once too, I assure you. But this is hardly the time and place. So let's move along, shall we?"

"No problem, Mr. Fletcher," Eric answered, putting his key into the ignition and starting the engine. "We'll leave right now."

"See that you do. This is a parking lot, not a lover's lane, you know."

Eric nodded as he rolled up the window. "I know, Mr. Fletcher. And don't worry. It won't happen again."

As they drove from the parking lot, Eric began to laugh. "Do you believe that? 'This is a parking lot, not a lovers' lane.' What's up with that? How lame!"

But Melissa wasn't laughing. She couldn't remember when she'd felt so humiliated. She only hoped that Mr. Fletcher wouldn't mention the incident to anyone else. It would be bad enough every time she had to face him, and she knew there was no way to avoid it. But if others found out, she didn't know how she could ever go back to school again.

"Well, that settles it," Eric said, heading down the road that led out of town, "no more parking at school. We should have just gone up to the hill in the first place. At least there we won't have to worry about anyone bothering us." He looked over at her and smiled. "We can be alone there, Melissa. And now that I know you feel the same as I do, that's just where I want to be—alone with you."

Melissa tried to return his smile, but she was shaking inside. What would happen now? How would she handle it if Eric . . . ?

She closed her eyes and took a deep breath. *Please, God, don't let it come to that. I just don't know what to do. Show me, please. Help me. I don't want to do anything wrong, I really don't. But you know how much I love him. And now I know he loves me too. What am I going to do?*

As the car began the ascent up the hillside, Melissa sat quietly and listened. But God didn't say a word.

CHAPTER 18

As they pulled up to their parking place overlooking the city, Melissa couldn't help but notice the gathering darkness, even though it wasn't even four o'clock yet. The overcast skies seemed to hasten the coming night, and suddenly Melissa found herself longing for sunshine.

Eric turned off the ignition and pulled on the parking brake, then turned toward her. His look was tender and inviting, but still Melissa hesitated. She knew once she slid across the seat and into his arms it would be that much harder to pull away again. Her stomach churned, and her breathing was shallow.

"What's wrong?" Eric asked, his voice soft and compelling.

"I told you," Melissa stammered. "I'm scared."

"You don't have to be," Eric assured her. "I would never hurt you. You know that."

Melissa nodded. "I know, but . . ."

"But what?"

She shrugged. "I'm still scared. I don't know what's going to hap-pen, now that . . ."

Eric reached over and took her hand. "Now that . . . ?"

"Now that we know we love each other."

"I already knew that. You did too, didn't you?"

Melissa hesitated, then nodded. "I guess so. I was just afraid to say it."

"But now you've said it, and so have I. So what else is there to be afraid of?"

"It's just that . . ." Oh, if only she could think of the right words to make him understand. It wasn't so much that she was afraid of him. It was that she was afraid of herself, afraid that she might love him too much, might get too involved, might allow herself to go too far in their relationship.

"I'm afraid of what might happen," she whispered. "Between us, I mean."

"Are you talking about sex, Melissa?" His voice was gentle. "Is that what you're afraid of?"

Melissa's green eyes opened wide. Now that he had actually said the word, she was more frightened than ever. She had never dreamed that something like this would come up in her life until after she was safely married. And yet here they were, still in high school. And instead of studying geometry together, they were talking about sex.

She swallowed and nodded. "Yes," was all she could say.

Eric moved closer to her on the seat—close enough that she could feel his warmth. "You don't have to be afraid, Melissa. I love you, remember? I would never, ever, do anything to hurt you." He lifted her chin, and their eyes met. Melissa felt the clash of desire and fear and . . . something else . . . warring inside her. What was it? What was the emotion that fought for control of her mind and her passions? Whatever it was, it was holding her back, like a large, unseen hand.

God, she thought. *It's you, isn't it? You didn't answer me when I prayed—not with words, anyway—but you're answering me now, aren't you?*

Again, she heard nothing, but her assurance of God's restraining presence was growing. And then April Lippincott's words began to echo in her mind: "*We all resist yielding control to God, no matter what area of our lives we're dealing with. Everyone wants to be the master of his own destiny—and in many ways we are. God allows us to choose— right or wrong, life or death, heaven or hell. But ultimately it all comes down to the same thing: Will we go his way or ours? Will we trust him or ourselves? He cares about every area of our lives, you know, including— and maybe especially—our relationships.*"

"This is wrong," Melissa blurted out, her voice shaking. "I can't . . ."

Eric frowned. "Can't what? I don't understand. We haven't done anything wrong."

"Not yet. But if we keep coming here together, spending time alone, and kissing, we will. Sooner or later, Eric, we will."

Eric cupped her face in his hand. "Of course we will. It's natural, Melissa. We love each other, so it can't be wrong. And I told you, I would never, ever, hurt you." He paused, then lowered his voice and said, "We were meant to be together; you know that, don't you?"

Melissa struggled to believe him. He was saying everything she felt in her heart. They were meant to be together. Yes, she was sure of that—at least, she wanted it to be true. And they loved each other, so maybe . . .

She shook her head. "No. Eric, we can't." Her voice still shook, and she spoke almost in a whisper, but she knew what she had to say. "I know we love each other, and I hope we were meant to be together, just like you said. But God says it's wrong for us to, you know, be together like that until after we're married."

Eric raised his eyebrows questioningly as he began to stroke her face. "I know you want me," he crooned. "And I want you. I've wanted you since I first saw you at school. The minute I laid eyes on you, I knew you were for me. You were the most beautiful girl I'd ever seen. Your long hair shining in the sun, your big green eyes, your sweet smile. Melissa, we love each other, and we want to be together—in all ways. How could that be wrong? And even though we're too young to get married right now, someday . . ."

His voice trailed off as his finger traced her eyebrows and then her lips. Melissa felt her resolve melting in the heat of her desire. Maybe he was right. After all, they did love each other.

She closed her eyes and let him pull her close, welcoming the taste of his lips on hers. Yes, they were too young to be married now, but someday . . . someday she would be Eric's wife.

And then suddenly it was Aunt Sophie's voice she heard, calling her back: "*It is a sad day when we marry outside our religion. It's inevitable. One will pull the other across the line, sooner or later. When two people marry, they become one. There is no closer human relationship than husband and wife. Only our relationship with God is more important. But when husband and wife don't agree on the most important aspect of life—that which is eternal, the spiritual dimension—there can be no true oneness. And so the two either divide, or one goes over to the other side. And so you can see why it so grieves the heart of Adonai.*"

But even as Aunt Sophie's words rang in her ears, Melissa argued with God. *You know how much I love him, Lord. And I can't change the way I feel about him. Even if I tried, I just couldn't.*

And then it was April's voice, speaking to her again. *God knows that, my dear. And he doesn't expect you to. But he does expect you to love him more. More than you love Eric, more than you love anyone. Loving God more than anything or anyone else is our first calling.*

Before Melissa could stop them, the tears began to roll from her eyes. Almost immediately Eric pulled back and looked at her quizzically. "What's wrong? Did I do something? Why are you crying?"

Melissa could scarcely speak, but she finally managed to choke out, "I'm sorry, Eric. It's not you. It's . . ." She looked up at him through her tears. "Please," she whispered, clasping her heart-shaped locket in her hand. "Take me home. I just want to go home."

~~~

Without a doubt it had been one of the best Mondays of Brad Anderson's life. Not only had he spent a large part of the weekend with Jeanine, but they had found the time to grab a quick lunch together today at work. And although they didn't have a date that evening, they were planning on going out to dinner on Wednesday.

Two more days, he thought, smiling to himself as he warmed a TV dinner in the microwave. *Plus I get to see her at work every day. How deaf, dumb, and blind could I have been that I didn't notice this fantastic lady before Melissa brought her to my attention?*

The bell dinged, and he pulled his bachelor's deluxe meal from the oven and plunked it on the kitchen counter, pulled up a stool, and flipped on the news with the remote. *Thank you, God, that this isn't all I've got to look forward to anymore.*

Waiting for his tasteless mound of generic meat and watery mashed potatoes smothered in some sort of rubbery gravy to cool, he flipped through his mail and half listened to the newscaster reporting on the latest political scandal to hit the nation's capitol. *That guy sure seems more excited about reporting bad news than I am about eating this wannabe dinner,* he thought, then smiled again. *All the more reason to plan something really special for Wednesday night. Jeanine mentioned that she really likes Italian food.*

The phone next to him on the counter rang, and he snatched the receiver from its cradle and pressed it to his ear.

"Hello?"

"Brad? It's Jeanine."

Brad's heart soared. "I was hoping it was you."

"Really? Well, I hope I didn't catch you at a bad time."

"Are you kidding? I'm trying to convince myself that I'm hungry enough to eat the world's worst dinner—à-la-prepackaged-TV style."

Jeanine laughed, and Brad realized how much he liked the melodic tone of her laughter. Wondering if she sang as beautifully as she laughed, he determined to find out one day.

"In a way, that's why I called," Jeanine said. "About dinner, I mean."

Brad's heart sank. Was she going to cancel their date?

"I know we have a dinner date for Wednesday, and I don't mean to be pushy, but, well, I'm having dinner with my mom tomorrow, and I wondered if you might want to join us."

Brad's smile returned as his heart made a comeback. "Seriously? You don't think she'd mind?"

"I know she wouldn't," Jeanine said. "In fact, I just got off the phone with her. I was telling her about you, and she said she'd like to meet you."

"Well, then, I'd sure like to meet her too. Where and when?"

"She likes to eat early. Would you mind terribly if we went over there right after work tomorrow?"

"Hey, I can eat anytime—especially if it's not a TV dinner."

Jeanine laughed again. "I don't know what we'll be having—it's Mom's turn to cook, and she fixes whatever she likes—but she's a great cook, and I can guarantee you it won't be a TV dinner."

"Then it's a date," Brad said, adding, "This doesn't change anything, does it? I still get to take you out on Wednesday? Because I was thinking we might have Italian, if that's OK with you."

"Sounds wonderful. I'll be looking forward to it."

Brad smiled. He didn't tell her that he would go to dinner with her every night of the week if she'd let him—even if TV dinners were the only thing on the menu.

~~~

Valerie Myers smiled at the tall, middle-aged man as he walked into her office on Tuesday morning. Robert Fletcher was a fairly new addition to their teaching staff, having just joined them in September, but he seemed to be working out well. The kids appeared to respond positively to him, and it was obvious he cared about them. That counted for a lot in Valerie's eyes.

Promoted from assistant principal to principal the previous year after the shocking exposure of the former principal's extramarital affair with a teacher, which eventually led to a tragic high school shooting, Valerie was totally devoted to her job. Divorced and with no children of her own, this middle-aged African-American woman had "adopted" each and every student at River View High and monitored their behavior like a mother hen, even though she tried not to cross the line on things that weren't her business.

"Sit down, Robert," she said, indicating the lone chair on the opposite side of her desk. "How are you? Things have been so busy around here, we haven't really had much of a chance to talk lately. Are you settling in OK?"

"You bet," Robert answered. "I couldn't be happier. The kids are great, and I feel at home already."

"Good for you. This is an excellent school, full of wonderful young people. I can't imagine a better place to work."

Robert smiled. "You're right about that."

Valerie saw his smile, but noticed a hesitation in his voice. Something was wrong. "You've come for more than a friendly chat, haven't you?" she asked.

Robert nodded. "You said when I came to work here that I should feel free to come to you with any concerns."

"And I meant it."

"Well, then, I have a concern about one of the students—someone I know is special to you."

Valerie raised her eyebrows questioningly. "All the students are special to me," she said.

"I know. But this one . . . Well, I understand you've been involved in her life in the past, particularly in light of what happened last year."

The alarm bells began to ring in Valerie's head. Her first thought was of Carrie Bosworth, the young girl who had been so seriously injured in the shooting and was even now in a wheelchair. "Is it Carrie?" she asked.

Robert shook his head. "No. A close friend of hers—Melissa Matthews."

Valerie was surprised. She hadn't heard of Melissa's having any problems recently. But then, she hadn't spoken to her in a while either. "What is it? Has something happened to her?"

"No, not really. It's just . . ." Robert took a deep breath. "I don't like to interfere, but you said I could talk to you about anything, so are you aware that Melissa is more than just slightly involved with Eric Fullbright, that new student who moved here from Nebraska over the summer?"

Valerie was more surprised than ever. "Eric Fullbright? Yes, I know who he is, although I haven't really spent much time with him. He's a good student, from what I understand. But Melissa Matthews? Involved with Eric? What do you mean exactly? I've scarcely seen Melissa, let alone spoken with her, since school started. I had no idea she and Eric even knew each other."

"Well, apparently they know each other well—maybe too well." Mr. Fletcher hesitated before going on. "I came across them in the parking lot after school yesterday, and they were more than slightly involved. I ran them off right away, told them the school parking lot wasn't a lovers' lane, but then I wondered if I'd made a mistake. From what I saw, they were well on their way to getting into trouble, if you know what I mean. And if they were that intimate in a public place, I'm concerned about how far the relationship may end up going in private—if it hasn't already. I know this sort of thing goes on with young people all the time, especially in today's so-called 'enlightened society,' but I also know, from what I've heard, that Melissa just isn't known for that sort of behavior."

Valerie was stunned. Not only had she been unaware of Melissa's relationship with Eric, but she would never have imagined her being involved to that extent with Eric or anyone else. Robert was right. This was definitely out of character for Melissa Matthews. Valerie couldn't help but wonder how much, if anything, Toni knew about all this.

She nodded. "You did the right thing in coming to me with this, Robert," she said. "I had no idea. I truly didn't. This is so unlike

Melissa—and I thought I knew her fairly well, especially after what happened last year. I'm the one who found her huddled over her friend Carrie Bosworth, who'd been shot and eventually ended up in a wheelchair, as I'm sure you know. Melissa was in complete shock. I helped her outside into an ambulance and later tried to follow up on her progress. I also got to know her sister, Toni, quite well, since we worked together to try to get to the bottom of that shooting incident.

"I don't know Eric Fullbright well enough to know whether this is unusual behavior for him, but it certainly is for Melissa. She's a sweet girl, and she's been through a lot of emotional turmoil and loss in her life, including the death of her father—all of which makes her extremely vulnerable right now. I wouldn't want to see her hurt again." Valerie sighed. "As much as I dislike interfering in my students' personal lives, I think I'm going to have to have a talk with Melissa—and maybe even her sister. I don't know if anything I can say will change Melissa's mind about Eric or head off a disaster in the making, but I'd never forgive myself if I didn't at least try. And there's not a doubt in my mind that Toni would want to know what's going on—if she doesn't already."

"Good," Robert said. "I'm glad you feel that way. I don't know Eric well either, other than seeing him in PE class a few times a week. And I don't really know Melissa at all, so I just thought it might be better if you handled it from here."

"You're right," Valerie said, her voice filled with resolve. "And I will look into it immediately, I promise you."

CHAPTER 19

It had been a while—far too long, Melissa decided—since she'd leaned against the huge pine tree that served as sentry over her parents' graves, far too long since she'd journaled her thoughts and prayers in this peaceful place. But now, on Tuesday afternoon, she sat here after school—alone—and was glad she had come.

Eric had wanted her to ride home with him, but she had declined, just as she had turned down his offer of a ride to school that morning. He had still shown up to walk her to her classes all day, but their relationship had been strained.

Melissa knew it was her fault, but she just didn't know what to do about it. And so she had decided to give it some time—and distance. But she hadn't yet found a way to explain that to Eric. Instead she had simply come up with an excuse for not riding to and from school with him that day, even though she knew that wouldn't work much longer.

Ever since she had insisted he take her home the previous afternoon, he had been looking at her strangely. She knew he was confused, particularly after she had just told him she loved him, but she had to sort things out in her own mind before trying to explain anything to him. She only hoped that she hadn't hurt him, which was the last thing she wanted to do.

The hardest part was that she missed him terribly. Each time she saw him, she wanted so much to respond to the invitation she read in his eyes. If only he could understand how much she wanted to get into the car with him and go to their parking spot and let him hold her and kiss her and . . .

She shook her head. No. That was exactly why she had refused to get back into the car with him. Her experience yesterday had literally shaken her to the core—the core of her emotions and the core of her faith. And so she sat on the multicolored fallen leaves that blanketed the ground of the cemetery, leaning against the faithful old tree, and writing out her thoughts and feelings—and prayers—on paper.

Oh, Dad, if ever I wished you were here, it's now. I know I've said that before—every time I have a problem. But I really mean it this time. I know I have Toni—and Abe too—but it's hard to talk to them. I guess it's because I know they wouldn't really approve. Not that you would, but . . . I don't know. You and I were always able to talk—about everything. Especially when we went fishing together. Remember? But I haven't been fishing since you died. I'm not even sure I'd like it anymore. It wouldn't be the same without you. But then, nothing is.

Melissa sighed, chewed the end of her pencil, and then continued. *I'm in love, Dad. At least, I think I am. His name is Eric Fullbright, and he's so handsome. Smart too. He's new in town. He and his family moved here from Nebraska during the summer, and now he's a senior at the high school. And he has this really cool car.*

In a way, that's a good thing, she wrote. *But in other ways . . . well, I think maybe it gives us too much time together. It's not so bad when we're at school, just holding hands and walking around the campus. I really like that part. And I loved it when he came to the house for my birthday dinner. He brought his parents, and even though I was really nervous, we ended up having a good time. His family seems nice. I think you'd like them—and Eric, too, of course. But then again, you liked everyone, didn't you, Dad?* She paused and smiled. *And everyone liked you. How could they help it? I still meet people everywhere I go that tell me what a great guy you were. I wish you and Eric could have met each other. It would be so much easier if you were here to give me advice. But you're not, and I just can't tell you how sad that makes me feel.*

I think maybe Toni has her feelings hurt because I haven't been talking to her about this, and I know I should, but I have been talking a little to April and Aunt Sophie. Do you remember April Lippincott? She's the lady who hired you to find her granddaughter, Julie. She's become a good friend—really, more like family—to all of us. And she's staying with us right now. I like talking to her because she really knows how to listen. And when she tells me something, I feel like it's coming from God. Does that make any sense?

You don't know Aunt Sophie, though. She's Abe's aunt. Abe is Toni's husband. I know that sounds weird, since Toni was still engaged to Brad when you died. But you'd like Abe. I know that for sure. He and Toni are perfect for each other, and they're really happy together. And Brad— well, he took it real hard, but I think he has a new girlfriend now, and I'm really glad about that.

Anyway, Aunt Sophie is a Jew—a devout one—and I like her a lot. She and April are friends now, too, and both of them have been giving me advice about how important it is to make sure I'm doing God's will, whether it's in my relationships or anything else. And now that my relationship with Eric is getting serious, I'm really trying to listen to God and find out what he wants me to do. She stopped, amazed at the thought that had just popped into her head. Trying to listen to God and find out what he wanted her to do? Who was she kidding? Certainly not God—and certainly not even her dad. He would be the first one to tell her what God's will was concerning her relationship with Eric. And it would not include parking in his car with him and crossing lines that God specifically said in the Bible were wrong.

She touched the locket that rested just below the hollow of her neck. How could she pretend she didn't know God's will about her relationship with Eric when it was as clear as it could be? If their relationship couldn't remain within acceptable biblical limitations, then she would have to stop seeing Eric completely. Period.

The sudden realization tore at her heart, even as it solidified in her mind. There were no two ways about it. She had to get the relationship on the right track—and keep it there—or end it.

As her eyes filled with tears, she wondered how she would ever find the courage to do what she now knew must be done. How would Eric respond? Would this be the end of their relationship? Would she actually have to give him up, or would he agree to honor the boundaries she knew God wanted between them?

Oh, Father, she wrote, as tears plopped onto the page, *it's you I need right now. You, my heavenly Father. Even my dad couldn't fix this for me if he were here. But you are here, Lord—right here in my heart. And you can do anything. So please help me. I want to love you most of all. I want to do your will. But I'm just not strong enough to do the right thing on my own.*

As a peace settled upon her, she recognized God's loving presence and assurance that he had indeed heard her prayer and he would help her. In spite of her broken heart, Melissa found joy in that knowledge.

~~~

Brad was amazed at how much Jeanine resembled her mother. Mrs. Simmons' short reddish hair was almost taken over by gray, but she had the same warm brown eyes as her daughter. And her ready laughter echoed with the same melodic tone. As Brad listened to them talk and laugh together, he thought he had never heard such a beautiful duet.

In addition, he found himself eating one of the best home-cooked meals he'd had in years—maybe ever, he thought, though he wouldn't dare say that to his own mother, who prided herself on her culinary talents. Brad found himself wondering if Jeanine had inherited Mrs. Simmons' cooking abilities. He certainly hoped so—and he hoped he would have a chance to find out soon.

As he helped himself to a second piece of homemade berry pie, he realized how comfortable he felt with these two ladies, one of whom he had just met and the other whom he had known for less than two months—and had almost overlooked entirely. How was that possible? How could he walk into this home for the first time and feel as if he belonged here? And yet that was exactly how he felt. Surely it was more than just their guileless personalities, their kind and gentle ways, or even their rock-solid faith in God. Was it possible that he felt this way because this was, after all, exactly where he did belong—with Jeanine Simmons and her family? Was God telling him that this was the woman with whom he would spend the rest of his life? Brad knew it was far too soon to be thinking along those lines, but the possibilities intrigued him.

He sipped his coffee as images of Toni invaded his thoughts. And then he smiled, realizing that those images no longer brought pain to his heart. He was over her, at long last, and he couldn't help but believe that the redhead sitting across from him at the table had at least something to do with that.

"What's so funny?" Jeanine asked, grinning as she reached over to touch his hand. "You look as if you're off in a daydream somewhere, but that smile is as real as that berry pie you seem to be enjoying so much."

Brad was startled for a moment, not realizing how far his thoughts had drifted. But Jeanine was right. The smile was real, and he was definitely enjoying the pie.

"Sorry," he answered. "I guess my mind was wandering. I was just thinking how really nice this is—the three of us together, the dinner. This is one of the best evenings I've had in a long time—and definitely one of the best meals."

Mrs. Simmons beamed. "Well, thank you, Brad. And believe me, flattery will get you everywhere around here. As far as I'm concerned, you have an open invitation to come for dinner anytime you like."

Brad laughed. "You'd better put some limits on that, Mrs. Simmons, or you're likely to have a permanent boarder. You are one excellent cook."

"Cooking is one of my favorite pastimes," she said. "I've always loved it. And I've passed that passion on to my daughter, as well as the talent. In fact, she may well outdo me in that area."

Brad raised his eyebrows. Could it get any better than this? A beautiful, intelligent, interesting woman who shared his faith and his love of the law, and who was also a gourmet cook—it was almost too good to be true.

"You look surprised," Jeanine said. " Are you having a hard time believing that I can cook like my mom?"

"Oh, no," Brad said quickly. "Not at all. I just—"

Jeanine laughed. "I'm teasing you. But I wouldn't want you to take my word for it—or even Mom's. I guess I'll just have to prove it to you. So forget taking me out to an Italian restaurant tomorrow. You come to my place, and I'll do the cooking. Then you can judge for yourself. Fair enough?"

Brad rolled his eyes and shook his head. "Any man who turned down an invitation like that should be locked away somewhere for the rest of his life. I'll be there. Just tell me what to bring."

"A healthy appetite," Jeanine answered, "and a large napkin. My spaghetti sauce is messy, but it's to die for."

~~~

Toni and Abe woke up early on Wednesday and decided to take a walk before work. As they left the house, the morning light was just beginning to streak the eastern sky.

"Looks like we might actually have clear skies today," Toni commented, zipping her jacket as they headed down the walkway.

"At least for now," Abe agreed. "But you know how fast that can change around here."

Toni nodded. "All the more reason to enjoy it while we can." She glanced at her watch. "We should have plenty of time to get a couple of miles in before we have to head back and get ready for work."

"Yeah, well, just don't forget that if we get two miles in before we head back, that means we have to get two more in before we reach home."

"Amazing. All those good looks and brains too. I really hit the jackpot with you, didn't I, detective?"

Abe chuckled but didn't answer. They walked on in silence for a block or so, and then he asked, "So are you going to call the church office today?"

"About signing up for those classes? You bet. We might as well jump in with both feet."

"OK by me. Do you know anyone else who's planning to go?"

Toni shook her head. "Nope. But I imagine there'll be several."

As they turned the corner, they were surprised to find themselves face-to-face with Valerie Myers. Toni hadn't talked to her in a while, but she knew Valerie was an exercise buff, so she wasn't surprised to see her out walking.

"Hey, you two," Valerie said, her attractive face lighting up in recognition. "I'd ask what you're doing out at this hour of the morning, but I guess it's fairly obvious, isn't it?"

Toni laughed. "Yes, it is. We don't get to do this as often as we'd like, but this morning we thought we'd at least get out and get some exercise while we had the chance. You do this regularly, don't you?"

Valerie's dark eyes smiled. "I try. Don't miss often. At my age it's important, you know."

Abe shook his head. "At your age? Let's see, that must be about twenty-nine, right?"

"Now how did you know that, anyway? Someone must have let you in on an otherwise well-kept secret." She laughed. "It's been so long since I've seen twenty-nine that I wouldn't recognize it if it came up and bit me." She paused. "So how's everything going with you two? And Melissa?"

"We're fine," Toni answered. "Staying busy at the agency. And Melissa's fine too, thanks."

Valerie nodded, but Toni noticed a line crease the dark skin of her forehead. Was something bothering her? Toni had become close with Valerie during the investigation into the school shooting the previous year, and she knew that even though this self-assured, no-nonsense, African-American career woman seldom let anything disturb her, something was up.

"What is it?" she asked. "I saw that look on your face. Is something wrong?"

"You don't miss much, do you?" Valerie sighed. "OK, have you got a minute?"

Toni and Abe exchanged a concerned glance, then looked back at Valerie. "Sure," said Toni. "What's up?"

"It's Melissa. Actually, I was planning to call you today and see if we could get together and talk."

"About Melissa?" Toni's heart was picking up speed, even though they were standing still. She didn't like the sound of this at all.

Valerie nodded. "Yes. One of the teachers—Robert Fletcher, the boys' PE instructor—came to see me yesterday. It seems he came across Melissa and Eric Fullbright sitting in his car in the school parking lot on Monday afternoon."

"I see," Toni said, her voice hesitant. "And was there some sort of problem?"

"You don't seem surprised that they were together," Valerie said, "so I assume you're aware of their relationship."

Toni looked at Abe before continuing. "We gave our permission for her to date him—reluctantly, I might add—but with some restrictions. Why do you ask, Valerie? What are you trying to tell me?"

"In Mr. Fletcher's words they were 'more than slightly involved' when he saw them. He interrupted them and sent them on their way, but he was concerned at the level of intimacy he witnessed between them. And, frankly, I'm concerned too. I have no reason to doubt Mr. Fletcher's assessment of their situation, and I'm surprised that Melissa would be involved with anyone to that extent."

Toni's mouth went dry and she heard a buzzing in her ears, just as Abe put his arm around her waist. "What exactly do you mean by *involved?*" she managed to ask. "Just how involved were they?"

"From what I understand, just hugging and kissing, but Mr. Fletcher felt that if their relationship had progressed to that level in a public parking lot, it might have gone even further in private. I certainly hope not, but I felt it was a serious enough possibility that it was worth addressing. That's why I was going to call you. Actually, I had planned to call Melissa in today and speak with her first, but now that we've run into each other . . ."

Toni nodded, trying to control her breathing. "I'm glad we did," she said. "It will give me a chance to talk to her before she goes to school this morning."

"Do you think that's a good idea?" Valerie asked.

Toni was puzzled. "What do you mean? Of course it's a good idea. I want to know exactly what's going on between her and that boy, and I want to know now. And besides that, I intend to put a stop to that relationship once and for all. I never should have—"

"What I mean is," Valerie interrupted, "maybe it would be better if I talked with her first. Would you trust me to do that? She might be more open that way."

"But—"

This time Abe interrupted Toni's protest. "I think she might be right, sweetheart. This might not be the best time to try talking to Melissa. You're upset right now—understandably so—but if you burst into her room and start accusing and questioning her, she's liable to clam up entirely. It might even push her further into Eric's arms."

"From the sound of things, she's about as far into his arms as she can get." Toni stopped herself and took a deep breath. "OK, you're probably right—both of you. I'm so angry right now I would probably just make the situation worse. I'll back off until you've had a chance to talk to her. But whatever happens, this Eric thing is over. I don't care what she says."

"All right," Valerie said. "I'll talk with her before the day's out, and then I'll call you. After that the three of you can deal with the situation however you see fit. Fair enough?"

Tight-lipped, Toni nodded. She didn't like it one bit, but she knew it was probably for the best. But by the time the sun went down tonight, Eric and Melissa would be over. On that point there would be no compromise.

CHAPTER 20

It was the first time in quite a while that Melissa had spent her lunch break with Carrie. But even as she realized how much she had missed long talks with her best friend and tried to ignore her guilt at having neglected her almost completely, her heart ached to be with Eric.

He had begged her to go with him during the lunch break to drop off his car for a much-needed tune-up, telling her he wanted her company on the six-block walk back to campus. But she had refused, using the excuse that she needed to get some studying done before an afternoon exam. She doubted if he had believed her, but he had gone on without her anyway. Now she sat on a bench across from Carrie at an otherwise empty table in the cafeteria, munching a tuna sandwich and wondering why she had turned him down. It would have been the perfect time to talk to him about the biblical restrictions they needed to impose on their relationship. And yet she knew in her heart that was the exact reason she had declined to accompany him. She was putting off the inevitable, for fear that he might not agree with her and break off their relationship entirely.

Suddenly she pulled herself back to the present, as she felt Carrie staring at her. Melissa smiled, trying to look as natural as possible. "This is nice," she said. "Having lunch together again. I've missed you."

"Really?" Carrie arched her eyebrows. "I'm surprised. To be perfectly honest, Melissa, I didn't think you'd thought about me at all—or anyone else, for that matter. Other than Eric, of course."

Melissa felt her face grow hot. She wished she had a comeback for Carrie's accusation, but she didn't. "I know," she said, her voice low. "I guess I've been kind of caught up with him lately."

"Kind of? Now that's an understatement. But it's OK, really. I'm not saying this to be mean; you know that. I've just been concerned about you."

Melissa nodded. "I know. Thanks."

Carrie's dark eyes were serious. "Are you all right, Melissa? Is everything OK between you and Eric?"

"Sure." Reaching up to touch her locket, she sighed and shrugged her shoulders. "I guess so, but I don't know. Maybe things are just a little too intense, if you know what I mean. I've been trying to keep my distance for a few days so I could think things through and try to decide."

"Decide what? Are you thinking of breaking up with him?"

Melissa felt tears pooling in her eyes, and she tried to blink them back. "I don't want to," she said, her voice cracking. "I really don't. I love him, Carrie, and he loves me. We want to be together, maybe even get married someday. But . . ."

"But he's pushing you?"

Melissa nodded again. "He says it's OK, that it's natural because we love each other. And when I'm with him, I want to believe it. I almost do, but then . . ."

Carrie's eyes were also watery, and Melissa knew her friend was hurting for her, though she said nothing.

"I've been doing a lot of praying lately," Melissa said, "and talking to Mrs. Lippincott and Aunt Sophie. And, Carrie, I know I can't cross the line that Eric wants me to cross. No matter how much I want to, I just can't. Believe me, I've tried to find a way to justify it, but I can't."

"That's because there isn't one," Carrie said softly. "You and I both know that. Sadly, Eric doesn't. In his mind it probably is OK. In fact, most people seem to think so. But we know better. And the Bible says that for those of us who know the difference between right and wrong—God's true standards that don't change—we're accountable to act on those standards. Anything less is sin. There's just no way around it, no matter how hard we try to find one."

Melissa sighed. Carrie was saying all the things she already knew in her heart, and she loved her for it—even if she still wished for another answer. "I've been thinking about how we've learned in some of our classes that there's no absolute truth, that everything is relative. But the Bible teaches otherwise, doesn't it?"

Carrie nodded. "And so we have to choose. Who will we believe—God, who never changes, or the world, whose opinions change with the wind?"

"You sound like April Lippincott," Melissa said.

"She's a wise lady. I'll take that as a compliment."

"I meant it as one."

By the time lunch was over, Melissa headed off to her next class with a stronger assurance than ever that she had to deal with her relationship with Eric quickly and firmly. She simply couldn't put it off any longer.

As she walked into the classroom, she was surprised to find a note on her desk, asking her to report to the principal's office at the end of the class period. Frowning, she stuck the note in her purse, wondering what the summons could be about. She hadn't talked to Valerie Myers in quite a while, and she had never before been called to the principal's office.

~~~

Spider had found that Jinx was not easily threatened, even when he realized there might be a serious price for noncompliance. Men like that, Spider believed, were either just plain stupid, or there was something they feared even more than Spider himself. In Jinx's case, Spider was sure it wasn't stupidity. Whatever the reason, Jinx's determined stance had brought Spider to the point of holding a grudging respect for the man. He knew he could easily pound Jinx into submission, but he'd decided to hold that option as a last resort, preferring to move slowly and try to gain the man's confidence. And now that he was beginning to figure out why the other three inmates were so interested in enlisting Jinx's cooperation, Spider had begun to think of it as a personal challenge. If anyone could get Jinx to go along with the plan, Spider was the one; of that he was certain. It was just a question of how and when.

And so he had begun to hang around Jinx, hoping the man would let his guard down enough to expose a weakness that could be exploited. Everyone had one, Spider knew, and Jinx was no exception. It was just a matter of identifying it.

When it happened, it had been so simple that Spider could hardly believe the circumstances that led up to it. If he believed in God, he might even have suspected his involvement in the situation. But, of course, he had long since given up believing in the God his mother had preached to him when he was a child. If there were a God, Spider reasoned, he wouldn't have allowed his mother to die at his father's hands while Spider—still known as Gerald then—was only seven years old. And God surely wouldn't have allowed a seven-year-old boy to be raised by an aunt and uncle who hated and abused him until he finally ran off at the age of fourteen to find a way to fend for himself. Since then Spider had learned to take care of himself, depend on himself, and trust no one other than himself. God had become a name he used only as a curse word, and he used it often and without apology.

But now he'd discovered what he'd been looking for—Jinx's weakness. And he couldn't be more pleased with himself. *Guess I was just in the right place at the right time*, he thought. *That no-good whining wimp Ernie might've got away from me before I could use him to mop up the cell floor but not before he left me with some useful information.*

So, Mr. James "Jinx" Landry, I've discovered your secret, haven't I? And don't think I didn't notice the look on your face when I told you your brother, George, was in River View looking for you. All I needed was to find out your real name, and all the other pieces fell right into place, didn't they? I may not know yet why you don't want your brother to know where you are, but the important thing is, you know that I know he's looking for you—and you definitely do not want to be found.

Spider smiled. He was feeling proud of himself, and he couldn't wait to see where this valuable newfound information would take him. He also wondered just how much that information would be worth to a certain group of three inmates that he was sure were making some promising plans—plans that he had no doubt would soon include him.

~~~

By the time school got out for the day, Melissa had run out of excuses to avoid Eric any longer. When she walked out of her last class, he was waiting for her, so she fell into step beside him, wordlessly agreeing to accompany him to pick up his car. As they walked along, her hand in his, she wondered if he could hear the thumping of her heart. She breathed deeply as they walked, praying and reminding herself of her lunchtime conversation with Carrie—and her meeting with Valerie Myers.

Her visit to the principal's office had been humiliating, though Melissa knew Ms. Myers had done her best to make her feel at ease, even as they discussed a difficult subject. Melissa had been horrified to know that Mr. Fletcher had told the principal about his encounter with her and Eric in the parking lot and even more horrified to learn that Toni and Abe were now aware of the incident. She didn't even want to think of the confrontation that awaited her when she got home. She had been able to convince Ms. Myers that she was going to talk to Eric about the situation and deal with their relationship—one way or the other. But she doubted she would have as easy a time convincing Toni.

"I've missed you," Eric said, squeezing her hand. "It's awful being away from you."

Melissa nodded. "I know. I've missed you too."

"I'm glad. Let's not do this anymore, OK? I know you've been trying to deal with what happened Friday night—although nothing really did happen, you know—but I hope you've worked through all that by now. Have you?"

They were still walking, and Melissa kept her eyes down. She didn't think she could say these words to Eric if they were looking at each other. "I think I have," she said, "but it hasn't been easy."

"I know that," Eric said, his voice soft. "I love you, Melissa, and I don't want to make things hard for you. But we can't help how we feel. I know we're young, but . . ." He stopped walking, and she stopped too, still gazing downward. Eric gently lifted her face to his and waited until their eyes met. "Can we sit down somewhere and talk?" he asked. "Please."

Melissa wanted to say no, that it was hard enough as it was, but she knew she owed it to him to agree. She nodded. "OK."

Eric led her to the nearby park, and they settled onto a bench. The sun that had shone so brightly that morning had since been obscured by thick clouds, and the cold wind promised rain before the night was over. Melissa shivered, as the chill seemed to pass right through her.

"Cold?" Eric asked.

Melissa swallowed. If she said yes, he would undoubtedly put his arms around her to keep her warm. But if she said no, she would be lying. Before she could answer, he took off his jacket and draped it across her shoulders. Immediately she regretted his act of tenderness. It only made her words that much harder to speak. *Help me, Lord*, she prayed silently.

"Thank you," she said. He didn't answer, but his eyes held hers, and she knew there was no more putting it off. "We have to talk about us. I know we said we love each other, but . . ."

She could read the hurt and uncertainty that had invaded his eyes, and she wanted so much to reassure him that everything was all right between them. But she had to press forward and finish what she'd started.

"I do love you, Eric. At least, I think I do. And I really want to be with you—that much I know for sure." The hurt and uncertainty were fading from his eyes as she continued. "But I'm a Christian. And that's more to me than just a label, more than a religion or a collection of traditions. It's a relationship between me and God, and it's the most important relationship of my life, now or ever." She was amazed that, as she spoke, her confidence grew. God was helping her, she was sure of it. "I love God, Eric. More than I love you. More than I love anyone. And if I'm going to honor that relationship, I have to keep my other relationships in line."

She hesitated, watching his reaction. A raised eyebrow was the only visible sign as he said, "Meaning you and me."

Melissa nodded. "Yes. God says that sex is wrong unless we're married. And we're too young for that. So . . ."

"So no sex."

She nodded again. "We have to promise each other, Eric. We have to stay out of situations where we might not be able to stop. We have to help each other."

"You're saying we can't have sex, not because you don't want to but because God says we can't."

"Yes."

"And how do you know God says that?"

"It's in the Bible. I can't tell you exactly where without looking, but—"

"Melissa," Eric said, his voice firm as he interrupted her, "I don't mean to make fun of your faith, but do you really believe everything that's written in the Bible? I mean, it's an old book, written thousands of years ago. What's it got to do with us today?"

"It's got everything to do with us," she said. "God wrote it so we'd know how much he loves us and how he wants us to live—always. And God never changes."

"If God loves us so much, why does he put so many restrictions on us? Doesn't he want us to be happy? If he knows we love each other, why wouldn't he want us to be together?"

"Because he knows a lot more than we do. We only know what we feel right now. He knows what's going to happen tomorrow and next week and next year, and ten years from now. Eric, he knows what's best for us—for each of us. And he wants that for us even more than we want it for ourselves. But we can only find it if we listen to him and obey what he says."

"And so, according to you, he says no sex until we get married."

Melissa nodded, their eyes still locked together. She saw Eric's jaw twitch before he asked, "Do you honestly think that you're going to go through the next few years of your life and never have sex until you're married?"

"I know that's what God wants from me," she said. "And I'm going to trust him to give me the strength to do it."

Eric's jaw twitched again, and his eyes narrowed. Then he stood and looked down at her. "I don't believe you," he said. "There's no way you can hold out, especially when you love someone. And if you really love me like you say you do, then you'll forget about all this crazy God stuff and prove to me that you're not just trying to dump me. Because that's what I think this is really about. You don't love me at all, do you, Melissa? You were just playing a game with me, and now you're tired of it and want to get rid of me."

Melissa's eyes filled with tears, and she jumped up and tried to take his hand, but he pulled away. "No, Eric," she protested, "that's not it at all. I do love you. I truly do. And I really want to be with you. But . . ."

"But . . . ?"

"But . . . I love God more. So I can't."

Eric nodded. "OK. You've made your choice, and I guess I know where I stand." He paused, then continued in a clipped, sarcastic tone. "Thanks for nothing, Melissa. See you around." Then he turned and walked away, leaving Melissa where she stood, shivering in the wind as tears coursed down her cheeks. Clutching her locket in her hand, she watched him until he was out of sight, and only then did she realize that his jacket was still draped over her shoulders.

CHAPTER 21

Toni had come home from work early, determined to be there when Melissa returned from school. She had already decided that the situation with Eric would be resolved that day, the relationship ended, and their lives returned to normal. No amount of tears or pleading on Melissa's part would change Toni's mind.

Still she couldn't be sure when her sister might show up. Since Melissa's relationship with Eric had begun, she tended to linger after school rather than coming straight home as she once had. Now, of course, Toni knew why.

As she waited, she tried to concentrate on writing the next chapter of *Storm on the Horizon*, but she finally gave up. Until things were settled with Melissa, she simply couldn't think of anything else.

She was both surprised and relieved when Melissa walked through the front door just after four o'clock. April hadn't returned from her church meeting yet, and Abe was still at the agency. This would give the two sisters an opportunity to talk things out in private.

Melissa appeared startled when Toni emerged from the kitchen and confronted her as the girl was headed through the living room in the direction of her bedroom. "We need to talk," Toni said, indicating the couch.

Hesitating only briefly, Melissa walked over and sat down carefully at one end. Toni took the other end and turned toward her. "I ran into Valerie Myers this morning."

Melissa dropped her eyes. It was obvious she knew what was coming.

"She told me about your run-in with Mr. Fletcher in the school parking lot on Monday."

"I know," Melissa said, her head still bowed. "She called me into her office this afternoon."

"I see. And?"

Melissa looked up. The vulnerability and bewilderment evident on her face tore at Toni's heart, but she steeled herself. This was no time to go soft, especially with Melissa sitting there wearing Eric Fullbright's jacket. She waited.

"We talked about Eric and me." The girl's voice was soft, shaking slightly. Again Toni resisted the impulse to soften her stance as Melissa continued. "I told her that I was going to talk to Eric and set boundaries on our relationship so we wouldn't ever get into that kind of situation again."

"And did you?"

Melissa nodded. "This afternoon. I told him that we have to have a biblical relationship, one that would be pleasing to God, because I love God more than I love him."

Toni raised her eyebrows. In spite of her resolve, she felt her heart melting. "How did he take it?"

Tears formed in Melissa's green eyes as she reached for the locket that hung around her neck. "He told me he didn't believe me. He said I was just trying to dump him, and that if I really loved him I would prove it by forgetting about all that 'God stuff.' And then"—she took a deep breath and swallowed—"when I told him I couldn't do that, he said I'd already made my choice, and he just walked away."

As Melissa's tears spilled over onto her cheeks, Toni felt her own eyes beginning to sting, and she reached over and gathered her little sister into her arms and pulled her close. It seemed that the relationship between Eric and Melissa had already been settled without her. It was also clear that the brokenhearted teenager was going to need a lot of love and support to get through the difficult days that lay ahead.

~~~

Toni had wondered if she should cancel their first training session at the church that evening, but Abe and April had convinced her otherwise.

Just minutes after Toni and Melissa had finished their cry and Melissa had gone off to her room, April came home. When she'd seen Toni's red eyes, she had, of course, asked what was wrong. Toni, her tears flowing once again, had told her the whole story. This time it was April who held Toni and comforted her while she cried.

Then, when Abe arrived home and the story had been repeated yet again, Toni announced that she would have to skip the prison ministry class and stay home with Melissa. April had immediately jumped in and assured her that she would take good care of Melissa while they were gone. When Toni still hesitated, Abe had reminded her of their mutual belief that this ministry opportunity was something God wanted for both of them. Finally she had agreed, knowing that Melissa was indeed in good hands with Mrs. Lippincott.

And so they sat in the conference room at church, filling out the preliminary papers and waiting for the class to start. They had been among the first to arrive and were somewhat disappointed at the small turnout. But as the clock ticked closer to the 7:00 p.m. starting time, other volunteers drifted into the room. Among them was the church janitor, John King, Abe's best man at his wedding and the unexpected hero who had rescued both Abe and Toni when they had been cornered at gunpoint in the church choir loft by the woman who had instigated the school shooting the previous year.

Toni was the first to notice the tall, lanky custodian when he entered. She nudged Abe, who looked up and smiled when he saw John. John returned the smile and sauntered toward them, paperwork in hand. "Anybody sitting here?" he asked, eyeing the empty desk beside Abe.

"Just you," Abe said as the man lowered himself into the seat and did his best to tuck his long legs underneath.

"I had no idea you were planning to get involved in the prison ministry weekend," Toni said, looking past Abe to the man she credited with saving their lives.

John looked embarrassed. "Well, I'd like to. I mean, I've thought about it a lot, and I think it's something God wants me to do."

Abe nodded. "Exactly the way we feel. It'll be great having you with us." He grinned. "Besides, we'll know whom to call if we get into any trouble while we're there."

This time John's face flushed a bright red. "Ah, you two always make a big deal about what I did. But it really wasn't much. I just came in to clean the sanctuary, and then when I heard voices in the choir loft, I went up to check. That's it, really. Like I said, it was no big deal."

Toni laughed. "Well, it was a big deal to us. We would have been in serious trouble if you hadn't come along when you did."

John shrugged. "I guess so." Then, in an obvious attempt to change the subject, he looked around and commented, "Looks like a pretty good turnout. Must be at least twenty people here."

Abe nodded. "Actually, there were only three or four when we first came. Guess we were the early birds." He glanced at the paperwork John still clutched in his big hand. "Sure is a lot of red tape for this thing, isn't there?"

John looked down at the papers. "No kidding. I'd better get busy filling everything out."

As the three of them concentrated on completing their forms, two more volunteers wandered in. Then the instructor, a man from Mark Johnson Ministries, walked in with the associate pastor, Jim Howell. They closed the door behind them, and Pastor Jim opened the meeting with prayer. As the class got underway, Toni felt a sense of excitement rising up within her. She didn't understand it all, but she was sure that this was the beginning of something much bigger than any of them could imagine.

~~~

Melissa was still fighting tears as she sat on her bed, her journal open on her lap. But she wasn't getting much writing done. Each time she attempted to make an entry, she started to cry. So she just sat there, praying silently and staring at the as-yet unconnected computer on her desk. Eric had offered to come over and help her hook it up. Obviously that was no longer an option.

Had she done the right thing? Yes, she was sure she had. There simply was nothing else she could have done—not if she wanted to stay true to her relationship with God. And despite the ache in her heart, she knew that was what she wanted most of all.

But now it was over—at least, she assumed it was. And yet, in addition to the locket he had given her for her birthday, she still had his jacket. Had he forgotten it, or had he purposely left it with her so they would have an excuse to contact each other again?

Melissa had asked herself that question over and over again, ever since Eric had left her standing alone in the park. Would he call her and ask for the jacket? Would he come by to pick it up? Would he wait and ask for it at school? Or should she just take it to him?

She shook her head. No. She wasn't ready for that yet. It would be too hard. She might even start crying and end up back in his arms, and then anything could happen. The jacket would have to wait.

The soft knock on the door startled her. She knew Abe and Toni had gone to a meeting at church, but she had forgotten that April was home. "Come in," she called.

Mrs. Lippincott opened the door and stepped quietly into Melissa's room. Her silver hair was swept up on top of her head as usual, and her pale blue eyes smiled sweetly from her gentle face. In spite of herself, Melissa smiled in welcome and patted the side of her bed.

"Come and sit down," she said. "Please. I'd love the company right now."

"I thought you might," April said, joining her on the bed. "Abe and Toni told me what happened with Eric. How are you doing?"

Melissa shrugged. "OK, I guess. Praying a little. Trying to journal. Crying, mostly."

April nodded. "I can certainly understand that. A perfectly natural reaction to what you've been through. You've had a rough couple of years, and this situation certainly doesn't help."

"But it's different this time. It's not like losing Dad. That was so final. And I really didn't have anything to say about it. It just happened. With Eric I had to make some hard choices—just like you and I talked about. And I'm glad I did, but . . ."

"But it hurts—a lot. And you miss him."

Melissa nodded. She didn't trust herself to speak.

April reached over and patted her hand. "You did the right thing. The only thing you could do under the circumstances. And as hollow as this may sound right now, God will bless you for it. How, I can't tell you. But he will. That much I know for sure."

"You know a lot about God, don't you?"

April smiled. "I'm not so sure anyone knows a lot about God, my dear. All we can really know about him in this life is what he has revealed to us through his creation and in his Word. And truly, that's enough. It's all we need to know for now. But I suspect all that knowledge is a mere drop in the bucket compared to what we'll discover when we finally cross that line into eternity and see him face-to-face." She closed her eyes, and her smile broadened. "It will be glorious," she whispered, "to finally see the face of our beloved Savior." She opened her eyes and looked at Melissa. "You know, my dear, the Bible says that when we see him, we will be like him."

"I don't really understand that," Melissa admitted. "I believe it, but . . ."

April nodded again. "None of us understands it. That's what faith is—believing even when we don't understand, when we can't see, when there seem to be no answers. And, of course, acting on that faith. It's not enough simply to believe God exists. We must act on our faith, live our lives according to God's instructions in his Word and his Spirit within us. Anything less is not faith at all. To claim faith without acting on it makes us the greatest of hypocrites."

"That's why I had to do what I did about my relationship with Eric, isn't it?"

"Yes, my dear. That's why. Jesus said we are truly his disciples when we obey him, not just when we claim to believe in him. And that's why I know God will bless you for your obedience. It wasn't easy for you— obedience to God seldom is. But when we take the first step, he carries us the rest of the way."

Melissa smiled. "I know you're right. It was so hard for me to talk to Eric about all this, but once I started, I could feel God helping me. He gave me the strength I needed, or I never would have been able to get through it. I sure wasn't strong enough to do it myself."

"None of us is, Melissa. And that's probably the greatest lesson you'll learn from this or any other trial of your life. When Jesus said that apart from him we can do nothing, that's exactly what he meant. Nothing. We need to trust him for absolutely everything, down to our next breath. And I promise you, my dear, he will never fail or disappoint you."

Melissa's heart still hurt, but she felt hope rising up inside her. April Lippincott was right. This wonderful woman had walked with Jesus for many, many years. She had been through a lot of pain and loss. But God had never let her down. He had always been there for her, and he would do the same for Melissa.

She smiled, thinking suddenly of April's late granddaughter, Julie. "I wish I'd had a grandma like you," she said.

"You do," April assured her. "God put us together when we needed each other most, and I will stay here with you as long as necessary."

"But don't you have to go back to Colorado soon?"

"I'll go back when God lets me know my assignment here is finished. Not a moment sooner, I assure you."

More than an hour later, as Melissa drifted off to sleep, she felt her pain slipping away as April sat at her side, stroking her forehead and humming "Amazing Grace."

~~~

The TV droned in the background, and a faint light peeked around the edges of the tattered shade that covered the motel window as George began to emerge from his two-day hibernation. He felt as if he were climbing out of a deep, dark pit. His eyes were full of sand, he was sure of it, and his swollen tongue felt too big for his mouth. It had been quite a party, lasting until the cocaine and the alcohol ran out and he and his new companion had fallen into a drug-induced sleep. He lay still in the semidarkness, afraid to move his throbbing head too quickly, trying to remember all that had taken place since he'd set out from his room on Sunday night in search of a little excitement in the form of some female companionship.

Sunday. How many days ago was that? He considered checking his watch, but there wasn't enough light to read it, and besides, the thought of lifting his arm was just too exhausting to attempt. The news seemed to be on. Maybe if he listened long enough he'd discover the day and time.

He strained to pay attention. Bits and pieces of world affairs filtered into his brain, interspersed with commercials and a sports update. Then, finally, it was time for the weather. He listened more intently and was shocked to discover that it was Thursday afternoon. The last he remembered it had been Tuesday evening, and he had collapsed, exhausted, onto the bed, his arm slung across the blonde he'd met at the bar on Sunday. She didn't have the long legs he'd hoped for, nor was she young, but she had made him laugh and had been more than willing to entertain him, so long as he supplied her with drugs and booze.

He smiled through his hungover haze at the memory of their two days and nights together. She might not have been a raving beauty, but she was a lot better looking than the prostitute Louie had brought him and a lot more fun. George decided he would keep her around a while longer.

Slowly he turned toward her side of the bed and reached out to touch her. The bed was empty. He opened his eyes wider and tried to focus, feeling around as if he would discover her hiding under the sheets.

"Hey," he called, the effort of it knifing through his head. What was her name? Millie? Mary? Maggie? Something like that. He pulled himself up to a sitting position. "Where are you?" he growled. Still no answer. At last he managed to drag himself from the bed and stumble to the lone light switch by the door. Flipping it on, he blinked his eyes in agony, covering his face with his hand until, slowly, he was able to peek from beneath his fingers and look around the room. No sign of her—not even the clothes she had tossed on the floor, or her purse, or . . .

He hurried as fast as he could to the bathroom. Empty. So much for keeping her around for a few more days. She must have gotten tired of waiting for him to wake up, he decided. Maybe she'd just gone out to get something to eat. Maybe she'd be back.

And then he glanced at the nightstand beside the bed. His wallet was gone. Frantically he checked the pockets of his discarded pants and tore through the jumbled sheets. Nothing. By the time he'd searched every inch of the motel room, he knew he'd been robbed— not just of his cash but also of his identity and credit cards.

He cursed the woman whose name he couldn't remember and then himself. How could he have been so stupid? This could ruin everything. He should have known better than to trust a woman. He'd never met one yet that was worth anything—with the exception of his mother, of course. And even she hadn't been straight with him, always favoring old Jimmy boy.

But that would soon be resolved, he reminded himself as he struggled to the shower, determined to sober up and go out and find that woman and his wallet, as well as the Matthews and Matthews detective team he'd hired to track down his brother. It was long past time that he got some answers from them, and he was in no mood to be put off any longer.

CHAPTER 22

When George stormed into the bar, he was angrier than he'd been since he'd discovered what his brother had done with the family money. If there was one thing George Landry couldn't tolerate, it was a thief. He had done a lot of things in his life—things he shouldn't have, he knew, and things he wished he hadn't but couldn't change—but he'd never taken anything that wasn't his. And now this blonde bimbo had stolen his wallet while he was asleep. But he was going to find her, and she was going to pay. Just like Jimmy boy would pay when he finally got hold of him.

After discovering his two-day companion gone, George had showered and dressed and driven to the Matthews and Matthews detective agency to confront them and discover what, if any, progress had been made on locating his brother. But the agency had already closed for the day, which only increased his anger. By the time he'd reached the bar, he was steaming.

He glanced around the seedy room as his eyes adjusted to the dim lights. No sign of her here, although he hadn't really expected her to return to the spot where they'd met four days earlier. But it was the only starting place he had, as he knew nothing about her, other than she was a sticky-fingered blonde—undoubtedly bleached—who couldn't be trusted and who was right now running around with his money and his credit cards. Someone was bound to know her, though, and he had no intention of giving up until he had his wallet back in his hands—and his hands around her throat.

He mounted a bar stool and glared at the man pouring drinks. "Whiskey," he said, "straight up."

The bartender nodded, finished waiting on the couple on George's left, then brought him his order.

"Thanks," George said, picking up his glass and sniffing the contents. Cheap stuff, he was sure, but it would do. He wasn't here to drink anyway, but he had to open the conversation somehow. He took a sip and nodded. "Good," he said, forcing a smile. "Thanks."

The bartender nodded in return and started to walk away.

"Say," George said, "maybe you could help me with something."

The bartender turned back and raised his eyebrows.

"I'm looking for a lady," he said. "Blonde and—"

A burly, middle-aged man to his right interrupted him. "Who isn't?" he asked, and laughed. The bartender laughed too. George forced himself to join in.

"OK," he said, glancing toward the laughing patron, "you got me on that one. But this is a particular blonde, about fortyish, maybe. Has a real loud laugh, lots of makeup. She was here Sunday night." He was eyeing the bartender again. "Her name is Mary, Maggie—something like that. You wouldn't know who she is, would you? Or where I might find her?"

George didn't miss the flash of recognition in the bartender's eyes before he shook his head. "Doesn't sound familiar," he said. "But then, we get a lot of people in and out of here all the time. Could be anybody."

George shrugged. "Sure. Just thought I'd check." He smiled. "I happened to see her here the other night, and I liked what I saw, if you know what I mean. Thought maybe I could hook up with her or something."

The bartender nodded. "Yeah, I know what you mean. Sorry I can't help you." He turned around and made his way to the other end of the bar, where he busied himself wiping up a wet spot with a dirty white towel. But George caught the look he passed to two guys seated adjacent to the bar where the man stood, still wiping up the now dry spot. Within minutes the two men left. George didn't doubt for a second that their departure had something to do with the blonde thief.

Picking up his glass, he downed the burning liquid in one gulp, plopped three dollars from his pocket on the bar, and headed for the front door, determined to follow the men and discover the whereabouts of his wallet. Once outside on the sidewalk, he pulled the collar of his jacket up around his neck. It had started raining, and it was cold. But George didn't care. His anger and the shot of whiskey would keep him warm.

He glanced up and down the street and scanned the parking lot. No sign of them. Then he heard the voices. They sounded as if they were coming from the alley behind the bar. Carefully he made his way to the end of the building and peeked around. He'd never heard the two men talk before, so he didn't recognize the sound of their voices.

But he heard enough to know that it had to be the two men from the bar and that he was on the right trail.

"Looking for Marilyn," a voice said.

"Can't let him find her," said another voice. "He's got to be the guy she told us about, and you know he's mad about his wallet."

The voices were moving away from him now, farther down the alley. George reasoned that they were heading for their car, maybe even going to the blonde to warn her. This was perfect. All he had to do was follow them.

He never saw the knife coming, but it slammed into his back with deadly accuracy. All he felt was a searing, agonizing pain that sucked his breath from his lungs and dropped him to his knees. Through the pain he could hear the bartender's voice, complimenting someone on a "good job," and then laughter ringing in his ears as he was dragged, lifted, and then tossed into a dumpster.

Thrown out with the garbage, he thought as darkness closed in on him. *And all over a woman. I should have known.*

And then he breathed his last.

❧❧❧

It was Friday morning, and Melissa and Carrie were making their way across the campus.

"Are you sure you're OK with this?" Carrie asked.

Melissa nodded, glancing down at her friend in the wheelchair. "It's for the best. Hanging on to it is just making it worse. I need to get it back to him. But what about you? Are you sure you don't mind taking it to him?"

Carrie smiled. "We talked about this last night, remember? For a long time. Of course I don't mind. And it's bound to be easier for me than you. After all, I don't have any sentimental attachment to it. For me it's just a jacket. For you, well . . ."

Melissa nodded again. "You're right. Hanging on to the jacket is like hanging on to him. And the way things are between us, there's just no sense in that. So go ahead and get it over with, please. I just hope he doesn't think I'm too much of a coward for not taking it to him myself."

"Hey, that's what friends are for, right?" Carrie smiled again. "And if he thinks you're a coward, that's OK. We know better. But there are some things that are just better done by a third party. And this is one of those things. It's not like you didn't talk to him face-to-face about your relationship. You tried to get him to agree to the only terms you could set if you were going to continue seeing each other. And he wouldn't agree, so that's that." Her face softened. "I know it's easy for me to say, Melissa, since I'm not the one with a broken heart. But it really is for the best. There just isn't any other way to deal with this."

Melissa's smile was tight. "I know," she said, wishing for what seemed the millionth time that there could be some other way—any other way—but knowing there wasn't. Her heart constricted as she thought of the locket, now safely tucked away in her dresser drawer at home. It had been a gift, so she had decided not to return it. But she simply couldn't wear it any longer.

As Carrie rolled away in search of Eric, the jacket resting on her lap, Melissa watched her go and once again found herself fighting tears. Would she ever be able to think of Eric without tears springing into her eyes? As much as she'd cried over the past couple of days, she thought the well should be running dry by now. But being here at school, where they'd first met and where they'd walked hand in hand down the hallways, only intensified the pain.

Maybe growing up isn't all it's cracked up to be, Melissa thought. Maybe life would be a lot better if she could just have remained a little girl forever.

~~~

It was mid-morning and Toni had scarcely walked through the front door of the agency before Abe jumped up and stuck the newspaper in her face.

"Have you seen this?" he demanded, his dark eyes wide.

She shook her head. She'd gotten up late and hadn't even had time to look at the paper, let alone read it. Abe knew that. In fact, he was the one who'd insisted she sleep in a little and come into work late because she'd had such a hard time getting to sleep the night before. What could possibly be in the paper that could be so important?

Taking the paper from him, she plunked down into her chair and began to scan the headlines on the open page Abe had handed her. Standing behind her, he reached over her shoulder and pointed to a relatively small article in the bottom left corner. As she read, her eyes opened wide, and she felt her heart beat faster. She set the paper down and looked back at Abe. "George Landry? Dead?"

Abe nodded. "I just called the station and talked to one of my contacts. It's George, all right. They identified him from his driver's license. It was in his wallet. No money or credit cards, though. Cops think it was robbery, plain and simple. They figure it happened sometime late yesterday afternoon or early evening. The only reason they found him so quickly was because some homeless guy was rummaging through the dumpster."

Toni was stunned. They hadn't been able to find out much of anything concerning George's missing brother, James, and they had been considering dropping the case. Now, she supposed, that was a moot point. But somebody was going to have to call George's sister.

"Unbelievable," she said, shaking her head as she stood and let Abe wrap his arms around her and pull her close. "This used to be such a quiet little town. But lately . . ."

"I know," Abe said, stroking her hair. "Crime rings, kidnappings, drug overdoses, robbery, and murder—sometimes I think the world's gone crazy."

"Sometimes I *know* it has," Toni murmured. "We get so caught up in our own personal lives—day-to-day crises with Melissa and Eric or just little things like where to go for dinner or what to wear to church. Those things suddenly seem so minor and unimportant when something like this happens."

Abe's hold on her tightened, and she thought again of the overweight, somewhat obnoxious man from Texas who had sat right here in their office asking them to help him find his brother. She had never really liked George Landry, and she hadn't trusted him or believed he was telling them the whole story, but now she felt bad about that. She really shouldn't have judged him, she told herself. She should have given him the benefit of the doubt, maybe tried a little harder to unravel the mystery of his missing brother.

"Stop beating yourself up," Abe admonished.

She lifted her head. "How did you know?"

His eyes smiled down at her, and he kissed her forehead. "Because I know you," he said. "I know your tender heart and how you take everything personally. You can't do that, sweetheart. Whatever happened to George Landry had nothing to do with us. Nothing, OK? Whatever he was doing in or near that bar was his business—his choice. And he paid for it with his life."

Toni nodded. She knew he was right. She also knew explaining it to George's sister was going to be difficult. But it had to be done, and she supposed she was the one to do it.

～～～

Sophie was restless. It had been a long day, and she was overtired. She knew she should have gone to bed sooner, but she had wanted to stay up and read just a few more chapters from *Yesha'yahu*, the prophet Isaiah. It had always been one of her favorite books in the *Tenakh*, but tonight chapters 52 through 54 especially had seemed so alive, so personal, as if Adonai himself were speaking directly to her, trying to tell her something important.

But finally, when her eyes could stay open no longer, she laid the precious book on her bed stand, turned off the light, and drifted off soon after closing her eyes. And yet her sleep was not deep, as she seemed to float in and out of consciousness, unable to distinguish between her dreams and reality.

And then she saw him—*Yeshua*. He had appeared to her in her dreams before, and lately she had found herself looking forward to his appearances. Tonight, as he walked toward her with outstretched arms and nail-pierced hands, she saw tears rolling from his eyes as the words she had read earlier echoed in her mind:

> Awake! Awake . . . !
> . . . Shake off the dust! Arise!
> . . . Loosen the chains on your neck,
> captive daughter . . . !
> For thus says Adonai:
> "You were sold for nothing,
> and you will be redeemed without money."

. . . Therefore my people will know my name;
therefore on that day they will know
that I, the one speaking—here I am!"
. . . Break out into joy! Sing together. . . .
For Adonai has comforted his people,
He has redeemed *Yerushalayim*!
Adonai has bared his holy arm
in the sight of every nation,
and all the ends of the earth will see
the salvation of our God.
. . . But he was wounded because of our crimes,
crushed because of our sins;
the disciplining that makes us whole fell on him,
and by his bruises we are healed.
We all, like sheep, went astray;
we turned, each one, to his own way;
yet Adonai laid on him
the guilt of all of us.
. . . Like a lamb led to be slaughtered,
like a sheep silent before its shearers,
he did not open his mouth.
. . . "By his knowing [pain and sacrifice],
my righteous servant makes many righteous;
it is for their sins that he suffers."
. . . "Sing, barren woman who has never had a child!
Burst into song, shout for joy . . . !"
. . . "For the mountains may leave and the hills be
removed,
but my grace will never leave you,
and my covenant of peace will not be removed,"
says Adonai, who has compassion on you.

When Sophie opened her eyes, they were wet with tears, and the image of *Yeshua* still burned in her brain. Redeemed . . . ransomed. Silent lamb . . . lamb of God. *Yeshua* . . . God's salvation. Words that had been going round and round in her brain for months now—key words, all of them. And yet . . . how did they fit together? And how did they apply to her?

Confused and excited, Sophie sensed she was only one puzzle piece away from understanding the whole picture. This time when she closed her eyes, her sleep was deep and sweet.

CHAPTER 23

It had been more than two weeks since George Landry's body had been discovered in the dumpster behind the bar. The prison ministry training classes were almost complete, and Thanksgiving was fast approaching. But still Toni couldn't forget her telephone conversation with George's sister, Mindy.

Toni had indeed been the one to call Mindy Jordan and inform her of her brother's death. Though the woman had seemed surprised and somewhat shaken by the news, Toni didn't get the impression that she was really shocked or even saddened.

"It was his lifestyle," Mindy had said in her slow Texas drawl. "George always lived on the edge, and it broke Mama's heart. She always said he'd come to no good. Course, Jimmy was the same way, I s'pose, but a lot sweeter about it. Not mean, like George—or Harley.

Jimmy and I got along real good, and Mama just adored him. Daddy, too, before he died. But that was a long time ago." Her voice drifted off, and Toni heard her sigh. "Guess they're all gone now," she said. "Daddy, Mama, George, Jimmy—even Harley. I ain't heard from him in weeks, even though he's still stayin' at our house. But he's got some new girlfriend livin' there with him, and I'm still here at Mama's, so I s'pose me and Harley'll end up gettin' a divorce. Guess it's a good thing we never had no kids after all." Her voice drifted off again.

Toni's heart had constricted with pain for the poor woman who seemed so totally and completely alone. Though Toni had lost her parents, she still had Abe and Melissa. And they were all so close, not divided and pitted against one another as Mindy's family had seemingly been.

"I'm sorry for your loss," Toni had said. "It must be hard to have to deal with so much all by yourself."

It was almost as if Toni could hear Mindy shrug as she answered. "Not really. To tell you the truth, Ms. Matthews, I don't miss Harley at all. And George and I never did get along. He and Harley were two of a kind—mean to the bone. It's hard to miss somethin' like that."

Toni imagined the woman was right, but before she could say anything, Mindy went on. "But now, with George gone and all, what does that mean about Jimmy? Will y'all keep on lookin' for him?"

Abe and Toni had asked themselves the same question and had come to the conclusion that they might as well let the case go. They hadn't been making much progress anyway, and they really didn't have any ideas about where else to look. Besides, they had recently taken on so many other cases that demanded their attention at the moment—and then there was the prison ministry, and Melissa. Toni had cleared her throat and tried to explain their decision to Mindy.

"I understand," Mindy had said when Toni finished. "And I can't blame y'all. I don't have no money to hire you myself, so . . ." Another sigh. "If y'all ever hear anything about Jimmy—anything at all—will y'all let me know? Please? He's really all I've got left."

Toni had promised to notify her if they learned anything about her remaining brother, though she cautioned her that she doubted that would happen. They had exhausted what few leads they'd had and had come up empty, and they wouldn't be actively pursuing the case anymore now, so it was unlikely they would ever hear the name of James Landry again. But if they did, they would certainly call her immediately.

Mindy had thanked her, and that had been the end of that. And yet Toni couldn't put it out of her mind. What had happened to James Landry? Where had he gone? And why? If he and his sister had been so close, as Mindy had indicated, why hadn't James stayed in contact with her? It was a strange situation—and a strange family—indeed.

≈≈≈

Spider was in control and he was reveling in it. Once he'd discovered Jinx's—a.k.a. James Landry's—weakness, the rest had been a cakewalk. Practically leading Jinx around by the nose, he'd handed the three inmates—whom he'd nicknamed Larry, Moe, and Curly—the exact information they'd been looking for to foolproof their plan. And now Spider was no longer just trying to learn about their plan so he could be a part of it; he was in charge of the entire operation. And it was huge. They'd even figured out the perfect time to pull it all off.

As he lay on his cot, staring at the ceiling, he smiled. *It won't be long now, Warden Schillo. You might as well start counting your days because the first weekend in December, they're over.*

~~~

Doug and Kelly Schillo held hands as they watched their three children scampering in front of them through the mall. It wasn't even Thanksgiving yet, and already the store windows were loaded with Christmas items. In fact, most of the shops had started advertising for Christmas right after school started in September. Though Kelly had no intention of doing any shopping while the kids were with them, she had thought it might be fun to bring the entire family to the mall for a short outing on this dreary Saturday afternoon. The weather outside was terrible, and this was one of the few places they could go to avoid the cold and rain. Of course, with the weather as bad as it was, she wasn't the only one to come up with that idea, so she and Doug fought their way through the crowds as they walked, keeping a close watch on the children and not allowing them to get more than a couple of steps in front of them at any time. They were a close-knit family and protective of their children.

"They're beautiful, aren't they?" Kelly asked, looking up at Doug, who nodded his agreement.

"They sure are. And growing like weeds."

Kelly wrinkled her nose at him. "I prefer to think of them as healthy little plants, not weeds, thank you."

Doug smiled. "I stand corrected. Plants they are. No weeds allowed in the Schillo garden."

They walked a little further, then Kelly took a deep breath and asked the question that had been on her mind all morning. "Is everything in place yet for the ministry weekend?"

"Sure is. It's going to be the first weekend in December. Between Mark Johnson's ministry team and the volunteers from some of the local churches, we're expecting about a hundred counselors—mostly men, of course, but a few women, too, to help out with the services. And of course we'll put extra officers on wherever we need them."

Kelly hesitated. She had been trying to work up the courage to broach this subject for weeks now. There was no sense putting it off any longer. "I'd like to come too," she said, hoping her voice sounded more confident than she felt.

Doug missed a step and looked down at her with a frown. "For the ministry weekend? You know I don't like your being around the inmates. Why would you want to do that?"

"I don't know. I guess I'm just curious about the ministry. I've heard so many good things about it. And you've told me yourself how much you admire and respect Mark Johnson and the work he does with the prisoners—how effective he is." Her voice trailed off, and she waited, letting her dark eyes do the rest of the talking for her. Doug never had been any good at resisting her pleading look.

Sure enough, she saw his resistance melting as she continued to gaze up at him. Suddenly he tore his eyes away and turned in the direction of their children. "Monte! Marianne! Madison! Get back here."

Obediently the three turned and scurried back to stand at their parents' feet. "Can we have ice cream?" Madison asked, her large blue eyes fixed on her father.

Doug laughed. "Ice cream? On a day like this?"

The kids squealed in unison, "Yes! Yes! We want ice cream! Please, Daddy, please!"

Doug shrugged and rolled his eyes exaggeratedly. "I'm outnumbered again." He sighed and looked at Kelly. "I suppose you're going to vote with them."

Kelly smiled. "Of course."

The kids began jumping up and down excitedly, obviously aware that their quest for ice cream had been won.

Doug was still looking at his wife. "What is it with the women in this family? Every time any of you looks at me with those big, beautiful eyes—brown or blue, it doesn't matter—I always cave in, don't I? Every time."

Kelly grinned and nodded. "You sure do. Every time. So does that mean I can come to the ministry weekend?"

Doug shook his head and sighed. "You're brutal, you know that? I just don't have a chance around here. OK, OK." He smiled and touched her cheek. "You win. You can come. But in between the services, I want you tucked away safe and sound in my office. Agreed?"

Kelly nodded. "Agreed."

Madison tugged on Doug's pants. "Can we get ice cream now, Daddy?"

"You bet. Let's go, half-pint," he said, bending down and scooping her up in his arms.

"I'm not a half-pint," Madison protested. "I'm a princess!"

Doug laughed. "All right, Princess Madison. Let's go eat ice cream."

Kelly smiled as she walked beside her husband, their youngest child riding happily on his shoulders, and their other two children pulling impatiently on her own hands. How grateful she was to God for her family and her many blessings.

~~~

When Brad woke up on Sunday morning, his heart was singing before he even got out of bed. It didn't bother him one bit that the wind was howling outside, pitting cold rain against his apartment windows while he showered and shaved. He was picking up Jeanine for church in less than an hour, and then they were going out for brunch afterward. They were, in fact, planning to spend the entire day together, taking a ride out to the coast after they ate. There was something romantic about the pounding surf on a storm-tossed day at the beach, Brad thought, something that made a person want to snuggle up with someone special.

And that, of course, was exactly what he had in mind. Jeanine was becoming more special to him with each passing day, and he didn't think he was being presumptuous in thinking that she felt the same about him. He saw it every time he looked into her soft brown eyes, which he did every chance he got. They were seeing each other almost daily now, and not just at work. They went to church together every Sunday, one week at her church, the next at his. Brad had been to visit her mother several times since his first dinner there, and Jeanine was fast becoming a part of the Anderson family, as she spent more and more time at their home. Brad had to admit that as deeply as he had always thought he was in love with Toni, he had never been happier than he was right now.

"Thank you, God," he said, picking up his keys and grabbing his jacket as he headed for the door. "Thank you so much for bringing that beautiful redhead into my life." Humming once again, he closed and locked the door behind him and hurried to his car. He scarcely noticed the rain pelting his head as he walked.

~·~·~

The weekend was over and the rain had finally stopped, although Melissa didn't really care. Monday mornings were always the toughest for her, as she steeled herself against running into Eric. No matter which direction she went on campus, there simply wasn't any way to assure herself of avoiding him, though she tried. But each time she saw him, the pain she was trying so hard to ignore would start up again in earnest.

As she rounded the corner, headed for her first-period class, she saw him. Only this time he wasn't alone. He was standing next to one of the most popular girls in the entire school—an attractive brunette named Sarah Lynch. Sarah was a senior, a cheerleader, and a candidate for homecoming queen. And she was looking up at Eric as if he were the most handsome guy who ever lived.

Melissa froze, devastated. She had known it could happen anytime. She had even tried to prepare herself for the occasion. But there was no preparing for such an emotional jolt. She felt as if her heart had just dropped to her feet. If only she could get away before he saw her.

But it was too late. Before she could move, Eric looked in her direction, and their gaze met. She saw the smile in his eyes before it touched his lips. But it wasn't a friendly smile. It was sarcastic, almost mean. And it cut straight through her.

He wanted me to see them together, she thought. *He's been waiting for this. Sarah Lynch, a senior, a popular girl that all the guys want to date. And he's got her. That's what he wants me to know. And he's glad that it hurts me.*

Willing herself to move, she was horrified to see him look back at Sarah and then remove his jacket—the same one he had draped over her own shoulders on their last day together—and place it over Sarah's sweater. Sarah smiled sweetly at him and kissed his cheek. Only then did Eric look back at Melissa, as if to be sure she was watching.

Swallowing her tears, Melissa turned and ran in the opposite direction. She might be late for class, but she wasn't going that way again until she was sure Eric and Sarah had moved on. Seeing them together—and realizing how much Eric wanted to hurt her—was just more than she could bear.

~~~

Melissa locked herself away in her room that night, determined not to let on to anyone about how bad she was feeling. She had struggled through dinner and then told everyone she had a lot of homework to do. Actually she had little that night, but she just couldn't face being around anyone at the moment. Her heart still hurt, and she was humiliated besides. There was no doubt in her mind that others had seen her reaction to the scene that morning, but there was nothing she could do about it. But at least for tonight she could hide away in her room.

She hadn't been there long when she heard a knock on her door. Melissa groaned. She really wasn't up to company, not even Toni or April. But a second knock told her that she would have to get up and answer it.

She was surprised when she opened the door and saw Carrie sitting there in her wheelchair. "Hey, Melissa," she said, wheeling herself inside without waiting for an invitation. "I thought I'd surprise you and come over and help you set up your computer. You haven't done it yet, have you?"

Melissa shook her head. "I didn't know you were coming."

"Of course you didn't. That's why I said I thought I'd surprise you. I couldn't very well do that if I called and told you I was on my way, now could I?"

Melissa closed the door behind Carrie and sat back down on her bed. "I don't know if I'm really up to tackling the computer tonight," she said. "Maybe you should've called first. I really do have a lot of homework."

"No you don't," Carrie said. "I know which classes you have, and I know you got a lot done during study hall today. I was sitting next to you, remember?" She wheeled closer to the bed and narrowed her eyes as she looked at her. "That's not what this is about, is it?"

Melissa didn't answer. She hadn't told Carrie about her run-in with Eric and Sarah, but news traveled fast on campus, so she probably knew anyway. Everyone probably knew. Melissa sighed. "I saw Eric today—with Sarah."

"I heard. Are you OK?"

"Sure. No. Not really. Everyone knows, don't they? They know about Eric and Sarah, and they know I ran away when I saw them together."

Carrie shrugged. "So what if they do? They'll get over it. And you have to get over it too."

"I know. But . . ."

"But it's hard. So what else is new? We've had this talk before, remember? Did you think life was going to be easy?"

"Not easy, but . . ."

"But not this hard. OK, this is bad. It hurts a lot. But six months from now you won't even remember it."

Melissa raised her eyebrows. She wished she could believe Carrie, but she didn't.

"OK," Carrie said. "Maybe it'll take a little more than six months. But you really will get past this, you know."

Melissa nodded. "I know. I just . . ."

"Forget about it. Try, anyway, at least for tonight. I've been praying for you ever since I heard, and I know you're going to be OK. And someday you'll be so glad that you're not still with Eric Fullbright. Honest."

Melissa sighed but didn't answer.

"Enough," Carrie said firmly. "I came over to help you with your computer, and that's what I'm going to do. Come on. I want to see this thing up and running as much as you do. More, maybe, since I don't have one myself. Where's the manual? Let's get started."

Grudgingly Melissa dug out the manual and sat down next to Carrie as they started reading through it. Maybe Carrie was right, she thought. Maybe it was a good thing her best friend had decided to surprise her and get her out of her pity party and on to something constructive. After all, she couldn't stay in her room and feel sorry for herself forever.

She forced a smile and looked at Carrie. "Thanks," she said. "I'm glad you're here."

"No problem," Carrie answered. "Now let's get to work. We haven't got all night. Dad's coming back to pick me up at nine. That gives us two hours. Do you think we can do it?"

"I think we can give it a serious try."

Carrie grinned. "That's good enough for me. Come on, girlfriend. Let's spread those parts out on the bed and see if we can figure out how they all fit together."

CHAPTER 24

Spider lay in his bunk on Monday night and reviewed the plan. It was foolproof—at least, as close to foolproof as anything could get. Reeling Jinx in had been the perfect touch to assure their success. True, Larry, Moe, and Curly were the ones who'd hatched the plan and realized they needed Jinx's involvement, but it was Spider who'd found a way to make it all happen. Jinx would never have agreed to such a huge risk without Spider's not-so-friendly persuasion.

The giant tattooed inmate shifted on his too-small bunk and smiled to himself. With continued good behavior Jinx had been hoping to get out in less than two years. He would never willingly have taken a chance at losing his fast-approaching parole to get involved with their scheme. But now he had no choice. For whatever reasons, Jinx did not want his brother to find him, and Spider had convinced him that all it would take was one phone call to let the other Mr. Landry know the whereabouts of his long-lost brother. In reality, Spider knew that it would undoubtedly take more than just one call to locate George Landry, but he also knew that he had enough contacts throughout the criminal world—both in and out of prison—that it wouldn't be too difficult, especially if the man was still in River View.

And so Jinx's cooperation was assured. The inmate who'd earned a trustee status and now had once-a-week janitorial access to Warden Schillo's office would gain Spider and his cohorts access to that office—and to freedom. The details had been worked out over the long Thanksgiving holiday when the warden had been gone for several days, and now all they had to do was wait for Friday night.

Spider smiled again. How ironic that all this should take place during a so-called "ministry weekend." The weekend had been announced and advertised in all areas of the prison, offering anyone interested the opportunity to attend one or more of the services and to receive one-on-one counseling with the volunteers. Even the inmates who were in solitary or under protective custody could sign up to speak with one of the counselors, even if they couldn't attend the services. Spider almost laughed out loud at the idea. He couldn't imagine what one of those pitiful volunteers could tell him that he hadn't heard a thousand times from his mother before she was murdered by his no-good bum of a father. But everything she'd taught Spider had died with her. There was no God, Spider had decided long ago, and there was absolutely nothing anyone could say to him to change his mind.

~~~

Even as Toni sat at her typewriter on Tuesday afternoon and tried to finish another chapter of her manuscript, her mind wandered to the upcoming prison ministry weekend. She was excited that the training sessions had gone so well and that the event was now less than one week away. With each passing day it was becoming more and more difficult to think of anything else. Besides the two of them and John King, there were fifteen others from their church planning to go in for the weekend. Combined with volunteers from the other churches in the area and the Mark Johnson ministry staff, there would be close to one hundred of them altogether. But ever since Thanksgiving, Toni hadn't been feeling too well and, in spite of her excitement, she wondered if she might be more nervous about such an undertaking than she realized.

After all, she reasoned, *out of all those volunteers going into the prison, only six of us are women, so maybe it's natural to be apprehensive. We're going to be way outnumbered! But the guys are the ones who'll be having one-on-one contact with the inmates, not us ladies. We're only going to be allowed to help out during the services, so why should I be nervous about that?*

But even as she tried to convince herself that there was absolutely nothing to be concerned about, her stomach churned and she felt dizzy. *That's it,* she decided, turning off the typewriter and heading for the bedroom. *I'm going to go lie down for a few minutes until this thing passes. The last thing I want to do now is get sick and miss out on going altogether.*

∾∾∾

Kelly Schillo could hardly wait for Friday night when the ministry weekend would begin. *Only two more days*, she reminded herself, smiling at the thought. Doug had promised that she could sit with the half dozen or so female volunteers during the Friday night and Saturday services. She had arranged for her mother to come to their house on Friday and spend the entire weekend so she and Doug would be free to be at the prison each time one of the services was being held. At the end of each service, she would be escorted to her husband's office to wait until the next one started. In the interim the male volunteers would counsel interested inmates on a one-on-one basis.

As she went from bed to bed that Wednesday evening, tucking in her three little ones, she smiled and wondered again what would come of the weekend ministry effort. She had heard many times of the positive and long-lasting effects of these ministry weekends, and she couldn't help but hope that she was going to be involved in something much bigger than any of them imagined.

∾∾∾

April was disturbed. She hadn't felt like this since just before Toni had that run-in with the high school teacher who had instigated the school shooting last year. That confrontation had almost cost both Toni and Abe their lives, but God had intervened by sending John King at just the right moment. Now, with that same feeling of apprehension and urgency to pray overwhelming her, April Lippincott went to her room that Friday morning, locked the door, opened her Bible, and sat down on the edge of her bed to talk to God.

≈≈≈

Abe was worried, and he couldn't figure out why. Granted, they
were scheduled to begin the prison ministry weekend that evening;
but they had been through the training, rehearsed their responsibilities, and been assured of their complete safety throughout the event.
He wondered if it might be that final paper they'd had to sign—the
one stating that each of the volunteers understood that, should they
be taken hostage while inside the prison walls, there would be no
negotiation for their release.

He shook his head. This was silly. After all, he had been trained in
law enforcement and knew that such a condition for entering the
prison was for their own protection. If the prisoners thought they
could use the volunteers as pawns, it would only increase the likeli-
hood of their being taken as hostages. The inmates understood all of
that, which should have made Abe feel secure.

But it didn't. He got up from his desk and walked to the doorway
between his office and the front office where Toni sat, her blonde head
bent over the books as she worked. *That's what it is*, he thought.
*If I were going in without her, this wouldn't bother me a bit. But my
wife . . .*

Still, he knew it would do no good to try to dissuade her at
this point. They had discussed and prayed about this together
for weeks and agreed that it was something God wanted for both of
them. And surely if God had called them to it, he would also protect
them.

Toni looked up then and smiled at him, the love in her blue eyes
tugging at his heart. *Please, God*, he prayed silently, *protect her. Please.
If anything ever happened to her . . .*

∾∾∾

April didn't know how long she had sat there on the bed, alternately reading Scriptures and praying, but she was becoming more and more convinced that she was to pray not only for Toni's safety but for Abe's as well. Obviously it had to do with the prison ministry weekend, so April also included all the other volunteers and the prison staff in her petitions.

Maybe that's all it is, she thought. *A call to pray for the protection of those going into the prison to minister. After all, I've been praying that way ever since I first heard about the event. But until now I never felt such urgency. Is it simply because it's only hours now until it all begins?*

Show me, Father, she prayed. *Show me how to pray. Give me wisdom, Lord.*

April flipped the pages in her Bible and began to read from Isaiah 43:1–5a:

> But now, this is what the LORD says—
> he who created you, O Jacob,
> he who formed you, O Israel:
> "Fear not, for I have redeemed you;
> I have summoned you by name; you are mine.
> When you pass through the waters,
> I will be with you;
> and when you pass through the rivers,
> they will not sweep over you.
> When you walk through the fire,
> you will not be burned;
> the flames will not set you ablaze.

For I am the LORD, your God,

the Holy One of Israel, your Savior;

I give Egypt for your ransom,

Cush and Seba in your stead.

Since you are precious and honored in my sight,

and because I love you,

I will give men in exchange for you,

and people in exchange for your life.

Do not be afraid, for I am with you." (NIV)

~~~

It had been a difficult week for Melissa, and she wondered if she would ever come to the point of being able to see Eric and Sarah together without wishing the ground would just open up and swallow her whole. But each encounter with the now almost inseparable couple pushed the heartbroken teen closer to God, forcing her to pray for strength to get through just one more hour, one more day.

And in spite of the pain, Melissa had to admit that she was enjoying being with Carrie and her other girlfriends again. She hadn't realized how much she had missed them when she was spending all her time with Eric.

As she and Carrie made their way down the hall on their way to lunch, Melissa turned to her friend and said, "Hey, how about coming over to spend the night tonight? Abe and Toni are going to be gone to that prison ministry thing, so it'll just be you and me and April. What do you think?"

Carrie smiled. "I'd like that. Now that we've got your computer hooked up, we can do our homework on that. Almost makes homework fun, doesn't it? And you know how much I like being around April. She really is a great lady."

Melissa nodded. "That's for sure. And it's never a problem to convince her to order pizza, so dinner's covered."

Carrie's face grew serious. "I hope we can stay awake long enough to talk to Toni and Abe when they get home from the prison. I'm so anxious to hear how it goes, but I imagine it'll be late, won't it?"

"Probably. I don't know what time their service will end tonight or how soon they'll get out of there once it's over, but then they still have an almost two-hour drive after that."

Carrie's smile returned as she rolled her chair to the cafeteria entrance. "Well, we are sixteen, after all. Surely two sixteen-year-olds can manage to stay awake a little later than usual on a Friday night, don't you think?"

"I hope so," Melissa said. "I know April will, and it'll be embarrassing if a woman in her seventies can outlast us."

The girls laughed as they got in line for their food, and Melissa found herself thanking God for giving her such a special best friend.

≈≈≈

Sophie had felt on the edge of tears all day, and she knew it was because of the dream. Seeing images of *Yeshua* in her sleep had become an almost expected occurrence lately, but this time he had spoken to her—called her, actually. "Sophie," he had repeated over and over again. "Sophie, come to me. I'm waiting for you. Come, Sophie."

His voice had been so compelling, the invitation so irresistible, almost as if she were being summoned for something, something too wonderful to imagine. But what could it be? She had thought she could shake the feeling, but as the day had progressed, it had grown stronger.

"What is it, Adonai?" she whispered. "What do you want from me? Are you calling to me through this *Yeshua?* Or am I being duped by the so-called god of the *goyim?*"

April. The thought came to her as clearly as if someone had spoken it into her ear. She was to go to April. Why, she had no idea, but if the woman could help her understand what all this *Yeshua* business was about, then she would go.

Sophie glanced at the phone. Should she call first? No. If it truly was Adonai directing her, then April would be there when she arrived. She picked up her purse from the dresser, grabbed a coat out of the closet, and headed for the front door, determined to settle this issue once and for all.

~~~

It was the continued ringing of the doorbell that finally brought April from her room. She glanced at her watch as she made her way to the front door. Two o'clock in the afternoon. She'd had no idea it was so late.

Surprised but pleased to see Sophie Jacobson standing on the front porch, April welcomed her inside. As the two embraced, April sensed that Sophie's visit was an important one.

"Come into the kitchen," April said, leading the way. "I haven't had any lunch today, and I just realized how hungry I am. How about something simple? Tea and toast maybe?"

Sophie nodded. "That would be nice, thank you." She sat down at the table and clasped her hands. April noticed she looked tense as she spoke. "I'm sorry I didn't call first," she said.

April smiled as she filled the kettle and placed it on the stove. "I'm just glad you came, Sophie dear. Truly, I am. And I hope you can stay a while. Abe and Toni will be gone to the prison ministry this evening—tomorrow too—so I'll be here alone with Melissa. We'd love to have your company."

"Thank you. I'd like that." Sophie continued to clasp and unclasp her hands as April prepared the toast and set the table. It was obvious she wanted to talk, but April felt she should wait and let the woman broach the topic that was obviously pressing her when she was ready.

She joined her at the table and smiled. "How was your drive down?"

Sophie looked surprised, as if her mind had been elsewhere. "My drive? Oh, it was fine, thank you." She picked up her tea and took a sip, then looked at April with narrowed eyes and lowered her voice. "April, I think that *Yeshua* is calling me."

April raised her eyebrows. So this was it. God had been working on Sophie's heart, and now he was about to give April the privilege of leading her the final few steps of the way. Maybe that was part of the reason she had spent so much time in prayer that day. While God was preparing Sophie to receive, he had also been preparing April to give.

"I'm sure that's true," April said. "In fact, I imagine he's been calling you for a long time. But his voice has become louder now, hasn't it? The invitation more insistent, more personal."

Sophie nodded. "How did you know?"

"All of us have to be called," April answered, "each in his or her own way, as God knows we will respond. But we can only come to him if he draws us. That's why it's so important to pray and ask God to call our loved ones to himself."

Sophie's dark eyes opened wide. "Have you prayed for me?"

"Many times. Abe and Toni have too."

"I thought as much. And I, too, have been praying—a lot. I've been searching the *Tenakh*—what you call the Old Testament Scriptures—trying to understand." Her voice trailed off as she set her cup down and reached across the table to take April's hand in her own. "He's been coming to me in my dreams—this *Yeshua*—over and over again. I could see his outstretched arms, the scars on his hands, the tears." She was almost whispering now. "But last night he called my name. It was like a summons, or . . ." She shook her head. "And then there's the word *ransom*. It keeps popping up, every time I open my *Tenakh*."

The verses April had read in Isaiah earlier that day came back to her with a clarity she could not ignore: "I have summoned you by name; you are mine. . . . I give Egypt for your ransom."

"Wait here," she said. "I'm going to get my Bible. There's something I want to read to you. And don't worry. It, too, is from the Old Testament Scriptures."

CHAPTER 25

The atmosphere crackled with excitement as worship music played in the background and lines of prisoners were escorted in by armed correctional officers. Toni was thrilled by the turnout. She knew attendance was optional for the inmates, so it was almost overwhelming to see them streaming in both doors and filling the pews to maximum capacity. She prayed it would be the same at all three services on Saturday, and she prayed that the prisoners' hearts would be open and receptive to God's message and his call.

Abe squeezed her hand, and she looked up at him and smiled. "This is wonderful," she said.

He nodded and returned her smile. "It's going to be quite an evening," he said and then looked around the room. Turning back to Toni, he whispered, "I have to admit that I was worried earlier today.

I'm not sure why but probably because you were coming in too. But now that I see how they've separated us from the inmates, I feel a whole lot better."

Toni glanced around again at their surroundings. He was right. All the volunteers had been seated in the large choir section, adjacent to but not among the inmates. Officers were posted in the aisles and at the doors. Although the volunteers could make eye contact with the prisoners, there would be no direct physical contact, even when the men counseled the prisoners individually. It had been explained to them on more than one occasion that they were not to touch the inmates under any circumstances, even when they were praying with them. *Another safeguard*, she thought. *And a necessary one, I'm sure.*

Just then an attractive dark-haired woman, who looked to be just slightly older than Toni, was brought in through the door behind the choir loft. At that point the only available seat in their section was at the end of the pew, right next to Toni and Abe. The lady walked up to her, then paused and smiled hesitantly before asking, "May I sit here beside you?"

"Of course," Toni said, scooting closer to her husband. "There's plenty of room. Please, join us."

As the woman sat down, Toni said, "I'm Toni Matthews, and this is my husband, Abe."

Extending her hand, the woman said, "I'm Kelly Schillo, Doug Schillo's wife. I'm glad to meet you both."

Toni was surprised. "You're married to Doug Schillo? The warden?"

Kelly nodded. "Yes, I am. And I'm so glad I was able to talk him into letting me come. He doesn't like for me to be around the inmates—wants to keep his work and family life separate, I guess. But I've heard so much about Mark Johnson Ministries that I just had to be here to see it for myself."

"I know what you mean," Toni said. "We're really excited about it too. Abe and I have been feeling for some time that God was calling us into jail or prison ministry, and this seemed like the perfect opportunity to get our feet wet."

"So, Mrs. Schillo," Abe said, peeking around Toni to look at Kelly, "is your husband here too?"

"Not yet," she said. "But he will be. He's in his office finishing up some paperwork right now. And please, call me Kelly."

As the woman smiled at them, Toni couldn't help but notice the warmth and sincerity in her dark eyes. *I like Kelly Schillo*, she decided. *She is a very nice lady.* "Well, Kelly, when your husband gets here, we can scoot down a little more and make room for him to join us," she offered.

"Thank you," Kelly said. "I'd like for him to be able to sit here next to me."

Toni could certainly understand that, as she slid her arm underneath Abe's and clasped his hand. She, too, was glad to be sitting next to her husband and sharing this amazing experience with him. She smiled as she thought ahead to all the exciting things that lay ahead for them as a family. Looking up at Abe, her heart swelled with love for him. *Later*, she reminded herself. *You can talk to him about it later.*

As the background music faded and the worship leaders took their place in front of the chapel, she closed her eyes. *Thank you, God*, she prayed, *for allowing us to be a part of this. Please fulfill all your purposes and be glorified in all that happens here tonight.*

~~~

It was quieter than usual in the cell blocks, now that many of the inmates had gone to the chapel service. *Fools*, Spider thought. *Do those idiots really think Bible thumping and praying is going to change anything? It's not like there's somebody up there listening.*

His cell mate also had gone to the service, and Spider smiled at the thought. *Anything to get away from me for a little while, right, chump? But don't worry. You're never going to have to deal with me again. By the time you get back tonight, I'll either be walking the streets a free man, or dead.*

Everything was in place, and it wouldn't be long now. The extra officers who had been brought in for the weekend were overseeing the chapel service, and the two left on duty in Spider's section would be no problem. They didn't know exactly what was going down, but they knew their part in it, and they would play it or pay the price. The renegade officers had been on the take for a long time, and the inmates had enough on them to force them into cooperating. All they had to do was let Spider and Jinx and their three accomplices out of their cells and then sneak them down to the corridor that led to the warden's office. Then the inmates would rough up the officers a little, enough to look convincing, and leave them tied up where they wouldn't be found right away. The officers would claim that one of them had foolishly allowed himself to get too close to Spider's cell, enabling the prisoner to reach out his long arm and yank him close, taking his gun and forcing the captured officer and his partner to let him and the others out of their cells. At least, that's the way the officers thought things were going to happen. But Spider knew better. He had no intention of leaving any witnesses alive, and he smiled at the thought. Snuffing out the life of those two losers was just an added perk on his way to freedom.

Holding his tiny mirror out between the bars, Spider looked down toward where Larry and Moe waited together in one cell, with Curly right next to them. They too had their mirrors out and were signaling a thumbs-up. The two officers should be here any minute.

~~~

Doug made his way from his office to the chapel with mixed emotions. He had long admired and respected Mark Johnson, both as a football player and as a believer, and he was completely confident that the ministry weekend would bring about some much needed positive changes within the correctional facility and its occupants. But he still didn't feel right about having Kelly there. Why had he allowed her to talk him into it? He would have felt so much better if she had stayed at home with their children, where he knew she would be safe.

He spotted her as soon as he entered the door behind the choir loft. Her shoulder-length brown hair shone in the overhead light as she joined in the singing that was just beginning. The pews were full everywhere Doug looked, and although a few of the inmates were looking around with either curious or bored expressions, the majority of the prisoners seemed intent on entering into the worship.

Doug slipped into the seat beside his wife and took her hand in his. She looked over at him and smiled in welcome, and Doug tried once again to reassure himself that everything would be fine. But the sense of uneasiness continued to haunt him throughout the service.

~~~

Even as the final strains of the closing worship songs faded away and the congregation stood for the benediction, Spider, Jinx, and the "three stooges" had ensconced themselves in the warden's office. The lights were out, and all they had to do now was wait. There was no doubt in their minds that Warden Schillo would return—alone—as soon as the service had ended. That was his MO, and he never broke it. It was common knowledge that at the close of any special event at the prison, the warden came to his office and filled out his report before doing anything else. He was a creature of habit, and they were counting on his predictable behavior. After that, everything would kick into overdrive quickly, with no letup until their objectives were accomplished or they all died in the attempt.

Jinx knew all that, and it certainly didn't make him feel any better. He'd been dragged kicking and screaming into this mess, certain that he was forfeiting his upcoming parole and his dreams of freedom and the good life to follow. If he got caught now, it would all be over—everything. His plans for the future, the money he'd stolen from the family and stashed away, he might as well kiss them good-bye. But if he'd refused and Spider had told George where he was hiding, Jinx would have been a dead man by now. He shook his head as he thought of the other four inmates hiding in the room with him. Jinx had been so sure he'd found the perfect place, the only place where his brother would never think to look for him. And then Spider and his buddies had come along and blown his dream to pieces.

All the long days and nights he'd spent in this prison, serving time for a crime he hadn't even committed, just to keep George away from him until things had died down and he could complete his plan. And even before that, how many years after his dad died had Jinx put up with George's sarcasm and put-downs and abuse, planning his revenge and the great escape he would someday make in order to spend the rest of his life in comfort, far, far away from his older brother? It had been hard to steal money from his mother and sister and then leave them behind, but he'd had no choice; it had been the only way. And so he'd done it, and everything would have worked out just as he'd planned, if only he hadn't broken down and called his mother before she died. There was no doubt in Jinx's mind that it was that phone call that had been his undoing, marking a trail for his brother to follow. And, through Spider, George had followed that trail all the way to prison. Now Jinx was tied up with these four goons who were going to blow everything.

"It won't be long now," Spider whispered from his place behind the door. "No noise, no movement. Got it?"

Jinx, along with the other three inmates, grunted in agreement. He just wished he could have talked Spider into letting him out of the plan once he'd done his part to get them inside the office, but Spider had refused. "Once you're in," he'd said, "you're in or you're dead. Got it?"

He'd gotten it. And so now he waited, wondering if he would live through the night and, if he did, if he would be able to get to the money he'd hidden and get away before George got his hands on him once again.

~~~

Abe had been relieved when Kelly had invited Toni to join her and Doug in her husband's office after the service while the men were counseling with the inmates. The other women would sit together and wait in the choir loft, which is what Toni had planned to do, but Abe felt better knowing that she would be in an even safer place, far out of the reach of any of the inmates. Besides, she and Kelly had seemed to hit it off, and it would give them a chance to get to know each other better.

"Just have one of the officers escort you to my office when you're done here," Doug instructed Abe. "The ladies and I will be there waiting for you."

"I can't thank you enough," Abe said. "I've been a little concerned about her being here."

"I understand completely. I feel the same way. That's why I made Kelly promise to wait in my office before and after each service, including tomorrow's."

As the ladies walked away, one on each side of the warden, Abe felt the tension ease in his shoulders. Now that he knew his wife was in good hands, he could get on with the next part of his ministry assignment. He turned and walked over to join the other counselors, who were being paired up with the waiting inmates.

~~~

Toni was amazed at the camaraderie she felt with Kelly Schillo. They had only just met, and yet it seemed they had been friends for years. They chatted as they walked, with Doug contributing little to the conversation other than an occasional smile or nod. By the time they reached the warden's office, Toni was sure that this was a relationship that would extend far beyond the prison walls and the ministry weekend in which they were both involved.

She wasn't paying attention to anything but her conversation with Kelly as Doug unlocked the door and reached in to flip on the light, then stepped back as the two new friends entered. He had scarcely put one foot into the room when a long arm reached beyond the women and grabbed him by his suit jacket, pulling him inside, then slamming and locking the door behind him.

"Not a word," growled the huge man clutching Doug, as he glared at Toni and Kelly who had also been grabbed and hands slapped over their mouths. "You three do exactly what I tell you, and no one will get hurt."

This isn't happening, Toni thought. *It can't be. Who are these men? What are they doing here in the warden's office? How did they get here? And what do they want with us? We're supposed to be safe in here.*

Toni tried to breathe deeply and stay focused, even as her hands were being tied behind her back and a gag stuffed into her mouth. She watched Kelly, whose eyes were wide with fear as she, too, was bound and gagged, and Doug, who watched helplessly as the two women were dragged off to sit in a corner.

"We hadn't expected any women," the large man said, pulling the warden toward his desk and plunking him down in his chair. "They might just be a problem that needs to be eliminated. But then again, who knows? Maybe I can find a reason for keeping them around. They're sure a lot better looking than you. And that could come in handy if I get bored or if you don't cooperate." The convict sneered. "But I can tell from the picture on your desk that the dark-haired one is your wife, ain't that right, warden? So something tells me you're going to cooperate just fine."

Doug jumped up from his chair. "You dirty—"

Before he could say another word, the giant had crashed his fist into Doug's face. Blood spurted from his nose as Kelly's muffled screams sounded in Toni's ears, but she knew it was useless for either of them to try to help the injured warden. Four inmates were standing over her and Kelly, and the other one who had just hit Doug was the size of a bear—and a lot meaner, Toni was sure. Whatever these men wanted, it was obvious they wanted it badly enough to do whatever was necessary to obtain it.

Oh, God, help us, she prayed silently, suddenly remembering the paper they had signed stating that they understood there would be no negotiating for their release should they be taken hostage. They were on their own. *Rescue us, Lord*, she begged. *You're our only hope.*

~~~

The pizza party was in full swing at the Matthews home, and April was thrilled that Sophie was so close to receiving Jesus. Sophie had even come to the point of acknowledging the possibility that maybe he truly was the Messiah, though everything in her religious upbringing had taught her otherwise. But still she held back, saying there were a couple of points she just didn't understand. Then, before the two ladies had been able to discuss the subject further, Melissa and Carrie had arrived, announcing their intended sleepover and requesting pizza for dinner. April had readily agreed, as had Sophie when she was asked to join them—although she'd requested no meat mixed with cheese, so as to keep kosher. And so the topic of Sophie and *Yeshua* had been put on hold for the time being.

But each time the conversation came around to Abe and Toni's involvement with the prison ministry that evening, the urgency to pray would again rise up in April's heart. *What is it, Lord?* she prayed silently. *Is something going on? Are they in some sort of danger? Oh, Father, keep them safe, whatever it is.*

CHAPTER 26

By the time the volunteers had finished counseling the inmates, word had reached the correctional officers in the chapel that there was trouble in the warden's office. Two officers had been found dead, their necks broken, and five of the prisoners from their section were missing, along with the officers' guns. It was assumed they were all holed up in the warden's office because a call had come from Warden Schillo himself, asking the police for five million dollars in unmarked bills, guns and ammunition, and a vehicle and driver to take five inmates and three hostages to a nearby airstrip. Everyone who knew Doug Schillo was confident that he would never make such a request except for one particular detail: his wife and another civilian hostage were in that office with him.

When Abe asked one of the officers to take him to the warden's office to pick up Toni, the man looked startled. The prison was quickly moving into lockdown status, and they had been ordered to concentrate on getting the remaining inmates back to their cells as quickly as possible.

"Your wife is in there? With the warden and his wife?"

Abe nodded. "They invited her to come with them after the service and wait there until I finished counseling. The warden told me one of you would be glad to take me to her."

The officer swallowed. "Come with me," he said. "There's something you need to know."

∾∾∾

Within minutes Abe was brought to the office of Rick Lupori, second in command at the prison. He too had sat in on the service but had planned to leave as soon as it was over. Before he could get to his car, however, he was called back and told of Doug Schillo's phone call. By the time Abe arrived in Rick's office, the prison's crisis team was also there, setting up a command center and mapping out a strategy to try to get the prisoners out without harming the hostages. Until Abe and his escort had shown up, no one had been sure of the identity of the third hostage. But after hearing Abe's story about Toni's having gone to the warden's office with Doug and Kelly Schillo after the service, it was obvious to everyone in the room who that previously unidentified hostage must be.

Abe was frantic as he paced back and forth across the small office. This was exactly the sort of thing he had been worried about all day. Why hadn't he listened to what he was now sure had been a warning? He knew he never should have allowed Toni to come into the prison. And now his greatest fear had been realized—his wife had been taken hostage by five ruthless inmates bent on obtaining their freedom at any cost, and he was powerless to help her.

Stopping midstride, he turned and slammed his fists down on Rick's desk. "There has to be something I can do," he cried. "You can't just expect me to sit here and wait quietly while my wife is trapped in there with those animals."

Rick looked up and stared straight into Abe's eyes. "That is exactly what we expect you to do," he said, taking Abe by the arm. "And if you can't, you'll have to leave. We have work to do here, and I can't have you interfering—"

Abe shook his arm free, and his voice rose in intensity as he spoke. "Interfering? Listen, this is my wife we're talking about here. My wife, do you understand?"

"I understand more than you think," Rick answered, his face still firm with resolve. But you were a cop, Matthews. You know the rules. No negotiating with prisoners. You knew that coming in."

Abe was glad the man didn't remind him that Toni also had known the rules, because he probably would have hauled off and smashed the guy right in the face. Yes, he knew the "no negotiating" rule; they all did. But rules applied to prison officials and correctional officers, not to husbands.

"Listen," he said, the idea forming even as he spoke. "I know none of you can negotiate with these maniacs. But what about me? What's to stop me from negotiating with them?"

Rick frowned. "What do you mean? How can you negotiate with them? What do you have to bargain with?"

"Myself," Abe answered. "I'll offer myself in exchange for the other hostages. You know as well as I do, if there's one thing prisoners hate more than anyone else, it's cops. And you just said I used to be one. Who knows? I even may have arrested one of those guys in there. Maybe they'd be willing to trade the hostages—the women, at least— to get their hands on me. What do you think?"

Immediately Rick shook his head. "It'll never happen," he said. "These guys aren't going to trade three sure hostages for one maybe, cop or no cop. They'll never go for it, I'm telling you. And besides, I can't let you do it." He shook his head again. "Sorry, Matthews, but the answer is no."

"Mr. Lupori, listen to me," Abe begged. "What have we got to lose? We don't know it won't work unless we try, right? Look, I'm willing to go in there, so why not call them and make the offer and see what they say."

Rick shook his head again, then stopped and eyed Abe quizzically for a moment before answering. "You know, I can't believe I'm saying this, but you might just have something. In fact, the more I think about it, the more I think you're right. And if you're willing, then it's worth a try. Because I have to tell you, Matthews, I sure don't have any other ideas. The situation is bad. They've got those hostages locked up in the one room in this institution that has its own direct exit to the outside, which makes their escape more plausible. Obviously they knew that. But if we try to get to them through either of those office doors, the hostages aren't going to have a prayer. I saw what they did to those two officers. And I know these guys, especially the one they call Spider. He's as mean as they come. When Warden Schillo called to present their demands, he said they were serious—desperate too. Desperate inmates who've already killed at least twice don't have anything to lose. And we know they have at least two guns, the ones they took off those officers they strangled to death. There's not a doubt in my mind they'll kill again without a second thought. Right now, as much as I hate to admit it, I'd say your offer is about the only thing we've got going for us."

Rick Lupori stopped and studied Abe's face. "You realize, Matthews, that even if they accept your offer and let the hostages go, your chances of coming out of there alive are just about slim to none."

Abe nodded. He knew that, but with Toni's life on the line, he didn't see how he could do anything else.

∿∿∿

Toni had resisted leaving. She had even begged—both Abe when he called and made the offer and her captors—to allow her to stay. But Abe had been adamant. And even the big inmate, the apparent leader of the group whose name was Spider, who had at first turned down Abe's offer, had finally changed his mind, particularly once the warden had told him it was the only way the prison officials would even consider their demands. As a result, Spider had insisted that the women leave, practically throwing them out the door once he knew that Abe had arrived and was standing on the other side, waiting for the hostages to be released. "There'll be plenty of good-looking women where I'm headed," he'd growled. "I don't need no women to slow me down now. Besides," he'd sneered, "I got me a warden and a cop, and it don't get no better than that."

Tearfully Toni and Kelly had stumbled out the door, pushed by one of the inmates as the two women made one final plea for their husbands' lives. But Spider's laugh as he reached out and pulled Abe inside and slammed the door was their only reply.

∿∿∿

Abe knew he was in serious trouble from the moment the huge tattooed inmate had picked him up with one hand and yanked him into Doug's office. But he had accomplished his primary goal—

getting Toni and Kelly out of there as quickly as possible. He only wished the prisoners would have agreed to let Doug go as well. From the looks of the warden's face, he had already been used as a punching bag. Abe imagined the only reason the poor guy was still alive was that his captors needed his help to escape.

And what do they need me for? he wondered. *Nothing that's going to keep me alive for long, that's for sure. But at least Toni is safe. Kelly too. Thank you, God.*

The phone rang and the big guy, whom one of the other inmates had referred to as Spider, indicated that Doug should answer it. "Speaker phone," he ordered. "I want to hear everything that goes on."

Doug picked up the phone, and Abe recognized Rick Lupori's voice on the other end as he explained to Doug that they were moving as quickly as they could. It would take a while, he said, to get that much cash together, but they were working on it. Abe, of course, knew that the police were just buying time. They had no intention of providing these criminals with a means of escape, but it was the only way to keep the hostages alive while they attempted to work out a plan of rescue.

As Spider hovered over Doug, listening to his conversation with the prison's second in command, another inmate sat down on the floor near Abe. There was something about the guy that seemed out of place to Abe—as if he didn't belong or didn't want to be there. If Abe was right, he decided, it might be an angle he could use to his advantage.

He continued to stare at the man, wondering what it was that seemed somehow familiar about him, as if he'd seen him before—or someone like him. Had he arrested him somewhere along the line? That was certainly possible. If so, that wasn't such a good sign.

By the time the phone conversation had ended, Spider was obviously agitated. "How do I know he's telling the truth?" he demanded.

"How do I know he's not just setting us up? I know about the 'no negotiating' rule, you know."

"Then why even try this?" Doug asked. "If you knew we wouldn't negotiate, what are you doing here?"

Spider backhanded Doug again, knocking him out of his chair. "You sure got a smart mouth," he said, reaching down to pick Doug up and throw him back into his chair. "Now listen to me, warden. Just answer my questions and no more smart remarks, got it?"

Doug nodded, wiping the blood that had begun to drip from his nose once again.

"Like I said," Spider continued, "I know about your 'no negotiating' rule. But I also know you got a family—one you care about a whole lot." He nodded toward Jinx, still seated on the floor beside Abe. "Old Jinx here—Mr. James Landry himself—he cleans up your office every week. Did you know that, warden? You know who cleans up after you? Well, Jinx is the man. And he told us about your family pictures and your kids' drawings. That's when we knew we'd found your weakness—one thing you'd negotiate for no matter what rules you might have. It's your family, am I right? Your wife and kids. You'd negotiate in a heartbeat if you thought they were in danger. And that was the original plan."

Spider laughed as a look of fresh fear filled Doug's face. "That's right," Spider said. "We were going to come in here and take you hostage and tell you that we know exactly where you live—which we do, by the way. All that information is right here in your office. And if you didn't meet our demands, we were going to have our accomplice—the guy that's waiting to fly us out of here as soon as you get us to the airstrip—go right on over to your house and hold your entire family at gunpoint until you decided to cooperate." He laughed. "You can't imagine how surprised I was when your wife came in here with you and I realized we didn't even have to send anybody to your house." He stopped and squinted his eyes at Doug. "But don't think we can't still send him over there if I find out you and the rest of the prison officials are playing games with us, you got it?" He reached down and grabbed Doug's shirt and pulled his face up to his. "I said, do you got that, warden?"

Doug nodded again, and his voice shook slightly as he answered. "I got it. But you don't have to worry. You heard the guy on the phone—Rick Lupori. He's acting warden while I'm in here, and he has authority to call the shots. They're working on meeting your demands, just like he said. But it's going to take a while."

"Yeah? Well, for all I know there's an army of armed officers standing right outside these two doors, just waiting to take us down when we step outside." Spider frowned and appeared to be thinking as he paced. With his size in such a small room, it took less than a half-dozen steps before he had to turn around and go back the other way. Suddenly he stopped and looked at Doug. "You know what I think? I think maybe I need to step out there and find out what's really going on—with you as my shield. What do you think of that, warden?"

Doug's face was expressionless behind his swollen, bleeding nose, and his left eye was starting to darken. "OK by me," he said. "They told me they weren't out there, and I believe them."

Spider grabbed him from the chair and shoved him toward the outside door. "Well, we're just going to find out. We're going to open that door first. If everything is clear there, then we'll go check out that hallway." He locked his massive bicep around the warden's neck and walked him to the door. When it was open and Spider had looked outside and decided it was all clear, he closed and locked the door again, then shoved Doug across the room toward the other exit. "The rest of you guys stay here until we get back," he called behind him, his arm still locked around Doug's neck. "Unless you don't think the four of you can handle one ex-cop." He laughed as they exited the office.

Is this the only chance I'm going to get? Abe wondered as he watched the door close behind the two men. He was glad to be rid of Spider, although he didn't know how long he would be gone, but he still didn't like the four-to-one odds against him. *You're going to have to show me what to do, God,* he prayed, *because I sure don't see any easy way out of this—not alive, anyway.*

And then it hit him. Jinx. James Landry. No wonder the man sitting next to him had looked familiar. The picture George had given him when he first came to the office looking for his long-lost brother was of a much younger James Landry, but it was him, no doubt about it. Spider had even confirmed it.

Abe turned to the inmate and found him staring straight at him. *OK, God,* Abe prayed, *if this is my way out of here, show me what to say.*

"So you're James Landry," Abe said, praying the other three inmates would stay out of the conversation and remain seated where they were, watching them from the other side of the room.

Jinx's eyes grew wide. "Why do you want to know?"

Abe made every effort to keep his voice even as he spoke. "Actually, I've been looking for you. Your brother, George, hired me and my wife to find you. I used to be a cop, but we're private detectives now. Anyway, George was looking for you to give you your share of your mother's inheritance." Abe hesitated. "You knew she'd passed away, didn't you?"

A brief flash of pain crossed Jinx's face at the mention of his mother, but it wasn't nearly as obvious as the fear Abe saw in his eyes each time he'd said the name George.

"I knew that," Jinx said. "At least, I assumed she was gone by now. She was in pretty bad shape when I last talked to her."

"When you called her from River View."

Jinx nodded. "Yeah. That was my big mistake, but I had to hear her voice once more."

Abe hesitated again, then went on. "What you probably don't know is that your brother is also dead. Happened just a few weeks ago, right there in River View. They found his body in a dumpster. He'd been stabbed and robbed. I'm sorry to be the one to have to tell you about it."

The man's eyes opened wide—with shock? Relief? When Jinx didn't say anything, Abe asked, "Are you OK?"

He nodded. "Fine. Just surprised, I guess. I was thinking that if I'd known this a few hours ago, I wouldn't be sitting here right now." He looked intently at Abe. "I didn't want to be a part of this," he said, "but Spider knew about George and said he'd tell him where I was." His voice trailed off, and Abe looked again at the three inmates across the room. They were glaring at them, but they hadn't moved.

"I stole the family inheritance when I left home a few years ago," Jinx said, his head bowed. "Close to half a million dollars. It was an awful thing to do, I know, but I just had to get away from there, and it was the only way I could figure out to do it. But I knew, once Mama died and George found out the money was gone, he'd hunt me down and kill me. The only place I could think of where he wouldn't look for me was in prison. So after I called Mama from River View, I went up towards Seattle and confessed to a crime I didn't commit—a convenience store robbery, just enough to get me a short sentence, since I didn't have a record. I stashed the money in a safety deposit box and paid the rent on it for five years. The key's hid in a safe place. That was my ticket out of the country once I got out of here. By then I hoped George would've given up looking for me. Everything seemed to be going according to plan; I was so close to getting out on good behavior. Then Spider showed up and told me my brother was in River View looking for me and that if I didn't cooperate, he'd tell him where I was." Still looking down, he shook his head. "I just wished I'd known George was dead."

As Abe listened to Jinx's story, he chastised himself for not having been more thorough in his search for the missing man. Although he'd checked the local arrest records in River View and had come up empty, he hadn't bothered to check the prison records across the state. Now he wondered if this entire scene could have been avoided if he'd followed through on the investigation. But this was no time for recriminations, he reminded himself. If any of them were going to get out of there alive, God was going to have to come through with a miracle.

He sighed, watching his companion closely.

"So that's how they roped you in," Abe said. "From what I overheard Spider saying, you have access to this office for cleaning once a week. That means your part was to get them in here."

Jinx nodded again. "They gave me the stuff I needed to make an impression of the key. I had to do it while the officer wasn't looking. I never come in here alone, of course. But it wasn't really too hard because the guard always gets bored and takes a nap while I'm working. And he never bothers to check me when I leave, so that's how we did it. I got the impression to them a few days ago, and they took it from there. I didn't ask about the details, but there are ways to get just about anything you want in here if you know the right people."

Abe didn't doubt the truth of that one bit. He'd often heard that it was easier to get drugs in prison than out, so it probably held true of other things as well—including keys. All Spider and his buddies needed was someone with access to the warden's office key for a short time, and they were in. The simplicity of it made Abe wonder just how safe anyone was here, even the volunteers in the chapel. But then he remembered how much prayer had been offered up during the preceding weeks, and he knew where their protection came from. *OK, God*, he prayed silently. *Now what?*

"I was just wondering," Jinx said, as Abe turned toward him. "What about Mindy? Have you heard from her at all?"

"My wife spoke with her a couple of times," Abe said. "She told her about George."

Jinx nodded. "She probably took the news about like I did."

"You're right. And she asked about you. She wanted to know if we'd keep looking for you, now that George was gone. She said she didn't have any money to pay us to continue the search, but she really wanted to know how you were. She said you were all she had left."

Jinx raised his eyebrows. "Really? What about her husband, Harley?"

"I guess that's over. Mindy is staying at your mom's place, and Harley stayed behind in their house with his new girlfriend."

"Can't say I'm too surprised about that. Never did like that guy much. My sister was way too good for him, if you ask me." He paused. "If we . . . if you make it out of here alive, will you tell her I miss her? That I thought of her and wanted her to be happy? And that I'm sorry about taking the money?"

"Sure," Abe said. "But let's hope we all get out of here alive. I'm not sure how, but—"

The door burst open then, and Spider shoved Doug back inside. "All clear," he announced, looking around the room before turning to Abe and pointing the gun straight at his head. "Good thing for you, Matthews. 'Cause it wouldn't take much for me to blow your brains out right about now. I never did like cops, and I sure don't like you. One false move from anybody—in here or out there—and you're the first one to go. Got that, Matthews?"

Abe nodded, his lips pressed together tightly. There was no doubt the man meant every word he said.

The phone rang again, and as all eyes turned toward it, Abe took what he imagined would be his only chance—however slight—to get out of there alive. He lunged for Spider and grabbed for his gun, but his weight scarcely moved the big man. As they grappled for the weapon, Abe felt Spider's other hand begin to close around his neck. He should have known better. The man was just too big and too strong. He didn't have a chance against him, but he'd hoped. . . .

And then he heard the gunshots. He expected to be hit any second, but instead he felt Spider loosening his grip. Abe looked up at the big man and saw his eyes roll back into his head just before he fell to the floor. And then there were more shots, and Abe threw himself down behind Spider. The hot pain in his side assured him that he had indeed caught one of the bullets, but maybe the giant's body would shield him from any further hits.

It didn't take him long, however, to realize that the three convicts on the other side of the room were not shooting at him, but at Jinx. Jinx was down, but still firing. One of the three hit the ground and didn't move. From the corner of Abe's eye he saw Doug pounce on one of the two prisoners still standing. Abe followed suit immediately, tackling the remaining convict with every bit of his body weight and grabbing for the man's gun. This time the prisoner went down, and in an instant Abe had him pinned to the floor. While Abe held the gun to the inmate's head, he saw that Doug too had gotten the best of the other prisoner and was now holding him at gunpoint as well. It was obvious that Doug was going to be all right, broken nose and all.

Abe looked back at Jinx. He was bleeding but alive. That's when he realized that it was Jinx who had shot Spider and saved his life. "Can you make it to the phone?" he asked.

Jinx nodded and pulled himself up, then moved slowly to the desk. *He's going to make it*, Abe thought as James Landry picked up the phone and dialed the command center. *And so am I.*

CHAPTER 27

Even with all that had happened, the ministry weekend went on as scheduled, with all three Saturday services filled to capacity. Hundreds of inmates received Jesus as Savior, some for the first time, others as a recommitment of an earlier decision long since abandoned. Warden Schillo, much of his face in bandages and with his wife at his side, attended all the services. Doug and the ministry leaders had decided it was the best way to proclaim to the prisoners that their faith in God could not be shaken by the events that went on around them. As a result of that decision, the prison's status had been changed to a modified lockdown, allowing the inmates out of their cells only to attend the services.

Abe, though he'd wanted to, had been unable to return to the prison on Saturday. He had spent Friday night and all the next day in the hospital, undergoing surgery to remove the bullet that had lodged in his side but, fortunately, had caused no serious damage. If all went well, his doctor had assured him, he could go home on Monday.

Toni, of course, had not left his side since he and Doug had emerged from the warden's office the previous night. Now, on Saturday evening, she sat beside his bed and watched him sleep, thanking God again and again that her husband was alive and resting comfortably. She knew many visitors were anxiously waiting in the lobby, but Abe had only recently been moved from recovery to his own room, so for now she was the only one allowed in to see him. If he felt well enough in the morning, the others could come in then.

Toni smiled as she brushed his dark hair from his brow. He had offered his life in exchange for her own, loving her as the Bible commanded a husband to love his wife and to lay down his life for her. How grateful she was to God for having given her such a strong and gentle man. He would make a wonderful father, and she couldn't wait to tell him.

~~~

Abe's side was sore when he awoke on Sunday morning, but his heart was singing. A baby. He and Toni were going to have a baby. She had told him when he had awakened during the night and found her dozing in the chair beside his bed. He had tried not to disturb her, but she had opened her eyes as soon as he stirred, grabbing his hand and pressing it to her lips as she gazed at him with grateful eyes. Within minutes she had given him the news, and they had held each other and wept with joy.

"I went to the doctor on Thursday," she had explained. "I hadn't been feeling well for several days, and I wondered if maybe I was pregnant, but I wanted to be sure before I said anything. Then, once

I did find out, I decided to wait until after the prison ministry was over so you wouldn't worry." She had smiled then and shaken her head. "Little did I know how all that was going to turn out. The entire time I was locked up in the warden's office, and then afterward while I waited outside wondering if you would get out alive, I kept praying, 'Please, God, rescue us so we can raise our baby together.'"

Now, staring at his breakfast tray with its lukewarm Jell-O cup and runny applesauce, he told himself that he had to eat it, no matter how unappetizing it looked. The sooner he got his strength back, the sooner he could go home.

Which was where Toni was right now. He had finally convinced her to go home and get a few hours sleep before coming back. He knew she was exhausted, but the only way he could persuade her to leave even for a little while was to remind her that she needed to take care of herself for the baby's sake. But he had to admit that it was lonely without her, and he was anxious for her to return.

When she came in an hour or so later, his tray had been removed and he had raised the bed so he could sit up a little.

"You look a lot better," she said, leaning over to kiss him.

"I feel better. Ready to go home if they'd let me."

"Tomorrow," she reminded him. "You heard the doctor."

Abe sighed. "I know. And I'm grateful to be doing so well, especially when I think of how things could have turned out."

Toni nodded. "When you told me last night about how that huge man named Spider almost killed you—"

"If it hadn't been for Jinx—James Landry—he would have. Isn't it ironic that George Landry's long-lost brother ended up being the one who saved my life?"

"I'm just glad James is going to be all right, although I imagine his sentence will be extended because of his involvement in that awful situation, even if he was there against his will. That's an amazing story he told you about the money he took from his family and how he decided to hide from George in prison."

Suddenly Abe remembered something else Jinx had told him just before they were all escorted from the warden's office. "You've got to call Mindy," he said. "James's sister. He wants her to have the money."

Toni frowned. "The family money that he stole?"

"Yes. No one's ever pressed any charges over that money, so James can do whatever he wants with it, now that his brother isn't around to take revenge. He told me the name of the bank here in River View where it's stashed in a safety deposit box, and he's going to get a letter notarized from prison, giving Mindy the rights to the box's contents. He said it was close to a half-million dollars, so I imagine it's going to come in handy for her, now that she and her husband are getting a divorce."

Toni nodded. "It'll be nice to finally have some good news to give Mindy when I call—not just about the money, but about James. I'm sure she'll be shocked to learn he's in prison, but at least he's alive and well, and they can be back in touch."

A rap on the door caught their attention, and they turned to see April and Sophie standing in the doorway. Sophie's eyes were red but shining.

"Can we sneak in for a few minutes?" April asked.

Abe smiled. "Absolutely. I'm so glad to see you both."

Sophie hurried to the bed, and Abe wrapped his arms around her as she started to cry. "Oh, Avraham! Praise be to Adonai that you are safe. When I heard what you did—that you had offered yourself in exchange for Toni . . ."

"I had to, Aunt Sophie," Abe said. "She's my wife. I love her. What else could I do?"

Aunt Sophie pulled back. "No, you don't understand, Avraham. What I mean is, when I heard that you'd offered up your own life to save hers, suddenly I understood why *Yeshua* had to die—for you and for me. For the Gentiles, yes, but also for Israel, even as was promised to us in the *Tenakh* from the beginning. He was our ransom, the payment for our sins so we could be redeemed from the evil one and reunited with Adonai. At last I understand. *Yeshua* is indeed the Messiah, and the ransom has been paid. We are free, if only we will recognize him as Messiah, the redeemer of our people. And I have, Avraham. After all these years, I finally have." She hugged him again. "Oh, Avraham, praise be to Adonai for sparing me from that plane crash and giving me the chance to recognize my Messiah."

~~~

Toni was overwhelmed at Sophie's revelation, as she realized what God had been doing behind the scenes, even as she had prayed for Abe's deliverance from the hands of his captors. As the four of them sat in the hospital room and rejoiced over Sophie's declaration of faith, April had explained that it had happened the night before as the two of them, along with Melissa and Carrie, had been waiting for Abe and Toni to return from the prison. As the night wore on and there was no news, they began to pray. Before long Toni had called on her cell phone and told them what had happened and that they were on their way to the hospital. When April relayed to everyone how Abe had offered himself as a hostage in exchange for Toni, Sophie had begun to weep, saying over and over again, "*Yeshua*, the redeemer. He has paid the ransom for Israel. He gave his life for ours. Oh, *Yeshua*. *Yeshua*."

She and Abe had still been digesting this wonderful news when Carrie and Melissa joined them in Abe's room. "You look great," Melissa said, kissing her brother-in-law on the cheek.

And then John King had arrived, clutching a bouquet of flowers and ducking his head as he walked through the door. He blushed when he saw the crowded room.

"Sorry," he said. "I should have called first."

"Nonsense," April said, hurrying to him and taking the flowers from his hand. "Here, I'll put these in water, and you go sit down and have a visit with Abe."

Awkwardly John pulled up a chair and sat down next to Toni, who smiled up at him from her own seat. "Isn't this great?" she asked. "A real celebration."

John nodded, looking from her to Abe. "I was worried when I heard what was going on. We all were. But we didn't stop praying till we knew you were safe."

"Thanks, buddy," Abe said, the emotion evident on his face. Then his expression changed, and Toni knew he was trying to make light of the situation. "What I want to know," he said, eyeing John, "is, where were you when I needed you?"

John laughed and was soon joined by everyone in the room. "Hey," he said, "you get one save per person per lifetime. I already rescued you once, so this time it was somebody else's turn."

"Well, I'm just glad somebody else was in the right place at the right time," Abe said, then shook his head. "I still can't get over the fact that it was James Landry who saved my life. Who would've thought?"

"Hello," called a familiar voice. Toni turned to see Brad and Jeanine standing in the doorway. "We won't stay," Brad said. "It looks like you've already got a full house. But we heard what happened, and we wanted to stop by and tell you how glad we are that you're OK."

Abe's smile was warm, and Toni knew this was a healing encounter for the two men who had at one time vied for her attention. It was obvious now, however, that Brad's romantic interests had been transferred to the petite redhead standing beside him.

"Hey, come on in," Abe said. "The more, the merrier."

Everyone scooted closer together to make room for the latest arrivals, as Brad quickly introduced Jeanine to the group. Melissa, of course, had already met her and smiled coyly at Brad, who winked and tousled her hair. "Way to go, bro," Toni heard Melissa whisper.

Just then the nurse showed up, a heavyset, middle-aged woman who stopped in the doorway and stood with her hands on her hips, shaking her head at the gathering in front of her. "Mr. Matthews," she said sternly, eyeing Abe, "I thought I specified short visits and only with immediate family members."

Abe raised his eyebrows in his most innocent look. "They haven't been here long," he said. "And they're all family—well, sort of."

The nurse nodded. "I've heard that story before. Didn't believe it then either. All right, five minutes, and then you've all got to leave—with the exception of Mrs. Matthews, of course—and let this man get some rest."

They were still chuckling after her departure when one final guest arrived. Mark Johnson, carrying a huge box of chocolates, poked his head in the door and asked, "Is this where the party is?"

"You bet," Abe said, motioning him inside and then introducing him to the others as the box of candy was opened and passed around.

"Wow," Melissa said when Mark shook her hand. "I remember when my dad used to watch you play football. You were great."

"Thanks, I think," Mark answered. "Were. Used to. Hmm. Why do I suddenly feel ancient?"

Everyone laughed as Brad rounded up some extra chairs, and they all managed to find a place to sit down.

"So," Abe said, addressing Mark, "how did everything go yesterday?"

"Great! Between the service on Friday night and the three on Saturday, we had close to five hundred men make commitments to Jesus. It was awesome. And, of course, we've already worked with the prison officials to set up follow-up discipleship classes and Bible studies for the new converts."

"Speaking of prison officials," Toni said, "have you heard anything new on Doug Schillo?"

"He's doing great," Mark answered. "He and Kelly were at all three services yesterday—although his face is pretty well hidden behind bandages."

"That's all right," Abe said. "He probably looks better now than he did the last time I saw him, right after Spider got through working him over."

Mark smiled. "That's what I came to talk to you about—Spider."

Abe nodded. "Yeah. He was really something, wasn't he? As mean as they come. And huge! I thought sure he was going to kill me. He would have, if James Landry hadn't shot him before he could finish me off. What a wasted life."

"True," Mark agreed. "But maybe not quite as wasted as you think."

Toni looked from Mark to Abe, who appeared as puzzled as she felt. What was Mark talking about? The oversized inmate had died when James shot him, so what could Mark possibly have found out about the man's life that would make it any less wasted and miserable than it obviously had been?

"He didn't die when James Landry shot him," Mark said, pausing while everyone absorbed his announcement. "In fact, he lived for almost an hour after the police and medics got into that office. He even regained consciousness for about fifteen minutes during his ambulance ride to the hospital."

"That's incredible," Abe said, amazement evident on his face. "I was positive he was dead. Are you sure? I mean, how do you know this?"

"Because I was in that ambulance with him. As I watched him being carried out on a stretcher to the ambulance, God spoke to my heart and told me to ride along with him. Believe me, I had to do some fast talking to get the EMTs and prison officials to agree, but they finally did. I prayed as we rode, and when he opened his eyes, I was right there beside him."

"What happened then?" Toni asked, her heart racing as she imagined the possibilities.

"He started crying," Mark said. "He kept saying, 'I saw Mama. I saw my mama. She said this was my last chance.' I asked him what he meant—his last chance for what? He said, 'To be with her in heaven.' That's when I knew why God had assigned me to ride with him in that ambulance. By the time we reached the hospital, Gerald 'Spider' Owens had prayed and asked God to forgive him. He had accepted Jesus as his Savior. Although he was pronounced DOA at the hospital, I can assure you he died with a smile on his lips and peace in his heart."

There was scarcely a dry eye in the room by the time Mark finished relating the story of Spider's deathbed conversion. Sophie seemed to be the most overjoyed at the news. "The ransom was paid for all," she said, nodding as the tears trickled down her face.

"I also found out a few more details about what happened Friday night," Mark continued. "One of the inmates in the warden's office definitely died during the exchange of gunfire. But it also seems the two correctional officers who got killed escorting the inmates to the warden's office were in on the plan—not willingly, I guess, but forced into it because they'd been involved with all sorts of illegal dealings in the prison for years. The inmates basically blackmailed them into helping, including getting them a couple of extra guns along with giving up their own and escorting them from their cells to the warden's office, although I'm sure they didn't expect to be killed in the process. But that's what happened. Apparently Spider finished them off once they'd finished their usefulness." Mark shook his head. "Hard to believe someone as cold-blooded as Spider could still turn to God with his last breath. We serve a merciful Lord."

Everyone murmured their agreement, and then Mark said, "On a more positive note, you'll all be relieved to know that the police picked up the outside accomplice who'd been waiting at a nearby airstrip to fly them out of the country. So it looks like all the loose ends are tied up—literally."

The nurse came back then, bursting into the room with a scowl that brought them all back to the present. "All right, that's it," she said. "I walk away for five minutes and the group just keeps growing. Everyone out—now. Shoo. Go on. Go home and leave this man alone for a while, will you?"

As they started to comply, Toni held up her hand. "Wait," she said. "Just one more thing."

All eyes turned to her as she took Abe's hand. "We have an announcement to make." They smiled at each other, then Abe nodded at her and she continued. "We're going to have a baby."

The room was silent for an instant, then everyone erupted into spontaneous applause and cheering—including the nurse. "All right," she said at last. "I give up. Go ahead and have your party. I'll see you people later." Laughing and shaking her head, she turned and left the room.

"*Baruch Hashem*," Sophie declared, clasping her hands together, then raising them in the air. "Praise be to God!"

"Oh, my dears," April exclaimed. "That's wonderful news!"

"A baby," Carrie said. "That's so exciting!"

"I'm going to be an aunt," Melissa said, grinning. "How cool!"

Brad, Jeanine, Mark, and John all joined in the congratulations as Abe squeezed Toni's hand. *Thank you, God*, she prayed silently. *Thank you, thank you.*

I am your Father.

The voice echoed in her heart, and she smiled. New life was springing up everywhere. He truly was her Father, the author of all life, and he loved them so much he had sent his Son to ransom their souls.

~~~

BE SURE TO START
AT THE BEGINNING OF THE
MATTHEWS MYSTERIES WITH
THESE OTHER BOOKS!

Obsession
A Novel
Kathi Mills-Macias
0-8054-2149-1, $12.99
Toni Matthews soon discovers that her father's fatal fishing trip and the Julie Green case were related. She then begins an investigation of her own in this fast-paced thriller.

The Price
A Novel
Kathi Mills-Macias
0-8054-2566-7, $12.99
The author reprises from *Obsession* with the creative plot twists and engaging characters that will keep readers on the edge of their seats.

BROADMAN
&HOLMAN
PUBLISHERS

www.broadmanholman.com